The Accidental Voyage

Also by Douglas Bond:

Mr. Pipes and the British Hymn Makers

*Mr. Pipes and Psalms and Hymns
of the Reformation*

Mr. Pipes Comes to America

Duncan's War

King's Arrow

Rebel's Keep

The Accidental Voyage

Discovering Hymns of the Early Centuries

Douglas Bond

P&R PUBLISHING
P.O. BOX 817 • PHILLIPSBURG • NEW JERSEY 08865-0817

Hymns are reprinted from *Trinity Hymnal* (Copyright © 1961, revised 1990, Great Commission Publications). Used by permission.

Page design and typesetting by Dawn Premako

Printed in the United States of America

Library of Congress Cataloging-in-Publication Data

Bond, Douglas, 1958–
   The accidental voyage : discovering hymns of the early centuries / Douglas Bond.
      p. cm.
   Summary: As they travel together in Italy, sail on the Mediterranean, and finally return to England, Mr. Pipes shares his Christian beliefs with Annie and Drew by recounting Christian history and singing hymns.
   ISBN-13: 978-0-87552-748-2 (paper)
   ISBN-10: 0-87552-748-5 (paper)
   [1. Christian life—Fiction. 2. Hymns—Fiction. 3. Travel—Fiction. 4. Italy—Fiction. 5. Boats and boating—Fiction.] I. Title.
   PZ7.B63665Acc 2005
   [Fic]—dc22

                                                        2005047186

For Brittany, Rhodri, Cedric,
Desmond, Giles, and Gillian

Table of Contents

Summary of the Mr. Pipes Adventures

In Annie and Drew's first meeting with Mr. Pipes, they discovered the odd little man playing the organ behind a curtain in the ancient church in Olney, England, where long ago John Newton wrote his hymns and preached. This kindly old man broke down their preference for all things new and popular by enchanting them with stories from the past, stories about fishing on The River Great Ouse, about sailing, about exploring the English countryside, and most of all about hymns and hymn writers from the British Isles. Accompanied by his cat, Lord Underfoot, Mr. Pipes taught the children to fish for barbel the Izaac Walton way and to hand, reef, and steer his little boat *Toplady*. But the greatest thing he taught them was how to know, love, and worship God.

The following summer, after a year of letter writing with Mr. Pipes, the children's parents finally agreed to let Annie and Drew fly back to England, cross the channel, and travel with the old man on a tour of the European continent. Dr. Dudley, Mr. Pipes's over-protective doctor and friend, strongly disapproved of such goings on. The threesome got locked in and spent the night in Martin Luther's castle, ate hamburgers in Erfurt and bratwurst in Wittenburg, rescued a nearly drowned kitten, went on a diet in Worms, sailed down the Rhine, toured a famous organ builder's factory—all the while shadowed by an elusive spy. They finally fled out an upper-story window in Tubingen under cover of darkness and made good their escape to Switzerland. They milked cows on an ancient dairy farm, and followed the cobblestone path of John Calvin in Geneva. Throughout the adventures, Mr. Pipes told them the stories of the psalms and hymns of the Protestant Reformation. Finally, on the steps of St. Pierre, Calvin's church, the spy is cornered and the mystery is solved.

Next Christmas vacation, Annie and Drew met Mr. Pipes and a reluctant Dr. Dudley in New England for a chilly visit to the landmarks of American history: Mayflower II near Plymouth Plantation, USS Constitution at the wharf in Boston, Nassau Hall and the battlefield at Princeton, all the while the biggest snowstorm of the winter brewing in their wake. They went rowing on the Delaware River, feasted on Atlantic salmon, and made a treacherous journey with Dr. Dudley behind the wheel of a rented pickup truck, driven mostly on the wrong side of the road. Throughout their travels, Mr. Pipes told the children the story of American hymn writers, Dr. Dudley mystified and resentful that anyone would have ever left England for the colonies in the first place. Finally, snowbound in Massachusetts and guided by Mr. Pipes, Annie put her pen to paper and wrote her own hymn, all the while attempting to tame a precarious new pet they called Monochrome. As lovely as the snow was, it seemed that they would miss Christmas because of it. In a break in the weather, Dr. Dudley confidently demonstrated his skill in snow skiing, but suddenly found himself in need of a doctor.

In their fourth adventure, Mr. Pipes and Annie and Drew are wholly unprepared for . . .

The Accidental Voyage!

How plentifully did I weep
in those hymns and psalms,
being touched to the very quick
by the notes of the Church
so sweetly singing.

—St. Augustine

When I was a kid, did I like singing about,
"We Are But Little Children, Weak"?
or "Jesus, Meek and Gentle"?
Not on your life!
I liked "Christian, Dost Thou
[See] Them?"—especially the bit about
"prowl and prowl around."

—Dorothy Sayers

1
So This Is Rome?

Shepherd of Tender Youth
(Clement of Alexandria)

Christ, our triumphant King,
We come thy Name to sing;
Hither our children bring,
To shout thy praise.

CLEMENT OF ALEXANDRIA
(TRANSLATION BY HENRY MARTYN DEXTER)

"*Pizza!*" thought Drew, breathing in the savory aroma of herbs, tomatoes, fresh-baked pizza crust, and heaps of melting mozzarella cheese. He licked his lips and rolled his eyes in anticipation as he raced—rather, putted—along the Via di Borgo on his blue moped. He inhaled again, and promptly sputtered and coughed as his lungs filled with the diesel fumes of a passing bus. Steadying his moped, he blinked several times, trying to see Mr. Pipes and Annie riding ahead of him through the smoky gray haze.

"Hey! Wait up!" he called, trying to coax more speed out of the tiny electric motor.

They raced on, unable to hear above the din of the city and the frantic buzzing of the electric bicycles. Drew pedaled furiously. He must have slowed down back there at the pizzeria. Glancing back over his shoulder, he decided it had to be pizza—pepperoni pizza.

A new scent filled Drew's nostrils as he raced around the next corner, still trying to catch up. Lining the streets under cover of rows of white canvas awnings, vendors waved bunches of colorful flowers and shouted at people to stop and buy. Though eager to catch up, Drew slowed down for a better look.

Without warning, a yellow Fiat coughed past him on the left, and with a squealing of tires and a sharp blast of his horn, the driver cut Drew off, narrowly missing his front tire.

Drew clawed at the brakes on the handlebars and swerved. His eyes wide with fright, he desperately tried to avoid a large bucket of carnations in his waggling path. With a *crash!* and a *sploosh!*, water from the bucket drenched him from head to toe, and he landed in a sodden heap surrounded by limp flowers, an empty bucket, his crashed moped, and a stomping-mad Italian woman.

"*Imbecilio!*" cried the woman, her black hair tied back in a red scarf, and her brawny arms on her hips.

Drew sat up and cleared a mangle of soggy pink petals from his face. In spite of the language barrier, he detected from her bulging eyes and expressive hands that the woman was less than happy with him. Something about her reminded him of an Italian opera he'd once seen on television. Had he understood the spoken part of Italian, he would have heard the following:

"Do I look like somebody who can afford to have a bucket of flowers wasted? No! My precious, *precious* flowers. What on earth are you doing in Rome, anyway? You came for the driving, no? I know, I know, you're a tourist—probably American."

Drew caught the word "American." But it had an "o" at the end; in fact, it sounded like most of her words had an "o" at the end.

14

"Whatever, whatever, I don't have to like the way you drive your moped. All right all right, anyway: I know, in Rome tourists are our bread and Gorgonzola. La, la, la. You come to see all our old stuff—we have the best crumbling old stuff in the world! And you come to eat our food—we have the best food in the world! And I had—*had*, mind you—the best flowers in the world until you smashed them into this heap of rubbish! Anyway, we have the best everything else in the world, right here in Rome (well, maybe not the best tourists)! Do you think I don't know all this? No. But why did you have to ruin *my* flowers? Why? Why not Luigi's or Signora Pellagrino's? Why me? Why?"

Drew stared dumbly back at the woman and wondered how she could say all that without taking a breath. She probably wouldn't understand if he apologized. But maybe if he spoke really slowly—

"I a-m s-o s-o-r-r-y," said Drew, speaking as loudly as he could. She just stared. He tried again, this time holding his hands, palms up, and shaking them for emphasis with each word.

The hands seemed to help. She answered in Italian:

"Yeah, yeah. So sorry, are you? Lot of good that does my poor flowers, no?"

Drew wished he could make her understand, but after another pleading look into her angry face, he fumbled in his pocket for a handful of lire—Mr. Pipes had told them that it took lots of lire to buy anything. He thrust the money into the flower lady's fist and disentangled himself and the moped from the flowers and bucket. Dripping wet, he yanked red carnations out of the handlebars and spokes, clambered back onto his moped, and urged it after Mr. Pipes and his sister.

So this is Rome, he thought, frowning and wiping a flower petal off his wet cheek. He strained to see Mr. Pipes and Annie through the weaving traffic. His sister's blond hair flashed in the sunlight as it streamed from under her helmet. He thought back on Mr. Pipes's first letter outlining his plan for an adventure in

Italy. Drew wasn't so sure about Italy; why not just go back to Olney and have another summer of adventures on The Great Ouse, sailing and fishing and exploring the countryside with Mr. Pipes and the Howard children? He did miss Bentley and even his sister Clara.

Ah, but then Mr. Pipes had mentioned Italian food. *It'd better be really good,* he thought, *after all this.* Then he remembered the wonderful smells of that pizza. *Give Italy a chance, give it a chance,* he told himself.

Meanwhile, Annie held on tightly behind Mr. Pipes and gazed from left to right at the bustling city. Her imagination raced back in time at the sight of an ancient arch or crumbling column, and the next moment she felt a smothering uneasiness at the chaos of surging, perspiring bodies and impatient motorists blaring their horns and hammering with their arms out open windows against the sides of their cars. Everyone seemed to be talking and gesturing at once, and traffic seemed to go round and round without ever getting anywhere. The racket was deafening.

Mr. Pipes had said that Italy involved some inconvenience to the foreign adventurer, but he assured Annie that they would not be disappointed and that perhaps the greatest adventure ever awaited them in the land of the early Christian saints—and martyrs.

Mr. Pipes rounded a corner, and Annie closed her eyes and breathed in the fragrant scents of carnations, gardenias, and a variety of roses. Row upon row of flower stalls lined the narrow street. She nearly turned all the way around on the back of the moped, taking in the heavenly panoply of color as she and Mr. Pipes rode past the flower market. She caught sight of Drew at the far end of the street and tapped on Mr. Pipes's shoulder.

"Drew's pretty far back!" she shouted next to the old man's helmet. She hoped he'd slow down or even stop so that she could look at the flowers—and Drew could catch up.

Annie felt their moped sputter to a stop as Mr. Pipes parked at the far end of the flower market. She hopped off and admired the rows of buckets overflowing with yellow, red, green, and white.

"I wish Rome was all like this; I could stay here all day," she said over her shoulder to Mr. Pipes.

"I understand perfectly, my dear," said the old man, his white hair glowing in the sunshine as he took off his helmet. "The Campo de' Fiori, or field of flowers market, is a refreshing relief from the otherwise rather sooty, gray stones and concrete jumbled about. It is like that in Rome, one-time capital of Western Civilization: dust, sweat, and general messiness give way around the next corner to beauty of the most extraordinary magnificence."

"Oh, but here comes Drew," said Annie.

Scowling, Drew stepped stiffly off his moped and squelched toward them, leaving a trail of water on the pavement.

"What on earth happened to you?" asked Annie.

"Oh, my dear fellow," said Mr. Pipes. "However did you manage to get so entirely soaked?"

"Crashed," said Drew, collapsing with a *sploosh* onto a bench.

"Into what?" asked Annie.

"A flower pot," he said simply. "Full of water. At least it was full of water before I hit it."

"I hope you didn't get hurt," said Annie with concern. "Did you crush any of the flowers?" she added, glancing at a nearby row.

"I didn't have time to check their vital signs," he said, frowning and rubbing his elbow. "How could I? The lady selling the flowers looked ready to feed me to the lions—she looked like one herself—and I thought I'd better scram."

Drew paused, looking at the street shimmering with heat and bustling with traffic. Voices rose and fell from the people on the sidewalk and in the market. Everyone seemed excited about something. He shook his head at the din.

"They call this place 'The Eternal City,' " he said doubtfully. "I must be missing something. All that seems eternal here is the noise and the heat."

In Drew's defense, he had spent more than a dozen hours on an airplane, where at every meal he had never had quite enough to eat. He had slept very little in the last twenty-four hours, his clothes were soaked, and his elbow hurt. The cumulative effect left Drew feeling out of sorts with the world.

"There is that, to be sure," agreed Mr. Pipes. "But my boy, what you need is refreshment—yes, refreshment is what you need."

Drew looked interested. The old man stroked his chin, and his generous white eyebrows worked up and down as he thought.

"I've got just the thing," said Mr. Pipes, after a moment.

"What?" asked Annie and Drew.

"Follow me to the nearest Italian soda stand," he said, strapping his helmet on. "Riding will dry your clothes."

"In this heat," said Annie, "they should be dry in no time."

"Do you think they'll have raspberry?" asked Drew, suddenly thinking more benevolent thoughts about Italy and Italians. He climbed onto his VeloSolex moped—not as powerful as Mr. Pipes and Annie's, but legal for someone his age to ride.

"Naturally they will have raspberry, Drew," said Mr. Pipes.

"Isn't that everybody's favorite?" said Annie, climbing on the moped behind Mr. Pipes.

*

Drew took a long pull on his straw and felt the bubbly sweetness of the creamy raspberry soda cooling his throat.

Mr. Pipes had led them to a sidewalk café on the Via del Colosseo. Framed by shops at the end of the street, the ruins of the ancient Colosseum loomed massive and menacing. Everything around it seemed small and insignificant.

"Ah," said Drew, smacking his lips. "That's better, much better. Say, did either of you smell that pizza back on the street? It was to die for."

"Perhaps for lunch," said Mr. Pipes with a laugh, "but it's far too early for lunch just now."

"Oh, just thought I'd mention it." Drew shrugged and took another sip of his soda. Then he sat back in his chair.

"It looks so big from here," he said. "It almost doesn't look real. You know, more like a giant sports arena in a movie."

"The Colosseum, you mean?" asked Mr. Pipes.

"I'm not so sure I like it," said Annie, her eyes narrowing.

"Why not?" said Drew.

"I don't know."

Drew shrugged and, looking again at the ancient ruins, asked, "Who built it?"

"A-and what did they use it for?" asked Annie.

"Ah, yes, the Amphitheatrum Flavium," said Mr. Pipes, setting his tall soda glass on the linen-covered table. "Begun by the Roman emperor Vespasian and opened for use by his son, Titus, in A.D. 80."

"But who actually did all the work?" asked Drew. "The thing's huge."

"The Romans used Jewish slaves taken captive when Jerusalem fell," replied Mr. Pipes.

"Slaves?" said Annie.

"Must have taken thousands of them," said Drew. He drained the last of his soda, slurping loudly with his straw to get every drop.

Annie frowned at him. "But what did they use it for?" she asked again.

Mr. Pipes looked from the Colosseum to Annie and adjusted the position of his gold-rimmed half-glasses on his nose before answering her.

"Well, now, that is not the most pleasant of topics, I fear, my dear."

"Why not?"

"Yeah," added Drew, "didn't they just play sports—football and stuff like that—in the Colosseum?"

"I fear not," said Mr. Pipes. "I'll tell you all about it whilst we go have a look."

After locking their mopeds together near the café, Annie and Drew followed Mr. Pipes down the sidewalk toward the Colosseum.

"So this place is almost two thousand years old," said Drew, as they came closer and the circle of the Colosseum loomed more massive above them.

"It's huge," said Annie, while they waited for a swirling wave of traffic to stop so that they could cross the street.

"You're right, Annie," said Drew. "I don't think I've ever seen anything so ginormous in my life."

" 'Tis a stupendous sight," said Mr. Pipes. "Many believe it is the most spectacular building in Rome; some believe it the most spectacular in the world."

Annie felt the urge to bite her fingernails. She couldn't explain it, but something about this place made her uneasy.

"Why all the arches?" asked Drew.

"The lowest row, along the street," said Mr. Pipes, "were entrances—eighty entrances and exits in all."

"How about the other rows?"

"Each upper arch originally framed a statue of one of the emperors or heroes of the empire," replied Mr. Pipes. "The entire structure used to be covered with glimmering marble, but the marble and the statues were plundered for use in many of the other buildings around Rome when the Colosseum fell out of use."

Mr. Pipes led them through the cool shade of one of the massive arches into the bright sunshine of the interior.

"This place could have held thousands," said Drew, as he took in the row upon row of ancient stone tiers rising in circles all around them. Lush grass now grew in places where emperor and commoner had been entertained together.

"Through the eighty arches streamed more than fifty thousand eager spectators," said Mr. Pipes. "With all those entrances it took only ten minutes to find a seat, and then the show began."

"Wh-what show?" asked Annie.

"Yeah, where's the field?" asked Drew. "I expected to see a big, flat, open field, you know, like a football field. But there's just all these old stone walls—reminds me of some kind of maze. You could get lost in there."

Mr. Pipes said nothing, but led them higher up the ancient steps for a better view.

"All those cages you see today," he said, stopping and sitting down on a slab of marble, "were covered in a heavy wooden floor with trapdoors, mechanical lifts, and winches, allowing the Romans to open and close cages—and dungeons—and to rearrange the entire arena."

"Sort of like stage sets?" asked Drew.

"Something along those lines, I suppose," said Mr. Pipes soberly.

Annie looked at the old man's eyes. She had grown close to Mr. Pipes on their adventures; she sometimes felt as though she could read his thoughts. He stared out over the ruined arena with a look that Annie had seen on his face before. They sat quietly for several minutes.

"What used to happen here—long ago?" asked Annie, sitting down next to the old man and slipping her hand into his. "It looks like you're watching it in your mind."

He smiled at Annie.

"The Colosseum was a place of horrible violence and cruelty," he began, "and all in the name of entertainment—but at such great cost. People flocked here for free bread and circuses to jeer and hoot as creatures died."

"Creatures?" said Drew.

"Y-you mean animals were killed here for entertainment?" asked Annie. "Cats? Like Lord Underfoot and Lady Kitty?" She thought back on Mr. Pipes's large gray cat, king of the castle at Mr. Pipes's old cottage on the river; and she remembered rescuing Lady Kitty under a bridge in Germany and later giving her to little Henri on the farm in Switzerland. She missed both of them terribly.

"Much bigger cats than they," said Mr. Pipes. "The Roman love of munera—blood sports—was legendary in the history of the world. Lions, tigers, elephants, giraffes, hippos, even horses were released from those cages under the movable floor, and gladiators—mostly slaves and prisoners—armed with sword and shield would fight the animals to the death. When Emperor Titus opened the Colosseum in A.D. 80, he held one hundred days of blood sports, wherein, it is said, five thousand animals died before a delighted mob."

"That's awful," said Annie. "I can't imagine anything worse. Didn't anyone feel sorry for the animals?"

"At first, no doubt, some still pitied them," replied Mr. Pipes. "One of our great poets described the slide into vice and decadence this way—"

"Is it a hymn?" asked Drew.

"Not this time," replied Mr. Pipes. "It is a poem about a monster."

"Cool!" said Drew.

"Wait," said Annie, opening her sketchbook and turning to a clean page. "I want to get it down."

Mr. Pipes smiled and then recited:

> Vice is a monster of so frightful mien,
> As to be hated needs but to be seen.
> Yet seen too oft, familiar with her face,
> We first endure, then pity, then embrace.

"So some folks," said Drew, "didn't like it—the blood sports—at first, but they put up with it, and after seeing it for a while, they eventually liked it. Is that how it works?"

"Yes, my boy," said Mr. Pipes. "But as they watched, they became bored with just seeing animals killed. It is always that way with entertainment; it dulls our appreciation of constant things whilst awakening an ever-increasing craving for passing thrills. Their lust for blood increased; they had to see greater violence and cruelty. Seeing animals killed was not enough."

"Wh-what do you mean?" asked Annie.

Mr. Pipes looked at Annie with sad eyes before he continued. He breathed a heavy sigh, and went on.

"The crowds demanded more blood—human blood. And soon gladiators with swords, nets, and tridents entered the arena to fight with one another."

"To fight with real swords?" said Drew. "Just to fight?"

Drew couldn't help himself; it all sounded kind of exciting. He gazed down on the arena and then back at their old friend. He could never admit his excitement to Mr. Pipes, though.

Mr. Pipes glanced at Drew and then gazed down at the ruins of cages and dungeons at the base of the Colosseum before continuing.

Annie stood up and followed Mr. Pipes's gaze. She turned quickly away.

"Mostly, they fought to the death," he said quietly.

"In front of all those people?" asked Drew, running his eyes around the massive circle and imagining it filled with a frenzied, jeering mob. "You see murder with actors on TV, but this was the real thing?"

"Oh, most real indeed, Drew," replied Mr. Pipes. "Blood and violence on TV and in movies grows worse in an attempt to satisfy exactly the same sinful craving for sensational thrills: blood—real blood—for the Romans, special-effects blood for us. But the net result is a dulling of pity for others and a dulling of wholesome desire.

"When the combat reached a stand, usually because one gladiator fell wounded," continued Mr. Pipes, "the screaming crowds raised or lowered their thumbs as a gesture of their will for him to live or die. More often than not, these stones echoed with, 'Kill him, kill him!' And if the emperor agreed, the poor soul was slain whilst the pitiless mobs derived their pleasure from the miserable suffering and cruel death of another human being."

"Let me get this straight," said Drew, blinking and shaking his head as if to clear some thought too awful to contemplate. "This all happened right here?"

Annie felt numb and bit her lip; she stared in revulsion at the ruined edifice.

"Oh, I'm afraid it is all very true, indeed," said Mr. Pipes. "But that is not all, my dears."

"What could possibly be worse than that?" asked Annie, barely trusting herself to ask.

"The Romans turned their appetite toward new victims," said Mr. Pipes quietly. "They called the followers of our Lord Jesus atheists because Christians refused to worship the many Roman gods. Worse yet, for their refusal to worship the emperor as 'Lord and God,' Christians were labeled traitors. Nero, sixth emperor of Rome, in A.D. 67 commenced the first wave of persecution of our brothers and sisters. Something of a madman, Nero burned the city of Rome whilst playing merrily on his fiddle, then proceeded to punish Christians for his misdeeds. His violence against Christians was so terrible that many otherwise loyal Romans were repulsed by it."

"Wh-what did he do to them?" asked Drew.

"He dressed some in robes dipped in wax; then he tied them to trees and set them on fire, like human candles, to provide lighting for the evening garden parties held at his extravagant palace, Domus Aurea, just across the way."

"Alive?" asked Drew. Mr. Pipes nodded.

Annie shuddered.

"Along with many nameless thousands," continued Mr. Pipes, "he also killed the apostles Peter and Paul here in Rome."

"That must have really hurt the spread of Christianity," said Drew. "I mean, who would be a Christian if he knew that the government could kill him just for being one?"

"Oh, quite the contrary, my boy," said Mr. Pipes. "Within a short time, the apostles and missionaries had carried the good news—on Roman-built roads—throughout the empire; Christianity often advanced most in the midst of great persecution. Whilst executing Christians, Roman military officers were converted because of the faithful witness of the persecuted; senators and slaves, people from every walk of life, came to faith in the risen, conquering Lord Jesus—all whilst hatred and cruelty against Christians raged on every side."

"Here?" asked Annie, hoarsely. "Were Christians actually killed here in this arena?"

"Yes, and in hundreds like it built for the same purpose throughout the Roman world," answered Mr. Pipes. "Old men, saintly women—even children were torn to pieces and devoured by lions and other wild beasts. Oh, yes, indeed; right here they shed their blood for their loyalty to Christ."

"Wasn't there any way out?" asked Drew.

"Certainly," said Mr. Pipes. "All they had to do was worship the emperor, but to do this meant denying Christ.

"A faithful Christian named Ignatius, leader of the church in Antioch, and the man who introduced antiphonal singing in church, was arrested and brought here. He said before his death, 'Let fire and cross, let companies of wild beasts, let breaking of bones and tearing of limbs, let the grinding of the whole body, and all the malice of the devil, come upon me; be it so, only may I win Christ Jesus!' They placed him down there, in the arena." Mr. Pipes nodded his white head toward the labyrinth of now-exposed dungeons.

"Even from where we sit, the mobs sprang to their feet, jeering and mocking Ignatius as they waited impatiently for his bloody death. Suddenly, with an ominous clattering, levers and winches ground into motion; the sand-covered floor gaped

open in several places; everyone held his cruel breath in anticipation. Then, roaring with delight, the brutal crowds watched
hungry lions bolt from their cages and fall upon the man whose
only crime was loyalty to King Jesus. Someone recorded Ignatius's last words, spoken moments before he was devoured: 'I
am the wheat of Christ: I am about to be ground with the teeth of
wild beasts, that I may be found pure bread.'"

Annie blinked, trying to see through the mist welling up in
her eyes. Drew ground his teeth together and breathed heavily.
He felt afraid—and ashamed.

Mr. Pipes went on and told them the story of the apostle
John's disciple Polycarp, arrested and ordered by the Roman
proconsul to "Reproach Christ. Swear, and I will release you."
The old man replied before they tied him to the stake, "Eighty
and six years have I served him, and he never once wronged me;
how shall I blaspheme my King, who has saved me?"

Drew gazed at the shimmering heat waves rising from the
ruins across the arena. He wanted to have that kind of faith—to
be able to say and do the right thing, no matter what. But it was
hard.

"You said women and children died for the Lord Jesus," said
Annie.

"Many thousands whose names, this side of heaven, we will
never know," said Mr. Pipes. "And some whose names and stories we do know."

He went on and told them of the slave girl Blandina, whom
none of the wild beasts would touch. He told them of her faithfulness to the end under unimaginable sufferings; of the death
of Ponticus, a boy of fifteen; of the virtuous woman Julitta,
tortured and killed along with her baby; of thirteen-year-old
Agnus, beheaded for her refusal to deny Christ.

Just then an American tour guide stopped nearby and spoke
to a cluster of tourists: "Now, I know you've all heard that Christians were thrown to the lions in Roman arenas. Well—" she
laughed—"well, let me assure you, more recent historical research

proves that reports of Christians devoured by lions have been greatly exaggerated. In fact, it's likely that no Christians ever met death here—probably Roman officials found that the lions preferred—ah, shall we say, more *tender* meals than Christians."

The group of tourists erupted in laughter as they moved down the steps and out of earshot.

Hot tears stung Annie's cheeks; she brushed them away with her hand and bit her knuckle until it hurt.

Drew clenched his fists and rose to his feet, still breathing heavily. He stared hard after the laughing crowd.

Mr. Pipes looked over his glasses at them both.

"It took great patience to suffer what so many did suffer for our Lord. We are not called at this moment to be misused by lions for our Savior, but we must patiently bear the misuse and mockery of the world. May we do so, my dears, with patience and so honor our Lord Jesus."

"How did they do it?" asked Annie.

"Do what, my dear?"

"Stay true to the Lord," she answered, biting her lower lip.

Mr. Pipes studied Annie's wide eyes. In them he saw pity for those who had suffered so terribly, and he saw flickers of terror as she thought about dying in such ways.

"Ah, my dear," he began, patting her gently on the shoulder, "those early Christians bore one another's burdens, strengthening each other in their mutual trials."

"But how?" she persisted.

"It was the church," replied Mr. Pipes. "God's children, from the days of the apostles, gathered faithfully on the first day of the week—the Christian Sabbath—to pray, sing, worship, and listen to the Lord's voice in the preaching of his Word, and to partake of the Lord's Supper. Honoring their Lord together on his day gave them the strength to honor him in their mortal pain on the day of their death."

"But how could they do all that," asked Drew, "when Roman officials wanted to arrest them and throw them to the lions?"

"When persecution was less severe, they met openly in churches. When that was unsafe, they met in house churches and even in caves and catacombs—quite literally underground."

"But it was still dangerous for them to meet," said Annie.

"Oh, very much so indeed, my dear," agreed Mr. Pipes. "But the greater the persecution, the greater the need to join together in prayer and praise before the Lord."

"But things like singing," said Drew, "would give them away, wouldn't it?"

"Sometimes it did, no doubt. Nevertheless, the early church sang, be sure of it."

"What did they sing?" asked Annie.

"Yeah, they didn't have Watts and Wesley," added Drew.

"Of course they sang the psalms, like God's people of old," replied Mr. Pipes. "And there are a number of passages of Holy Scripture in the New Testament that must surely have been hymns sung by those earliest Christians."

Mr. Pipes got up and began climbing higher up the steps toward the upper tier of the Colosseum. The children followed.

"What Scriptures did they sing?" asked Drew, wiping perspiration from his forehead.

Mr. Pipes paused on the steps in thought and then, resuming his steady climbing, said, "Revelation 15:3-4, a very psalm-like text, most surely was sung. Imagine these sacred strains rising from those cages. Moments before our Christian brothers and sisters faced the rage of evildoers and their entrance into the heavenly city." He turned and gestured below to the arena, then lifted his hands heavenward and said,

> Great and marvelous are thy works,
>> O Lord God Almighty;
> Righteous and true are thy ways,
>> Thou King of the ages.
> Who shall fear, O Lord, and glorify thy name?
>> For thou alone art holy;

For all the nations shall come and worship before thee;
For thy righteous acts have been made manifest.

Annie looked down at the broken arena, trying to imagine it all. "So do you really think they sang from their prisons before," asked Annie, "well, you know, before they were killed?"

"Surely they did," said Mr. Pipes. "When Paul and Barnabas lay chained to their guards, they sang hymns through the night. And Christians, in trial or in triumph, have sung their praise and worship ever since. Maybe they sang responsively, as Ignatius taught his congregations in Antioch before his death here in Rome."

Annie gazed at the arena and imagined Christians' voices rising in song from dungeon to dungeon. "What about hymns that aren't in the Bible?" she asked. "Did the early Christians actually write poetry to the Lord and sing it?"

"Ah, Annie, a poet's question, indeed," said Mr. Pipes, smiling tenderly at her.

Before answering, he led them along a curving row of grass near the top of the Colosseum. The circle of the ruined edifice yawned widely, and the tourists looked like ants crawling around on the ruins far below. From around a bend in the ancient stone bleachers, a black wooden cross came into view. A moment later, Mr. Pipes stopped at the base of the cross and carefully took off his tweed jacket.

Annie stared at Mr. Pipes's clean white shirt and black necktie. Proper Mr. Pipes never took off his tweed jacket, no matter what activity they did with him—even fishing. But then, she couldn't remember its ever being this hot on their other adventures.

"We must find shade," said the old man, wiping his brow again. "Dr. Dudley will give me what-for if I remain in this sun any longer."

"Are you feeling sick?" said Annie, taking his arm and frowning with concern.

"Here, I'll carry your shoulder bag and coat," said Drew, glancing uneasily at their old friend.

"Now, don't you two go doting on my frailties," he said with a chuckle and a dismissive wave of his hand. "I feel perfectly fine—fine, that is, for my years."

They settled on the grass under the shadow of the worn stones of a nearby arch. Annie leaned against the warm stones and studied Mr. Pipes's face.

"I say, this is much better," he said, folding his jacket and using it for a pillow against the base of the stone arch.

"You're sure?" asked Annie.

"Truly, my dears," insisted the old man. "I forbid you to worry over my health."

"We're way up here!" said Drew, squinting down at the arena.

"These would have been the cheap seats," said Mr. Pipes. "Where the plebeians strained to see the gory spectacle far below."

"If I had to come," said Annie, shivering in spite of the heat, "I would have liked it better up here—it would seem less real."

Drew looked at his sister, then at Mr. Pipes.

"We'd have been down there," he said simply, nodding at the arena.

Annie bit her lip but made no reply.

Mr. Pipes looked at Annie's face and continued: "Christians from Jerusalem to Antioch, from Rome to Alexandria, faced dying for their faith. And one important way they united their hearts to bear their sufferings was by singing hymns."

"So maybe persecution actually encouraged poets to write hymns," said Annie.

"Indeed it did, my dear," said Mr. Pipes.

"Alexandria." Drew said the name slowly. "Was that a city named after that guy, what's-his-name? Alexander the—the Big?"

"The Great," corrected Annie.

"Someone called him Alexander the Pig," said Mr. Pipes with a laugh, "for the way he gobbled up other nations and states—Shakespeare, I believe it was. But yes, Alexandria was founded by Alexander the Great in 332 B.C. Eventually, Alexandria developed the greatest library of the ancient world and became the center of learning, with schools formed to teach every major philosophy and religion in the empire."

"So is that where the first poet learned to write poetry?" asked Annie.

"Some historians consider Alexandria the birthplace of noninspired hymnody. And sometime after A.D. 170, during a lull in persecution, a young man named Clement, yearning for knowledge, arrived in the city. He unexpectedly fell under the teachings of Christ at a school, and found his hunger for knowledge satisfied in the fear of the Lord—the beginning of wisdom. Later, he was appointed to be headmaster of the Christian school, where many students came under his teaching, including the early church father Origen. Clement wrote a book called *The Tutor*, wherein he described Christ, the ultimate teacher, and the children whom Christ teaches and his method of teaching them. After detailing considerable guidelines on Christian conduct for children, he concluded with a poem called 'A Hymn of the Savior.' Many consider it the oldest Christian hymn not taken directly from the words of the Bible."

Mr. Pipes paused and smiled at Annie and Drew.

Annie looked up at him from her leather sketchbook, a gift from Mr. Pipes last Christmas. And what a Christmas that had been. Mr. Pipes persuaded their parents for the first time to actually listen to the gospel. And she knew he prayed faithfully for her family. For this and so much more, she had come to feel a growing sense that Mr. Pipes was more than just a friend to them; he had become like a spiritual grandfather. She knew that Drew felt the same way.

"Oh, don't stop there," she begged. "How does it go?"

The old man opened his leather shoulder bag, drew out his hymnal, and, after adjusting his glasses, opened to the hymn. Drew looked over his shoulder at the words, and Annie studied Mr. Pipes's face as he began reading. She loved the way he read poetry, especially poetry filled with passionate praise. Mr. Pipes read in what Drew had come to call his all-or-nothing voice:

> Shepherd of tender youth,
> Guiding in love and truth
> Through devious ways:
> Christ, our triumphant King,
> We come thy Name to sing;
> Hither our children bring,
> To shout thy praise.

Eyebrows raised, he looked over the tops of his glasses at Annie and Drew. "Hither our children bring . . ." he mused to himself. Could they know how much he cared for them, he wondered, how fond he had become of them?

He continued reading:

> Thou art our holy Lord,
> The all-subduing Word,
> Healer of strife:
> Thou didst thyself abase,
> That from sin's deep disgrace
> Thou mightest save our race,
> And give us life.

> Thou art the Great High Priest,
> Thou hast prepared a feast
> Of heav'nly love—

He stopped and said: "Now, my dear ones, think of those martyrs—men and boys; the matron and the maid—who faced dying in this place, and in hundreds of arenas like this one, and called on the Lord for help and found him ever faithful.

> While in our mortal pain,
> None call on thee in vain:
> Help thou dost not disdain,
> Help from above.
>
> Ever be thou our Guide,
> Our Shepherd and our Pride,
> Our Staff and Song:
> Jesus, thou Christ of God,
> By thy perennial Word,
> Lead us where thou hast trod;
> Make our faith strong.
>
> So now and till we die,
> Sound we thy praises high,
> And joyful sing:
> Infants, and the glad throng
> Who to thy church belong,
> Unite to swell the song
> To Christ our King."

They sat silent for several moments, letting the words sink into their souls.

"It sounds like a hymn a Christian teacher would write," said Annie at last.

"He does sound pretty interested in kids," agreed Drew, digging in his knapsack distractedly.

"But it would be unfair to give Clement all the credit; he received considerable help from his American translator, Henry

Martyn Dexter," said Mr. Pipes. "Dexter, not only a good theologian, was clearly a gifted poet. In 1846, whilst preparing a sermon on the early church, he wrote this tender hymn using Clement's Greek poem as the basis."

"B-but what finally happened to Clement?" asked Annie, afraid to hear the answer.

"I fear that we do not know," replied Mr. Pipes. "Persecution of Christians resumed around A.D. 202, of which he wrote, 'Many martyrs are daily burned, confined, or beheaded, before our eyes.' He apparently fled Alexandria soon thereafter, but beyond that, very little is known of him."

Annie read the last lines of the hymn over again to herself: "Infants, and the glad throng / Who to thy church belong"—*what could that mean?*, she wondered. But before she could ask, Drew groaned:

"Oh! I'm dying of hunger! My stomach thinks my throat's been cut. Oh, Mr. Pipes, it's just gotta be past lunchtime—way past."

Mr. Pipes smiled at Drew as he wiped his glasses on his handkerchief and mopped perspiration from his brow. Drew, who was almost always dying of hunger, was no reliable measure of mealtimes.

"Yes, my boy, and we've lost our shade. Let us find a cool place for our first Italian midday meal."

"Lead the way!" said Drew, helping their friend to his feet.

*

In the courtyard of a nearby pizzeria, Mr. Pipes and Annie and Drew listened to the music of water gurgling from the mouth of a stone fish as it fell into a small pool. Above them, the muscular arms of wisteria seemed caught in a perpetual wrestling match with the trellis that filtered the sun and shaded the garden dining area from the afternoon heat.

Annie closed her eyes and inhaled the perfume dropping from the purple blossoms overhead.

"Oh, those flowers smell like heaven!" she said.

Drew glanced at his sister.

"Yeah, it smells like heaven," he agreed. "But that's *pizza* you smell."

He closed his eyes and sniffed the air: basil, tomato sauce, baking cheeses, and fresh pizza crust wafted from the brick ovens in the kitchen. His mouth watered and his stomach growled. Maybe Italy's not so bad after all, he decided. Staring hungrily at the table covered in starched linen and laid for serious eating, he fidgeted with his fork.

Then it arrived. A waiter set a plate-sized pizza in front of each of them. Drew swallowed several times as he stared in anticipation at the mozzarella and Parmesan cheeses, browned to perfection, smothering thick slices of Italian sausage.

Mr. Pipes folded his hands, bowed his white head, and offered thanks:

> Thou art the Great High Priest,
> Thou hast prepared a feast
> Of heav'nly love . . .

The children joined Mr. Pipes in a hearty "Amen!" Mr. Pipes lifted his head and, tucking his linen napkin under his chin, took up his knife and fork.

Drew dove into his pizza like someone who hadn't eaten for weeks.

Nodding at Annie's plate, Mr. Pipes said, "Do fall to, my dear. I fear what might befall us if Drew finishes eating before we even make a beginning!"

2
In the Catacombs

Hail, Gladdening Light

We hymn the Father, Son and Holy Spirit
  Divine
Worthiest art thou at all times to be sung
With undefiled tongue,
Son of our God, Giver of life, alone!
Therefore in all the world thy glories, Lord,
  they own.

(TRANSLATED BY JOHN KEBLE)

The next morning, Annie gripped Mr. Pipes's hand and
strained her eyes unblinkingly into the darkness. The morning
sunlight of the Via Appia now behind them, she inched her
feet forward into the black recesses of the narrow tunnel. The
only sound came from the scraping of their feet on the sandstone floor of the cavern. She heard Drew breathing heavily
behind her.

"Better watch out around the next corner," he hissed in her ear. "I'm sure I saw something sort of wispy peeking out at—at you."

"Kn-nock it off, Drew," said Annie, poking him in the ribs with her elbow.

Drew snickered. "Tut, tut. Remember, 'She who hates her brother walks in darkness.'"

"Now, Drew," Mr. Pipes's voice scolded out of the darkness, "one mustn't tamper with the text of Holy Scripture."

Annie reached out with her free hand to steady herself; her fingers touched the clammy dampness of the subterranean passage. She pulled back in alarm.

"I-is there going to be a light down here?" Her voice quavered and sounded hollow against the stone walls.

"I see a little light just ahead," said Drew, looking past his sister. "In fact, it looks like things open up into a bigger cave."

"Until then, I shall switch on my torch, my dear," said Mr. Pipes, fumbling in the blackness for his flashlight. Then he added to Annie, "My dear, you will need to relinquish your grip on my fingers, if you please, for only a moment, whilst I discover where I've stowed it."

Annie reluctantly let go. Mr. Pipes opened and closed his fingers until the blood began circulating and he regained some feeling in them. With a click, a shaft of light shone down the crude walls of the tunnel, casting eerie shadows on every side. They shuffled forward.

"I-it's so still." Annie attempted a laugh, but it sounded higher-pitched and louder than she had hoped.

"Quite still, indeed," agreed Mr. Pipes. "The English novelist Charles Dickens found the catacombs 'so sad, so quiet, so sullen; a desert of decay, somber and desolate.'"

With these words, he turned toward Annie, hoping to reassure her. Quivering light from his flashlight struck his face from below, casting grotesque shadows above his chin and nose. But worse yet, spidery shadows from his bushy eyebrows stretched menacingly onto his forehead.

Annie threw her hand up in an only partially successful attempt at stifling a squeal. Her hand knocked Mr. Pipes's arm. The flashlight clattered to the floor and went out.

"Nice work, Annie," said Drew. "Now we don't have any light."

"Surely we might use one of your torches," said Mr. Pipes, feeling on the cold stone floor for his flashlight.

Annie groaned. "I left mine back at our hotel by my bed."

"Hold the phone," said Drew. "I've got mine!"

Foil from chocolate bars rustled out of the darkness from where Drew stood, and Mr. Pipes and Annie heard the muffled thudding of contents from Drew's knapsack landing on the floor of the tunnel.

"Drew, my boy," said Mr. Pipes, "do be careful. All your portable property will lie strewn about the cave, never to be recovered."

"Whew! I hope he *does* lose some of it. What's that smell?" asked Annie. "We've only been traveling for a few days, and your backpack already smells like dirty socks. How do you do it?"

"Here it is!" Drew sang out in the darkness, ignoring his sister.

He flicked on his flashlight, and a dull amber light ventured a few feet into the darkness.

"Oh," he said. "I guess I sort of used it up last night."

"Reading under your blanket?" asked Annie.

"Fact is, I was writing a poem," said Drew, defensively.

"Indeed, I must see this poem," said Mr. Pipes. "That is, when light returns. Now, then, gather your things, Drew, join hands, and we shall make our way carefully toward Drew's hint of light. Yes, yes, I do believe I, too, see light just ahead."

*

"Ah, is this not better, Annie, my dear?" asked Mr. Pipes, smiling at her moments later.

Annie did feel better in the warm glow of the terra-cotta lamps shining on the decorated walls of the tiny underground chapel into which the tunnel had opened.

With a sigh of relief she smiled in return. "And it's so pretty here with all these wall paintings. Who did them, and what do they mean?"

"Yeah, and they've got to be really old," added Drew, running his hand along a painted ledge with words Drew couldn't understand etched into the rock.

"Do you see the three symbols adorning that archway?" asked Mr. Pipes. "The early Christians painted them as visual reminders of the foundations of their faith and of Christian virtues taught and practiced by Christ and his followers."

"The cross must have reminded Christians of Jesus' death for their salvation," said Annie. "But what does the bird mean— looks like it might be a dove?"

"You will remember from your reading in Scripture," replied Mr. Pipes, "that the Holy Spirit descended like a dove upon Jesus after his baptism. The dove symbol also reminded early Christians of eternal rest, inspired by the psalmist's longing, 'Oh that I had the wings of a dove! I would fly away and be at rest.'"

"How about the anchor painted next to the cross?" said Drew. "It's shaped a bit different from *Toplady's* anchor, but it must be an anchor." Drew thought of fishing and sailing back in England on the quiet waters of The River Great Ouse in Mr. Pipes's little boat.

"Indeed, it is an anchor," replied Mr. Pipes. "Early Christians suffering for their faith in the Lord used an anchor to symbolize their sure and steadfast hope in Christ and the promises of eternal glory with him."

"I get it," said Drew, remembering how Mr. Pipes had taught them to set *Toplady's* anchor securely in the mud along the banks of the river. "If you don't have an anchor, you lose the boat with the current."

"Yes, my boy. And when a storm descends on a ship anchored in harbor, the anchor keeps the ship from smashing to pieces on the rocky shore. Important things are anchors. Yes, the Christian's hope was sure and certain when firmly set on Christ's redeeming work alone."

"How about those fish?" asked Drew, brightening as he pointed to a pattern of fish drawn above a shallow alcove set in the wall. "What do they stand for?"

Setting his shoulder bag down on a worn shelf, Mr. Pipes smiled at Drew.

"I knew you'd ask," said Mr. Pipes. "For your answer I must give you a Greek lesson."

"Huh?" said Drew.

"Greek?" said Annie.

Mr. Pipes laughed. "You see, the fish symbol is in part based on the Greek word for 'fish': *Ichthys.*"

"But what's so important about fish?" asked Annie.

Drew frowned at his sister.

"But there must be some other reason why they used a fish," said Annie.

"Indeed, there is," said Mr. Pipes. "Several theories predom-inate, but most likely it stems from many of the apostles' making their living as fishermen."

"And didn't Jesus tell them," added Drew, "to be fishers of men? I like that part."

"He did," replied Mr. Pipes. "And St. Augustine explained this most beloved symbol as derived from the parallel of Christ living 'without sin in the abyss of this mortality as in the depth of waters.' In any case, the symbol may have first appeared in Alexandria and was often mentioned by Clement. As you can see," he said, turning around slowly in the decorated chapel and pointing at the many fish symbols, "Roman Christians used this symbol throughout their catacombs."

Annie turned around, gazing at the dim ceiling and crude arches adorned with simple paintings commemorating the per-secutions and triumphs of the early saints.

"What did they do in these caves?" asked Annie.

"From time to time they met underground for worship," replied Mr. Pipes. He looked carefully at Annie as if trying to decide if she was ready for what he had to say next. "But the hundreds of miles of catacombs zigzagging underneath Rome were principally tombs where Christians, who rejected the pagan practice of cremation, buried their dead loved ones."

Annie moved closer to Mr. Pipes in the dim cavern.

"So they buried dead people down here?" asked Drew, slowly.

"Thousands upon thousands of them, and for several centuries," replied Mr. Pipes.

"Did you say hundreds of miles of tunnels?" asked Drew.

"You could get lost," said Annie in hushed tones, "d-down here."

"Did the Romans let them do it?" asked Drew.

"Yes and no," said Mr. Pipes. "They were happy for Christians to dispose of their own dead; that saved the Romans the trouble of doing it. But worship of Christ was forbidden and of course Christians worshiped the Lord when they buried their dead."

"How did they find their way in all those miles of caves?" asked Annie.

"That's where the fish symbol helped out again," said Mr. Pipes. "When a Christian met another person but wasn't sure if he was a follower of Christ, as they talked, the Christian might casually draw part of a fish in the sand with his foot; if the other man responded by finishing the symbol with his foot, they talked openly. Plans could be discussed and directions given for where Christians would be meeting. Some of the gatherings in the catacombs were marked with a fish, its head pointing which way to turn in the dizzying labyrinth of tunnels."

"Wow! It would have been fun to live back then," said Drew, his eyes sparkling in the light of the terra-cotta lamps.

Annie and Mr. Pipes turned and looked at him incredulously.

"Drew, you mustn't forget their suffering," said Mr. Pipes.

"Oh, I suppose that would take some of the fun out of it," said Drew.

They sat silently in the cavern for several moments. Then Annie asked, "Did they sing—when they buried people?"

"These very walls rang with their singing, my dear. I imagine that when a mother and father laid their young child to rest in a burial niche along these walls, they might have sung 'Christ our triumphant king, we come thy name to sing, hither our children bring. . . .' "

Annie and Drew hummed along with the old man as he sang several lines from the hymn.

In the stillness that followed, Annie sighed. She looked around the simple cave chapel and decided that it wasn't quite so scary down here as she had first thought. She, too, imagined the cavern filled with grieving loved ones, whispering condolences and not quite meeting the eyes of the mourning parents; she felt something of their hope in the Lord Jesus who rose from the dead. Then, as she studied the walls of the cave, she caught sight of another crude drawing.

"I know it's dark in the catacombs," she said, "but what does that lamp symbol represent?"

"Yeah," said Drew. "Just painting one on the wall doesn't help with the lighting problem down here."

"I believe you might know the answer to your own question, my dears," replied Mr. Pipes. "What were God's first words recorded in the Bible?"

"Let there be light!" said Annie.

"And didn't Jesus call himself the Light of the world?" added Drew.

"Yes, to you both," said Mr. Pipes. "And of the Bible the psalmist wrote, 'Thy word is a lamp to my feet and a light to my path.' Throughout Scripture Christ dispels the darkness and sin of the soul, just as the light of a lamp dispels the darkness in a room."

"Or in a catacomb," added Drew.

"Early Christians celebrated Lord's Day evening worship services," continued Mr. Pipes, "on some occasions right here in the catacombs, with a symbolic lighting of the lamps. Ministers and elders lit a candle and passed its flame to the unlit candle held by each member of the congregation, thus symbolizing the flame of the gospel of Christ passed from one sinner to the next through the preaching of the good news, and so throughout the world."

"Oh, I can just see it," said Annie. "The warm glow of candlelight filling these chambers—and that dark tunnel we came through. It must have been lovely."

"No doubt it was a most moving ceremony," agreed Mr. Pipes.

"What did they do while lighting all those candles?" asked Drew.

"Ah, they sang," replied Mr. Pipes.

"With instruments?" asked Drew. "I can't imagine there ever being an organ down here."

"No organs in the catacombs," agreed Mr. Pipes with a chuckle. "Organs came later when Christians gained the freedom to build churches and worship openly without persecution. No, those early saints sang unassisted by instruments. But cast your mind back to a service, perhaps here in this chamber. What with the solemnity of the tombs of the martyred dead lining the walls, the quivering flames of candles, the worshipers uniting their voices in praise—it must have seemed, very much indeed, like heaven."

"What did they sing?" asked Annie.

"Most scholars agree that the hymn 'Hail, Gladdening Light' must have been one of the very earliest written. It was most likely sung by rich and poor, senator and slave, united in the worship of Christ, as each Lord's Day drew to its close throughout the empire."

"How's it go?" asked Drew.

Mr. Pipes hummed a chantlike melody that began softly and then rose and fell, steadily getting louder until his voice seemed to soar.

"Now let us blend the melody with its grand words," he said, clearing his throat. "But to sing as our early fore-bears did, one must learn to chant several syllables on the same note. Do listen first, and then we shall sing together," he said.

Annie and Drew listened as Mr. Pipes chanted the first six words without any note change; his voice then rose and fell with the simple melody.

> Hail, gladdening Light, of his pure glory pour'd
> Who is th'immortal Father, heav'nly, blest,
> Holiest of Holies, Jesus Christ, our Lord!
> Now we are come to the sun's hour of rest—

He broke off and explained, "These next lines grow louder, ris-ing with real energy to 'We hymn the Father,' and so forth." He demonstrated:

> The lights of evening 'round us shine;
> We hymn the Father, Son and Holy Spirit Divine.

"This next line is chanted more softly, then swells to 'Son of our God . . .' And the last two lines rise to an ecstasy of praise calculated to thrill the very soul.

> Worthiest art thou at all times to be sung
> With undefiled tongue,
> Son of our God, Giver of life, alone:
> Therefore in all the world
> Thy glories, Lord, they own."

"I can almost hear them singing," said Annie.

"This is a grand expression of worship, indeed, and most worthy of its object," agreed Mr. Pipes. "Now, shall we join our voices with theirs?"

"Oh, yes. I only wish we had candles," said Annie, her eyes sparkling in the dim light of the lamps.

"And an organ wouldn't hurt," said Drew.

For several moments, the ancient sandstone cavern rang with their singing. When they had sung through the hymn several times, Annie asked, "Who wrote the poetry?"

"We do not know, my dear," replied Mr. Pipes, shouldering his leather bag. "With persecution pressing them on every side, early Christians wrote none of their hymns down until much later. But who actually wrote these psalmlike words remains a mystery."

"Too bad," said Annie. "But it is a lovely hymn."

"You know," said Drew, falling in behind Annie and Mr. Pipes as they walked back into the dark tunnel, "the words talk about the Father, Son, and Holy Spirit, but mostly about the Son, I think. Why is that?"

"Well observed, my boy," said Mr. Pipes, nodding his white head approvingly. "The hymn-writer wanted to clarify the important doctrine of the deity of Jesus Christ—that he is fully God, a truth rejected by Jews and Roman pagans."

Annie's grip on Mr. Pipes's hand tightened as they left the light of the underground chapel behind. With a sigh of relief she caught sight of a spot of sunlight against the wall. And moments later they stepped out into the remains of the Villa Quintili, the bone-white ruins of the ancient town warm from the late-morning sun.

"Furthermore," said Mr. Pipes, resting against the fluted remains of an ancient column, "those who have made it their life's work to study the great hymns have observed three important functions served by them. The first is codifying doctrine, in this case, that Jesus is God—giver of life alone."

"You told us about the importance of doctrine in hymns last Christmas, remember?" said Annie.

"Yeah," said Drew. "Wasn't it Ray Palmer whose hymns included important doctrinal truths when much of the church didn't like the doctrinal part of Christianity anymore?"

"Yes, indeed, it was Palmer," said Mr. Pipes. "Most of the hymn-writers of the Reformation, along with Watts, Newton, and so many others, understood that without the objective doctrines of Christianity, we have no basis for our praise. And one of the strengths of hymns is their ability to adorn—to show the beauty of—the great and high doctrines of Holy Scripture."

"What else do hymns do?" asked Drew.

"Hymns should be able to be sung by everyone," said Mr. Pipes, "not only those living at any given time. In fact, great hymns will be sung by generations of Christians, thus unifying the body of Christ from age to age."

"Like we just did in the catacombs," said Drew, rifling through his knapsack.

"And as I trust you will continue to do throughout your lives," replied Mr. Pipes. "One hymn-writer put it like this: 'In lofty songs exalt his name, in songs as lasting as his love.' Do not settle for whimsical praise, enslaved to the changeable tastes of a moment."

"Drew, what are you looking for?" asked Annie.

"Oh, nothing. Only I think I might just keel over and die from hunger, that's all," said Drew, wincing as he rubbed his stomach. "D'you have anything in your knapsack?"

Annie pulled out three sandwiches wrapped in plain brown paper, three bottles of mineral water, and three apples. She arranged the little picnic on a slab of ancient marble.

"Now, what was it you and Mr. Pipes were going to eat?" asked Drew, grinning as he sat down on the grass near the food.

Annie rolled her eyes.

"Any chocolate?" asked her brother.

"After we've eaten the real food," said Annie.

Then, turning back to Mr. Pipes, she said, "Now, let me see if I can guess the last function of hymns." She narrowed her eyes in thought. "Would it be glorifying God?"

"Precisely," said Mr. Pipes. "Hymns must be written in such a way that the glory of God is their clear object. Thus, timeless hymns, ones that endure and should endure, lift our mind and heart above ourselves to God."

"'To lead us from ourselves to thee,'" quoted Annie, leaning against a warm slab of marble and gazing at a wispy cloud passing lazily overhead. "That was in one of the hymns you taught us last Christmas at Whittier's house."

"Which phrase almost perfectly expresses," agreed Mr. Pipes, "the third function of great hymns: they are written to help worshipers turn away from themselves and to the Lord."

"Mr. Pipes, I'm afraid that if we don't eat lunch, Drew's going to pass out—or pretend to," said Annie.

"I believe you might be correct, my dear," said Mr. Pipes, smiling as he looked at Drew's fluttering eyes and feigned agony.

When Mr. Pipes finished leading them in prayer, Drew asked, "What kind of sandwiches?"

"Pig," said Annie, grinning and looking directly at her brother.

"That's my kind of sandwich," laughed Drew, unwrapping his and taking a bite.

"I almost can't get my mouth around it," said Annie, turning the thick slices of bread this way and that, looking for the thinnest part.

"Oh," said Drew, "this bread is so fresh and crumbly. And the ham is just right: stringy with lots of mustard."

"You might want to use a napkin on some of that mustard," said Annie, pointing at a smear of yellow on Drew's chin.

"*Porchetta*, I believe Italians call roasted pig," said Mr. Pipes, swallowing and dusting breadcrumbs off his lap. "And it does make a lovely luncheon for us."

"An' for them!" said Drew, his mouth full as he pointed excitedly at three or four bright green lizards scurrying across the marble and darting away with the crumbs.

"Eek!" cried Annie, nearly spilling her bottle of mineral water. "Do they bite?"

"No, indeed," said Mr. Pipes, gently lifting one and studying it in his hand. "They are most friendly creatures and nearly as tame as my dear cat, Lord Underfoot."

"Really?" said Drew, cupping both hands and inching toward one of the lizards. "Gotcha!" he said, lifting one by its long green tail.

"Oh, don't hurt it," said Annie, torn between revulsion and curiosity.

"Here, Annie," said her brother, "you can hold him—he's not even slimy."

Annie shuddered, but held out her hand hesitantly. Drew slid the little green body onto Annie's hand. The lizard lay prone on her fingers, only its throat moving in and out as it breathed. She cautiously brought the little creature closer to her face to get a better look.

"Oh, you're so cute!" she said softly.

Mr. Pipes looked at Annie's face and stopped smiling. He looked back at the lizard and blinked several times. A slight frown crept over his face.

"And most happy, I am sure," he said, clearing his throat, "when left to his own devices in the wild."

Drew caught two more lizards and wrapped them loosely in his sandwich wrapper along with a mound of bread crumbs recovered from their picnic.

"These guys like us," he said. "Did you see how easy it was to catch them?"

"I think they might be hungry," said Annie, lightly stroking her lizard with her finger.

"Surely not, my dears," said Mr. Pipes, blinking rapidly now and looking from side to side like a cornered animal trying to escape.

"And I'll bet you don't ever get enough food here in the wild," continued Annie, in her best wounded-victim tone of voice, her nose nearly touching the lizard's. "Oh, you sweet little thing."

Drew looked at his sister and then back at the lizard. He scratched his head.

"They're *lizards*, Annie," he said.

"I know. Oh, Mr. Pipes, can't we take them with us?" begged Annie. "It'll be way easier than a kitten. Please?"

"Your kitten found in Germany last summer," said Mr. Pipes, "if I may remind you, proved to be considerable trouble—as did your pet skunk last Christmas."

"Oh, I do hope the caretaker at Whittier's house," said Annie, "is taking good care of Monochrome."

"But Mr. Pipes, you said lizards make good pets," said Drew.

"Surely I said no such thing!" said Mr. Pipes. "But my dears, lizards? It could prove most inconvenient."

"So you'll let us?" said Annie. And without waiting for an answer, she handed Drew her lizard and threw her arms around Mr. Pipes. "Oh, thank you!"

The rest of that afternoon they spent making a lizard cage. Drew found a scrap of wire screen in a garbage can behind a shop that repaired windows. And, with many gestures, Annie asked the owner of another shop for a small wooden box they found discarded in the alley behind his wine shop. Protesting all the while, Mr. Pipes soon found himself making suggestions and then actually assisting Annie and Drew as they constructed a portable home for four green lizards.

3
Crash and Burn!

O Light That Knew No Dawn
(Gregory of Nazianzen)
Of the father's Love Begotten
(Prudentius)

from sin thy child in mercy free,
And let me dwell in light with thee.

"Might I make so bold as to suggest," said Mr. Pipes, next morning at their hotel as they packed their knapsacks for another day of adventure in Rome. He looked hard at the awkward lizard cage that Drew held in his hand before continuing. "I say, might I suggest that we leave the little darlings here, by the open window. Jostling about on mopeds is just not the thing for lizards; I am most certain they would not enjoy it in the least."

"But won't they starve?" asked Annie, holding the cage at arm's length and then clucking her tongue piteously at their new pets.

"Thus far in life, they do seem to have done rather nicely looking after themselves," observed Mr. Pipes. "Furthermore, I

50

do wonder if eating establishments—" he broke off, looking sideways at Drew. "That is to say, if eating establishments will not frown on our dinner guests being four writhing green lizards—perhaps frown on it to the extremity of disallowing us a table."

"You mean," said Drew, looking worried, "not—not let us eat?"

"Precisely my meaning, dear boy," said Mr. Pipes, shaking his head.

"That settles it, Annie," said Drew. "The lizards stay. We've already put lots of food in their cage. It'll be best for them all around."

Annie agreed and they set off on their mopeds.

"Mr. Pipes," said Annie, fifteen minutes later as they locked their mopeds against an iron grating rimming the promenade that followed the banks of the Tiber River. "I've been thinking about what you said yesterday."

"Yes, my dear?" said Mr. Pipes.

"He said a lot of things yesterday," said Drew. "Could you narrow it down a bit?"

"About hymns being written to glorify God," continued Annie, ignoring her brother, "and the other characteristics of hymns."

They paused to watch a young street artist as he set out his chalk and sketched an outline on the sidewalk.

"Oh, this looks interesting," said Annie. "Could we stay and watch him for a few minutes?"

"Certainly," said Mr. Pipes.

They sat on a nearby park bench and watched the artist as he wrote the word *Grazie* in large letters on the pavement. He plunked a tin bowl down beside the word, rubbed his hands briskly together, and then walked around the outlined space, stroking his chin in thought.

"He will be at his drawing for some time," said Mr. Pipes. "What was it you were thinking about, Annie?"

"Well, we sing some things at the worship center with our neighbors, the Smiths," she continued, "that I'm just not sure fit those functions of hymns you told us about."

"Oh, yeah," agreed Drew. "I'm beginning to see more and more differences with the hymns you teach us and the stuff we sing in church. And you know something, it makes it kind of hard to invite our mom and dad to church; sometimes I'm not sure they'd hear quite the same message."

"I do pray often for them," said Mr. Pipes, "and that you, my dear ones, might faithfully shine the light of Christ's gospel to them. But are they any more willing to discuss the things of God with you?" he asked.

"Oh, yes," said Annie. "Since your talk with them last Christmas, at least, sometimes now they will listen. And Dad reads each of your letters, Mr. Pipes, over and over again. I've even heard him reading parts of them out loud to Mom."

"I shall continue to write him, then," said Mr. Pipes, smiling. "But what songs are sung at your church that you don't want your dear parents to hear?"

"Remember that one, Drew?" said Annie. "How did it go? 'You are my wholeness, you are my completeness ...' Something like that."

"Sounds a little mushy to me," said Drew.

"Well, now, Drew," said Mr. Pipes. "Don't be too quick to throw it out. Let me hear more."

Drew wrinkled his brow, frowned up at the blue sky, and began reciting:

In you I find forgiveness,
Yes, in you I find release.
It's a wonder you take all those blunders I make
And so graciously offer me peace.

"Blunders, is it?" said Mr. Pipes, his white eyebrows splaying upward.

"I wondered about that, too," said Annie. "'Blunders' doesn't sound so bad as 'sins,' does it?"

"No, indeed," agreed Mr. Pipes. "Do go on; surely it improves." Annie continued where Drew left off:

> And in you I find true friendship,
> Yes, your love is so free of demands
> Though it must hurt you so,
> You keep letting me go
> To discover the person I am.

Mr. Pipes's brow furrowed. "Do repeat that; surely I misunderstood."

Annie repeated the lines.

"You actually sing this in a Christian church?" asked Mr. Pipes, getting the words out with some difficulty. "This quite clearly turns things all around: God is *man's* completeness on *man's* road to self-discovery."

"I'm not sure the poetry's so good, either," said Annie.

"Oh, if I heard you correctly, you are most right, Annie," said Mr. Pipes, running his fingers several times through his white hair. "All truly great poetry makes us *less* self-referential and gives us an enlargement of perspective. But in this chorus, the one singing seems much more concerned with self-fulfillment than with worshiping God."

"Yeah," said Drew. "The Bible doesn't sound like this."

"Indeed," agreed Mr. Pipes. "What is more," he continued, "I doubt Christian martyrs could have sung the line, 'Your love is so free of demands,' considering all that following Christ cost them."

"Oh," said Annie, biting her lip. "That makes singing this almost a mockery of their suffering."

"So much for unifying the church," said Drew.

"Indeed," agreed Mr. Pipes. "The persecuted church now or in any age could not and I daresay *would* not sing this—forgive me, children—this *rubbish.*"

"And there's not much—if any—doctrine," said Annie. "There's really not much said about God at all."

"Are you quite certain you didn't just hear this on popular radio?" asked Mr. Pipes incredulously. "I fear that it sounds much more like its author found his inspiration in a psychology textbook than from the pages of Holy Scripture. Oh, surely this is not sung in the high worship of God. I am almost afraid to ask, but is there more?"

" 'Fraid so," said Drew. "Maybe you ought to sit down?" he suggested before reciting:

And like a father you long to protect me,
Yet you know I must learn on my own
Well, I made my own choice,
To follow your voice
Guiding me unto my home.

"Shocking, truly shocking!" said Mr. Pipes, shaking his head.

"Eject! Eject! We're going down!" yelled Drew, extending his arms like wings and making the sound of a bomber plummeting to the earth. "This one sure crashes and burns on the doctrinal function of hymns."

"I fear for Christians who would sing this," agreed Mr. Pipes, furrowing his brow. "When we praise ourselves for making our own choice of God instead of praising God for making his sovereign choice of us, we turn the Bible's message all around. I am simply all astonishment that true Christians would sing this kind of spiritual treachery and not realize that they, alas, no longer sing to the glory of God but to the glory of themselves."

"Pretty much loses on all fronts," said Drew. "Hey, I never noticed before, but it doesn't ever mention the name of God or Jesus."

"A rather serious omission, I should think," said Mr. Pipes.

"I wonder if the Romans would have killed Christians if the church had just worshiped and sung like this," said Drew. "You know, they wouldn't have actually been breaking the law by worshiping Christ as God; you could plug in any god for the pronouns. I'll bet this wouldn't have offended anyone, not even those pagan Romans."

"There isn't much left," agreed Annie. "But I do think lots of people sing these choruses and still love the Lord Jesus."

"Yes, for now they still do, no doubt," agreed Mr. Pipes. "But why allow this kind of man-centered mumbo jumbo to erode the high worship of God? It can only dilute and eventually destroy true faith. That is why sung worship must codify doctrine, unify the body of Christ in all ages, and have as its object the glory of God, not the glory of man. It has been observed that church music in which any one of these essential functions goes missing 'will have the short life of all rootless things.'"

"Hey!" said Drew. "I've got a good way to remember this: codify, unify, and glorify! How's that?"

"Very clever, Drew," said Mr. Pipes.

"But this one doesn't do any of that," said Annie.

"And thus, may this unworthy chorus," said Mr. Pipes, "and all like it, have the shortest possible existence."

"He's still walking around rubbing his chin," said Drew, nodding at the street artist.

"Waiting for inspiration, no doubt," said Mr. Pipes.

"It looks like there's another artist working just down the river," said Annie. "Maybe he's actually drawing something."

Moments later they stared dumbly down at the sidewalk. This artist sat cross-legged and barefooted in the middle of his work, his pants all smeared with blue, red, and yellow chalk. Gripping several pieces of chalk in each hand, he made multicolored circles, jagged lines, or twisted shapes apparently as the mood suited him. With blotches of chalk on each cheek, he smiled up at them and continued vigorously moving his arms. Then he paused and carefully placed chalk in between his toes. Staring soberly up at them, as if this next technique required deep concentration, he randomly swirled his feet and arms, leaving a trail of colored scribbles behind on the sidewalk. Drew decided that the man looked like a land crab crawling over a garbage dump.

Grinning and nodding, Mr. Pipes and Annie and Drew backed cautiously away and quickened their steps down the promenade.

"Now, this is real art!" said Annie in wonder a few minutes later as she squatted down for a better look.

Mr. Pipes dropped several lire into this artist's bowl.

"*Grazie!*" said the artist, without looking up.

"He's really good," said Drew, fishing in his pocket for some coins.

"He's got every muscle just right," said Annie, gazing at the drawing.

"He sure does. Who's he drawing?" asked Drew.

"This young artist," began Mr. Pipes, "has got it right. He is using the great master artists' work for a model. He's drawing the *Creation of Adam*, the central scene from Michelangelo's Sistine Chapel."

"So if that's Adam, there on the left," said Annie slowly, "that'd be God on the right? Is it okay to paint God?"

"That is an important question disputed by the church for centuries," replied Mr. Pipes. "The Roman Catholic Church came down on the side of the argument that says it is wrong to make icons—images of God—and to pray to the images. Roman Catholics, nevertheless, make images of saints and bow down and pray to them. Michelangelo, the great Renaissance artist, painted three hundred figures in a chapel, retelling biblical history from creation to the last judgment. The *Creation of Adam*, reproduced skillfully here, is the most magnificent of all."

"So they didn't worship it, did they?" asked Annie.

"No, not officially," replied Mr. Pipes. "But in the Renaissance a growing number of people elevated man's splendor above God's; they turned things around as many do today."

"I love the hands extended like that," said Annie. "It looks so lifelike."

"But the artist didn't get it really right," said Drew, scowling at the drawing.

"What do you mean?" asked Mr. Pipes.

"Well, he's got Adam helping out in his own creation. You know, extending his hand out to meet God's. That's not how it happened."

"How right you are, my boy," said Mr. Pipes, smiling and looking intently at Drew. "Nor does the light of grace and salvation come with our participation. It is all God's doing, his gracious gift."

"It reminds me of the first thing God said in the Bible," said Drew.

"Let there be light," said Annie, dropping a handful of coins into the bowl.

They turned and made their way back along the Tiber. Drew looked intently at the river, the great dome of St. Peter's and Vatican City reflecting dully in the muddy waters. He wondered if the fishing was any good.

Mr. Pipes drew a quick breath. "That reminds me of another important hymn of the early church, long before all this was around." With a frown he stretched his hand toward the domes and spires, and the noise and bustle of the city. "Another hymn on the all-important theme of light."

As they unlocked their mopeds, Mr. Pipes said, "Would you care to find a quiet place and have a snack?"

"Would we ever!" said Annie and Drew.

"I do believe they sell Italian gelato there," he continued.

"Don't know what *gelato* is," said Drew. "But it sounds like something good to eat." He strapped on his helmet. "Lead the way; I'll do my best to keep up."

"Watch out for flower pots!" called Annie to her brother as they buzzed out into the traffic.

Half an hour later they found themselves surrounded by tree-lined pathways and marble statues guarding the shores of a little lake, their white reflections shimmering in the quiet water.

"Now, this is the part of Rome I like," said Annie, her eyes shining as she took in the beauty all around them.

"Is that an island?" asked Drew, pointing to a cluster of trees flanking a sixteenth-century temple.

"More properly called an islet, I should think," replied Mr. Pipes.

"And those look like boats!" said Drew. "They don't have sails, but do you think we could rent one and row out to the island?"

"A lovely idea, indeed," said Mr. Pipes.

Moments later, Drew smiled as he fitted the oars into place and scooted to the exact middle of the rowing thwart. He braced his feet and opened and closed his hands on the oars in anticipation. The boat bobbed from side to side as Annie and Mr. Pipes stepped on board and sat on the wide stern thwart.

"Everybody set?" he asked.

"Carry on, Drew," said Mr. Pipes, casting off the mooring line.

Drew dipped his oars carefully into the water and pulled.

After several strokes he said, "She's a bit sluggish." He glanced over his shoulder and then turned back and sighted along Mr. Pipes's white head and the top of a tall poplar tree. He took several more strokes, straightening out waggles in his course by lining up the tree with Mr. Pipes's head.

"She's not *Toplady*," said Annie, remembering the graceful lines of Mr. Pipes's boat tied snugly to the stone pier in front of his cottage back in England.

"Hired boats are built to withstand the hazards of the reckless and inexperienced," said Mr. Pipes. "But for all that, she's not bad."

"I suppose not, but she's not *Mayflower II* or *Old Ironsides*," said Drew, thinking of their tour of those famous American sailing ships. "You know what I'd like to do someday?"

"Tell us, Drew," said Mr. Pipes.

"I'd like to actually go to sea on a sailing ship." Water dripped from the oars as Drew halted for a moment; a faraway expression came over his face.

"Me, too," agreed Annie, a little less enthusiastically.

"Perhaps some day you shall," said Mr. Pipes. "But meanwhile, we have a seaworthy little craft beneath us and a lovely lake to explore. No wishing needed here. Let us enjoy."

Annie closed her eyes and felt the warm Italian sun on her face. She trailed her fingers in the lake and listened to the chattering of the water against the stout wooden planking of the boat.

Drew adjusted course by making two strokes with his starboard oar; he smiled as he grew more used to the heavy old vessel.

The trees along the shore of the lake were alive with songbirds, and Mr. Pipes breathed deeply and joined them, humming several bars of music.

"What are you humming?" asked Annie.

"Is it the other hymn about light you mentioned?" asked Drew, without missing a stroke.

"Indeed it is," said Mr. Pipes.

"Do you know who wrote this one?" asked Annie.

"Yes," replied Mr. Pipes, sitting back, adjusting his glasses and looking at the sky. "Fellow by the name of Gregory: Gregory of Nazianzen. Born around A.D. 325, his saintly mother, Nonna, a woman renowned for her life of prayer, taught him early in life to know and love the Bible. Eventually, Nonna's faithful witness led to the conversion of her husband, who one day became a bishop.

"In school, Gregory was a classmate of Julian, a future emperor of Rome. Later, after studying in Alexandria for several years, he took ship for Athens, planning to continue his studies. Whilst crossing the Mediterranean Sea, however, a violent storm arose with such fury that even the seasoned sailors gave up hope of saving the ship or anyone on it."

"You can sail on the Mediterranean Sea from Italy, can't you?" asked Drew.

"Yes, of course," replied Mr. Pipes.

"Does it often have storms?" asked Annie.

"From time to time," said Mr. Pipes. "But just when all seemed lost for Gregory, the storm ended and the ship made it safe to Athens."

"Sounds like John Newton's storm," said Drew.

"And like Newton," said Mr. Pipes, "Gregory gave God the glory and came to see his deliverance as a fresh call to live a life devoted to God. Though all around him urged him to go into the Christian ministry, he preferred the life of an ascetic—a life of solitude and prayer. Eventually, unable to resist the urgings of his father and church leaders, Gregory became the Bishop of Constantinople."

"That name sounds sort of familiar," said Annie.

"Constantine . . ." said Drew slowly. "Wasn't he an emperor of Rome?"

"Very good, Drew; he was," said Mr. Pipes. "But unlike earlier emperors, he was more sympathetic toward Christians. In A.D. 312, after claiming to see a vision of the cross the night before a battle fought just north of Rome, he defeated his last imperial rival. He gave the Christians' God credit for the victory and issued an edict the next year granting freedom of worship to Christians."

"After all they'd suffered," said Annie, "that must've made all the Christians very happy."

"No doubt it did," agreed Mr. Pipes. "The Edict of Milan removed any 'let or hindrance' to worship and now made it a crime for anyone to trouble or molest Christians."

"So Gregory was a bishop after the persecution ended," said Drew.

"Yes, but now trouble came for the church in the form of doctrinal attack," continued Mr. Pipes. "A group called Arians denied that Jesus was fully God. But God raised up many champions to defend the truth of Scripture at just this point of attack. Christians defended the doctrine of Jesus' eternal existence—'begotten of the Father before all worlds'—and the Arians insisted that Jesus' life had begun at his birth in Bethlehem."

"But if the Arians were right," said Annie, "Jesus' death on the cross couldn't do any of us any good."

"That is true," said Mr. Pipes. "But in the Nicene Creed, the defenders of the truth declared Jesus 'Light of light, very God of very God . . . being of one substance with the Father.' The entire creed has been set to a rousing melody and may be sung as a glorious declaration of faith in our triune God—the three in one."

"I've never really understood," said Annie, frowning, "how that works."

"Do you mean the Trinity?" asked Mr. Pipes.

"Yes, I just don't understand how God can be one and three at the same time."

"'Tis a great mystery," agreed Mr. Pipes. "But it is a mystery clearly taught in Scripture and essential to the Christian faith. In John chapter 10 Jesus declared 'I and the Father are one—'"

"Hey, that's bad grammar," said Drew.

"Ah, and it is in Jesus' grammar," said Mr. Pipes, "where lies the key to the mystery: God is one, and Jesus and the Holy Spirit—co-equal, co-eternal, the same in substance, yet separate—are also one with him."

"That still leaves a lot I don't understand," said Annie.

"Scripture declares the mystery in the clearest light that we mortals can grasp," replied Mr. Pipes. "What we cannot see, dim as our mortal eyes are to eternal truth, we accept by faith. And thus, while Arians worked hard at bringing God down to the level of our understanding, Gregory and others helped lift our understanding to the praise of a God who is gloriously and infinitely above us."

"So what did Gregory do to fight against the Arians?" said Drew.

"Ah, he wrote a great hymn," said Mr. Pipes, "a poetic adornment of the doctrine of the Trinity."

"Can we hear it?" asked Annie.

"You shall. Notice how Gregory begins with a defiant salvo against Arian heresy."

The old man ran his hand through his white hair, and Drew rested on his oars so that he could hear better. Mr. Pipes hummed softly for a moment and then sang the first verse in his clear voice:

> O Light that knew no dawn,
> That shines from endless day,
> All things in earth and heav'n
> Are lustred by thy ray;
> No eye can to thy throne ascend,
> Nor mind thy brightness comprehend.

He paused.

"The light would be Jesus, right?" said Annie.

"And shining from endless day," said Drew, "would be a direct hit against Arians, who said Jesus' life began in Bethlehem."

"Precisely," said Mr. Pipes, smiling at them. "In the next two verses the poet asks the Father for grace and consecrates himself to hearing and serving God. He then boldly offers worship to Christ as God. The final verse goes like this:

> Thy grace, O Father, give,
> I humbly thee implore;
> And let thy mercy bless
> Thy servant more and more.
> All praise and glory be to thee,
> From age to age eternally.

"There's that phrase again," said Drew, resuming rowing. "From age to age."

"Praise and glory from age to age," repeated Annie. "It's almost like Gregory's reminding us that the church must always offer worthy praise to God—always."

"From age to age," said Drew.

"And I implore you, my dear ones," said Mr. Pipes, looking soberly from Annie to Drew, "make this yet another hymn you sing to God, now and always."

He looked at his watch.

"However," he went on, "I hate to say it, but we did not rent this rowboat from age to age. Our hour's almost up."

"Ramming speed," said Drew, digging his oars in.

"Don't forget the crabs, Drew," said Annie, grinning as she remembered Drew's first rowing lesson two summers ago in *Toplady*. He'd caught a crab—sailor's language for pulling too hard on the oars before the blades are fully in the water—and flipped, feet in the air, on his back.

" 'Twould be most embarrassing," agreed Mr. Pipes, "all eyes on you as we draw closer to shore—most embarrassing, indeed."

*

"I get it! *Gelato* means 'ice cream'!" yelled Drew as Mr. Pipes led them from the shore of the lake toward a covered shop labeled *Gelaterie*.

"I'll have three scoops in a waffle cone," said Drew.

"Andrew the P—" began Annie. "No, I won't say it, but *Drew*."

"How about four scoops, then?" he said, pretending not to understand.

They found a small round table in the shade, and with very little talking they licked and crunched for several minutes.

"So what does 'Giardino Zoologico' mean?" asked Drew, frowning at a nearby sign. He bent his head back and licked melting ice cream trickling from the pointed end of his cone.

"Zoo Garden," replied Mr. Pipes. "Mm-mm, Italians make wonderful ice cream."

"A zoo with animals?" asked Annie.

Drew looked at his sister but said nothing.

"Over one thousand of them," replied Mr. Pipes. "Shall we go have a look?"

"I'd sure like to see the lions," said Drew.

Annie wasn't at all sure that she wanted to see real lions after visiting the Colosseum, but she followed Drew and Mr. Pipes past the ticket collector, through the turnstile, and into the sprawling zoo. Drew picked up a map and, acting as navigator, led them to the lion pens. A deep-throated growl grew into a snapping roar as they watched two lions argue over a joint of pink and red meat. The bigger of the two lions, his mane bristling, twitched his tail irritably as he sank his teeth into the meat, one eye on his rival.

Annie shuddered and turned away. Mr. Pipes and Drew looked on soberly. Mr. Pipes put his hand on Annie's shoulder and recited:

> "They met the tyrant's brandished steel,
> The lion's gory mane;
> They bowed their necks the death to feel:
> Who follows in their train?"

"I-I'm so glad it all finally ended," said Annie. "It did end, didn't it?"

"The persecution, you mean? Well, yes, in a manner of speaking, it ended." Mr. Pipes measured his words. "Thanks in large part to a Spanish poet named Aurelius Clemens Prudentius. Emperor Theodosius called Prudentius, a gifted young man and student of the Latin poets Virgil and Horace, to Rome to help establish the new religion. Christianity was now the official religion of Rome, but pagan practices remained and infested the church. Prudentius's job was to fight against this paganism."

"How did he do it?" asked Annie.

"One way," said Mr. Pipes, "was by appealing for the ending of blood sports in the Colosseum. Though Christians were no longer the victims in these gruesome games, men and beasts still died for sport. One zealous Christian named Telemachus went to the arena and was so overwhelmed by the violent fighting that he vaulted over the barricade and attempted to stop the gladiators; he was struck and killed. This tragedy and Prudentius's eloquent appeals led to the end of blood sports in the Colosseum in A.D. 404."

Annie looked back at the lions eating their dinner. She sighed.

"I'm glad the persecution is finally all over," she said.

Mr. Pipes looked at Annie and stroked his chin in thought.

"Annie, I must tell you, many Christians suffer terrible persecution for their faith—today. Oh, yes, blood sports in the Colosseum ended, but today many of our dear brothers and sisters—and even their children—are persecuted for their faithfulness to Christ."

"Today?" asked Annie, biting her lip.

"Can't anybody do anything to stop it?" asked Drew.

"We must pray for them," said Mr. Pipes. "And we must be content, and determine to use our freedoms to help them when we can."

The lion licked its paw and began bathing its face.

"You said Prudentius was a poet?" said Annie.

"Yes, and he, like Gregory of Nazianzen, wrote a hymn calculated to expose the Arian heresy, and thus to honor Christ as God."

Mr. Pipes leaned his elbows on the iron fence separating them from the lions.

"It is set to a lovely twelfth-century plainsong melody and is often sung at Christmas, though it is appropriate any time."

"From age to age," said Drew, grinning.

"Evermore and evermore," agreed Mr. Pipes with a chuckle.

"Notice the echoes of the Nicene Creed in the first line. It goes like this:

> Of the Father's love begotten
> Ere the worlds began to be,
> He is Alpha and Omega,
> He the Source, the Ending he,
> Of the things that are, that have been,
> And that future years shall see,
> Evermore and evermore!

"Prudentius goes on to speak of Jesus' birth and of the prophets' foretelling of his coming to redeem sinners. And concludes with a doxology of praise to the Trinity:

> O ye heights of heav'n, adore him;
> Angel hosts, his praises sing;
> All dominion, bow before him
> And extol our God and King;
> Let no tongue on earth be silent,
> Every voice in concert ring,
> Evermore and evermore!

> Christ, to thee, with God the Father,
> And, O Holy Ghost, to thee,
> Hymn, and chant, and high thanksgiving,
> And unwearied praises be,
> Honor, glory, and dominion,
> And eternal victory,
> Evermore and evermore!"

Mr. Pipes's voice rose to a crescendo on the last verse. He no sooner finished than the lion lifted his bushy head and gave a great roar. Annie looked startled; then a smile crept over her face.

"I think he was joining you, Mr. Pipes," she said, looking intently at the great beast. "That was his hymn, and chant, and high thanksgiving."

4
High Fashion in Milan

O Trinity, Most Blessed Light
(Ambrose of Milan)
Te Deum (Niceta)

O Trinity, most blessed Light.

O Unity of sov'reign might,

As now the fiery sun departs,

Shed thou thy beams within our hearts.

That night back at their hotel, Annie sat gazing out the window at the sparkling lights of Rome. Though Mr. Pipes and Drew were sound asleep, racing engines and blaring horns kept her awake, and she wondered where on earth everyone could be going at this time of night. *Didn't they ever sleep in this city?*

She heard a rustling sound from the lizards on the windowsill and peered closer into the makeshift cage. Reaching her finger through a small gap, she stroked one of the lizards on its tiny head. She had tried to come up with names for them, but—she squinted critically at the four green lizards—frankly, they all

68

looked exactly the same; it was hard to give different names to creatures that looked so much alike. So far she hadn't liked any of the names: "Liz" seemed a little too obvious, and anyway, she had no idea which one might be a girl, if any. Drew had suggested "Elizabeth," "Lizard-breath" for short, but Annie was afraid it might hurt their feelings. He had argued that, being lizards, they obviously had lizard breath, so how could calling them "Lizard-breath" hurt their feelings? There were times when Annie wondered about brothers. *Oh, well,* she thought with a yawn as she crawled back into her bed, *maybe lizards are the kind of pets that don't need names.*

*

Every morning after breakfast Mr. Pipes opened his Bible and read to the children, usually from two or three passages. Though often impatient for each day's adventures, they had come to love hearing his voice rising and falling as he read the sacred words. Annie longed for the day when their parents might read the Bible with them; it still seemed a long way off.

"Now then, Annie and Drew," said Mr. Pipes, when he finished reading that morning, "especially Drew, do be sure you don't leave anything lying about. Our taxi will arrive shortly and we depart by train for Milan in"—he checked his watch—"in precisely one hour; we shall have no opportunity to retrieve it."

"I'll get the lizards," said Drew.

Mr. Pipes inwardly groaned. "Of course you will," he replied.

Moments later, looking bewildered, Drew bolted back into the room, holding the makeshift cage.

"Gone, they're all gone!" he said, wiggling his finger through a gap in the wire screen. "And just when I was starting to feel attached to them."

With considerable effort, Mr. Pipes avoided breaking out in an enormous sigh of relief.

Annie braced herself for a wave of sadness and a sense of great loss to flood over her; none came. In fact, she, too, secretly felt relieved. Squirmy green lizards with ratlike tails and slithering tongues had somehow failed to truly endear themselves to her. But she did feel bad for Drew.

"Oh, I'm so sorry," she said. A nagging fear that she might in some way have contributed to their escape tugged at her mind. Her heart skipped a beat; she looked around the hotel room.

"But where did they go?" she asked, a shudder rippling up her spine as she thought of a lizard darting out from under the bed and scurrying onto her leg. Or, worse yet, what would she have done if one had crawled in bed with her last night?

Mr. Pipes looked at his watch. "We find ourselves somewhat precariously positioned I fear between the proverbial rock and hard place. We simply cannot leave four lost lizards to be discovered by the maid; poor dear might simply die of fright. We must try to find them."

Ten minutes later, a young man wearing a hotel uniform entered the room and saw two children and an elderly white-haired man on their knees crawling around on the floor.

"Ahem, your taxi has arrived," he said in perfect English.

Frowning, Mr. Pipes rose stiffly and ran his fingers through his white hair.

"Ah, yes, of course, our taxi," he said, dusting the sleeve of his jacket. "Drew, gather our things together." Then turning to the hotel porter, and clearing his throat awkwardly, he said, "I regret to inform you . . . Ah, that is to say, well, we have . . . misplaced our . . . our lizards."

The boy suddenly looked interested. "Here, in the room?" he asked.

"Yes, regrettably, in the room," confessed Mr. Pipes.

"I collect lizards," he said, his eyes searching the walls enthusiastically.

Mr. Pipes blinked several times before replying. "You collect lizards?"

The boy looked at Mr. Pipes incredulously. "Every boy collects lizards, sir. The way I see it, some just lack opportunity. But you have to be careful." He stopped and poked his head into the hallway, looking carefully both ways before continuing. "There's a pretty militant bunch of quacks around here who are always talking about saving the whales, or ending the enslavement of dogs, and they put food out at night for cockroaches; you know the type. They'd chain themselves together in front of the hotel, singing all mournful-like, if they knew you had lizards in here."

Drew ran to the window.

"They must not be on to us," he said, a hint of disappointment in his voice. "No protesters down there."

Annie and Mr. Pipes looked relieved.

"Expert that you clearly are," said Mr. Pipes to the porter, "perhaps you would be so kind as to collect our lizards for us, else we will miss our train."

"Don't forget to give him the name of our hotel in Milan," said Drew, slinging a knapsack over his shoulder. "So he can send them to us."

"Oh, you wouldn't want that," said the porter soberly, his eyes narrowing. "If they caught me, they'd torture me until I gave 'em your address. Then they'd know how to get you, too. Nasty bunch, really. Around those animal-huggers, I'd rather be a lizard than a kid who likes lizards."

"Yes, well, and furthermore," said Mr. Pipes. "I am afraid the Italian postal service would not approve." Digging in his pocket, he handed the boy a wad of lire. "Not only shall you have new lizards for your collection, accept this with our gratitude. But do find them before the cleaning staff arrives—promise me you will. And now for our train and Milan."

"Make sure *they* aren't following you," the porter called after them.

*

Mr. Pipes and the children arrived at the station with only moments to spare. They waited, then waited some more. Finally, more than an hour late, their train arrived.

"This often happens with trains in Rome, my dears," explained Mr. Pipes. "We must be thankful it arrived at all."

Occasionally looking out the train window at the Italian countryside, Annie and Drew mostly talked with Mr. Pipes and wrote in their sketchbooks. Several hours later, they arrived in Milan.

"Boy, everybody sure looks all dressed up and fancy," said Drew, after gathering their luggage and walking out onto the street.

"Milan is the fashion capital," said Mr. Pipes, "of a considerably fashion conscious country."

"Should have worn my tuxedo," said Drew, buttoning up all the buttons on his polo shirt and tucking his shirttails into his jeans.

Annie stole a glance at her reflection in a shop window as they passed. Smoothing her long blond hair back, she frowned at her freckles and at the wrinkles in her jumper from sitting on the train most of the morning.

"You look simply lovely, my dear," said Mr. Pipes, taking her arm.

"So if it's the fashion place," said Drew, "does that mean everything's going to be all new-looking?"

Mr. Pipes smiled. "How your tastes have changed, Drew. But have no fear; Milan is a most ancient city."

Mr. Pipes suddenly waved his arms at a passing taxi.

"Ah, he has stopped. Come, my dears, we must run for it or we shall lose him."

Once in the taxi, Mr. Pipes explained that he was taking them to one of the oldest churches in Italy where long ago the Father of Western Hymnody had ministered.

"It sure looks old," said Drew moments later as they got out of the taxi. He stared up at the towers of the Church of St. Ambrose.

"Oh, it is quite old," said Mr. Pipes, leading them along the columns and arches of the portico. "One of the very oldest."

"How old?" asked Annie.

"Well, some of the original columns in this church," explained Mr. Pipes, "were actually salvaged from ancient Roman buildings."

"As old as the Colosseum?" asked Drew.

"Perhaps. Although much of what you see was built about nine hundred years after Christ, there are several significant features from the fourth century."

"Wasn't that when Constantine made the Edict of Milan?" asked Drew. "313, wasn't it?"

"Very good, Drew," whispered Mr. Pipes as they passed through a high rounded arch, through bronze doors over a thousand years old, and into the dark interior of the church.

"It sure is different from the catacombs," whispered Annie, taking in the gold-gilded altar screen and the elaborate stone-carved capitals on the columns.

"It doesn't look like Christians needed to hide anymore," agreed Drew, slapping his hand against the massive stones, an echo reverberating through the ancient sanctuary. "Not if they met openly in a place like this."

"So, was this church built," asked Annie, now gazing further up at the dim, rounded vaults of the ceiling, "as a result of the freedoms won for Christians in the Edict of Milan?"

"In a manner of speaking, yes," replied Mr. Pipes, pausing in front of the high, boxlike pulpit. "Ah, yes, under the pulpit, guarded by those lovely stone arches, do you see the carvings on that sarcophagus?"

"Sarcapha what?" asked Drew, sticking his head through one of the arches for a better look.

"Stone casket," said Mr. Pipes, smiling.

"Someone's buried in there?" asked Annie, halting.

"Yes, some prominent early Christians who died sometime soon after the edict," replied Mr. Pipes, "though historians are not in agreement as to who they were."

"Who built the original church?" asked Drew.

"Ah, of that we know more," replied Mr. Pipes, sitting down on a rough wooden bench and crossing his legs. "Construction began on this site in A.D. 379 and was consecrated by the Bishop of Milan, fellow named Ambrose, in A.D. 386. Fact is, that fresco on the wall hard by the third column on the left is a painting of St. Ambrose. You'll find carvings and mosaic episodes pictured on the dome—you can see it just there above the altar screen— and many other relics memorializing his life and ministry throughout the church and throughout the entire city of Milan."

"Must have been an important guy," said Drew.

"Oh, he was indeed," replied Mr. Pipes.

"Tell us about him," said Annie, sitting down next to their old friend.

Mr. Pipes smiled, clasped his hands around one knee, and, after gazing up at the colorful mosaic pictures of St. Ambrose, began the story.

"Ambrose was born around A.D. 340 and lived in France for his early years. His father was Roman Prefect, a sort of governor, of the western provinces of the empire, including my beloved Britain."

"That makes his dad a big shot," said Drew.

"Yes, but like all big shots, as you call them, Ambrose's father died."

"While Ambrose was still young?" asked Annie.

"Yes."

"What did his mother do?" asked Annie.

"She moved the family to Rome, where Ambrose went to school, studied law, and was eventually appointed consul or governing official of Northern Italy because of his eloquence and scholarship."

"And let me guess," said Drew. "He lived right here in Milan."

"Precisely," said Mr. Pipes. "But these were not easy times to be in government service; Rome was decaying and smarting under increasing threats from invading barbarians. Far more dangerous, however, was the Arian heresy infecting the church. Sometime after Ambrose's arrival in Milan, the Arian bishop of the city died."

"That's good," said Drew.

"It was theologically a hopeful providence," agreed Mr. Pipes. "However, the Christians and Arians began protests in the streets in their enthusiasm to appoint the next bishop. No one could agree, and tension mounted. When election day arrived, angry mobs crammed the streets and filled the church. Governor Ambrose, fearing full-scale violence, stood up before the shouting crowds and, using his persuasive eloquence learned in the law courts of Rome, urged them to make a wise and peaceful choice. When he finished speaking, silence filled the church. Then a voice broke the stillness: 'Ambrose is bishop!' The warring factions soon joined their voices in the chant: 'Ambrose is bishop! Ambrose is bishop!'"

"What did he say to that?" asked Annie.

"He resisted the appointment," said Mr. Pipes. "But even though Ambrose was not yet a baptized member of the church, the people insisted; he finally agreed. Ambrose took this new and unusual appointment seriously. He presented himself to the church for baptism, resigned his consular appointment, sold all his wealth and distributed it to the needy, and devoted himself to the study of the Bible."

"He gave up everything," said Drew.

"But did he turn out to be an Arian or a real Christian?" asked Annie.

"He proved to be a devoted worshiper of Jesus Christ as God," replied Mr. Pipes, "and because of his devoted service, many believe Ambrose was the ideal Christian bishop."

"What did he do to make them think that?" asked Drew.

"Many things," replied Mr. Pipes. "But like all great men, he was willing to act against his own self-interest in the higher interest of doing what was right. For example, he once refused to allow the emperor to come to church and participate in the worship of God."

"But why would he do that?" asked Drew. "Isn't coming to church a good thing?"

"Of course it is, but not for the unrepentant. This emperor, worried over riots in Thessalonica, ordered his soldiers to quell those riots by a general massacre of the whole town. Ambrose would not let the emperor come to church until he truly repented for this mass murder of innocent people."

"Boy, Ambrose wasn't afraid to stand up to an emperor!" said Drew.

"Did the emperor submit?" asked Annie.

"Yes, he professed his crime publicly and sought forgiveness."

"So Ambrose did the right thing, and it worked," said Drew.

"Doing the right thing always works, regardless of what might happen to you in this life. Ambrose feared God more than the emperor."

"What else did he do to be so loved by his followers?" asked Annie, sketching part of the mosaic on the dome.

"That takes us back to the Arians, who fought on against Ambrose. They wrote propaganda hymns filled with taunts and insults against the Christians and taught their followers to sing them in the streets, often throughout the night. Ambrose and the true believers battled back with hymns refuting Arian heresy and extolling the biblical doctrine of the Trinity. Faithful Christians gathered in candlelit processions and marched through the streets of Milan and other cities singing to one God: Father, Son, and Holy Spirit."

"Did they ever turn down a street and face Arian singers?" asked Drew, his eyes wide. "I'll bet the feathers flew when that happened."

"Oh, yes, confrontations—sometimes violent ones—ensued," said Mr. Pipes. "In one such riot, the leader of the Christian hymn-singers was beaten to death by the Arians. Many Christians, now fearful for the life of their beloved bishop, gathered around the basilica church where Ambrose lived and guarded him through many nights; he taught them to sing hymns through these long vigils. Monica, the praying mother of St. Augustine, later the great champion of the doctrines of grace in the early church, joined the faithful protectors of Ambrose. In his *Confessions*, Augustine said of their hymn-singing, 'The voices flowed in at my ears, truth was distilled into my heart, and the affection of piety overflowed in sweet tears of joy.'

"The violence against Christians eventually led to an imperial edict making Arian singing illegal. But Christians kept singing, and more and more they gathered in the evening at the churches, thus further establishing the rich heritage of 'even song,' evening singing in the worship of God."

"That reminds me of Thomas Ken's Evening Hymn," said Annie.

"Yes, and all such hymns especially appropriate to evening worship may find their heritage in the singing of Ambrose and the faithful churches in Milan."

"But did Ambrose actually write the poetry for the hymns?" asked Annie as she concentrated on drawing Ambrose from the mosaic overhead.

"He wrote some of them, and so many others wrote hymns under his sweet influence that he is rightly called the Father of Western Hymnody. Thus, many hymns are ascribed to him that he may not have actually written himself but others wrote while sitting under his guidance."

Mr. Pipes got up and led them down a flight of stairs. Annie gripped the iron railing and placed her feet carefully: the steps were worn from hundreds of years of use into a swooshing dip at the middle of each stone tread.

"This is the crypt," he said, after they had descended the stairs, his voice sounding eerie against the low barrel vaulting and red marble of the walls and columns.

"There's nobody down here," said Drew, his voice ringing against the stones. "Wouldn't music sound good against these walls?"

"Perfect for singing a hymn," said Mr. Pipes. "I am reminded of one of the greatest hymns of all time; legend says that Ambrose and Augustine sang the *Te Deum* in antiphonal praise right here on this site when Ambrose baptized Augustine."

He dug in his shoulder bag and opened his hymnal.

"It is best sung to the common-meter Scottish tune *Dundee*, and goes like this."

Mr. Pipes hummed for a moment to get the pitch right. He rubbed his hands together and wiggled his fingers.

"I do wish I was at liberty to use that fine organ up above us—did you notice it, Drew?"

"I sure did."

"Well, we shall sing without it. You follow along:

O God, we praise thee, and confess
That thou the only Lord
And everlasting Father art,
By all the earth adored."

As their voices resounded in the ancient crypt, Annie imagined how wonderful it must have been when hundreds of Christians sang this same hymn on this same spot more than fifteen hundred years ago.

The holy church throughout the world,
O Lord, confesses thee,
That thou eternal Father art,
Of boundless majesty.

Thine honored, true, and only Son;
And Holy Ghost, the Spring
Of never-ceasing joy: O Christ,
Of glory thou art King."

When the last echo of their voices had drifted into silence,
Mr. Pipes said, " 'Tis a wonderful legend: Ambrose singing a
verse, then the new Christian, Augustine, responding with the
next verse, and so forth, making up the words for the very first
time as they sang."

"I can just hear it," said Annie, her face glowing in the dim
light.

"I do so hate to disappoint you, my dear. However, wonderful hymn that it is, the legend is simply not true," continued Mr.
Pipes. "It was surely written during Ambrose's life, but most
likely from the pen of a missionary to ancient Serbia, named
Niceta, who, it is said, 'spread Christianity among barbarians by
his sweet songs of the cross.' The barbarians of early England
heard the *Te Deum* sung on their rocky shores in A.D. 597, when
Augustine of Kent, sent by Pope Gregory, came to spread Christianity throughout the land."

"Hey, that's sort of like how you spread Christianity to us,"
said Drew, remembering that first summer when they had met
Mr. Pipes in Olney. "I guess if the hymns worked on barbarians
hundreds of years ago they work on American kid barbarians
like us, too."

Mr. Pipes laughed.

"It was the hymns you taught us, Mr. Pipes," said Annie,
putting her hand in his. "That's what did it."

"And God be praised," said Mr. Pipes, squeezing Annie's
hand. "It was his truth, adorned in the hymns, that sweetly drew
you both to our blessed Lord Jesus. And yes, Drew, grand hymns
like this one can lift barbarians out of the mire of sin and darkness into the light of truth and understanding in every place
and—"

"—From age to age!" both Annie and Drew chimed in with him.

"Well said, indeed."

Mr. Pipes led them down one of the five aisles of the crypt and stopped before an elaborate railing.

"Wow! What a fancy jar!" said Drew, looking at a large silver and glass urn protected behind the railing.

"What's in it?" asked Annie, admiring the beautiful vase.

Mr. Pipes looked carefully at Annie before answering.

"It is generally accepted to be the dust of St. Ambrose," replied Mr. Pipes.

"His d-dust?" said Annie.

"Decomposed body," said Drew, matter-of-factly. "You know, when someone dies, over time their body turns back into dirt. Pretty fancy container for dirt."

Annie looked at Mr. Pipes. He nodded.

"I would not have put it quite so bluntly, my dear," he said. "But the Urn of the Patron Saints is said to contain what remains in this world of St. Ambrose."

"But he is with the Lord Jesus now, and will be forever, right?" said Annie.

"Oh, most certainly, my dear," said Mr. Pipes, reassuringly. "And on the Judgment Day his earthly body, made perfect, will rise, and we with him will sing the glorious praises of God."

"And never get tired of singing," said Drew. "I think that's a line from one of the hymns you taught us."

" 'And hymns with the supernal choir incessant sing and never tire,' " quoted Annie.

"Good job, Annie," said Drew. "That'd be Mr. Ken."

"Can you teach us one of St. Ambrose's hymns?" asked Annie, light reflecting off the polished silver of the urn sparkling in her eyes.

"With pleasure, my dears," said Mr. Pipes. "St. Augustine gives us good reason to believe that Ambrose wrote the hymn 'O Trinity, Most Blessed Light.' "

"Sounds like a good first line," said Drew, "for a guy who spent a good chunk of his life fighting off those Arian madmen like Ambrose did."

"Indeed," agreed Mr. Pipes. "Shall we sing it together, here on the spot where Ambrose consecrated this church?"

"Yeah, and right here with his remains," added Drew, nodding at the urn.

Mr. Pipes stood between them, holding the hymnal as they sang. Later that evening at their hotel, Annie tried to describe the experience in her journal, but all she could write was: "I never felt as close to someone who lived so long ago; it is as if I now know Ambrose."

Before going to bed that night, Drew borrowed Mr. Pipes's hymnal so that he could write out the words of the hymn in his journal. Maybe they would help him with the hymn he was trying to write—*after all*, he told himself, *Annie wrote one, so why can't I?*

O Trinity, most blessed Light.
O Unity of sov'reign might,
As now the fiery sun departs,
Shed thou thy beams within our hearts.

To thee our morning song of praise,
To thee our evening prayer we raise;
Thee may our glory evermore
In lowly reverence adore.

All praise to God the Father be,
All praise, eternal Son, to thee,
Whom with the Spirit we adore
Forever and forever more.

5
A Gargoyle's Point of View

Let All Mortal Flesh Keep Silence
Christ Is Made the Sure Foundation

All that dedicated city,
Dearly loved of God on high,
In exultant jubilation
Pours perpetual melody;
God the One in Three adoring
In glad hymns eternally.

Annie took longer than usual getting dressed the next morning. First she braided her hair. Turning from side to side, she frowned at herself in the mirror—and took the braids out. *How about leaving it down and just pulling a few strands back and tying it behind with a ribbon; hmm-mm, that looks a little more—well, fashionable*, she decided. Next, she dug through her limited wardrobe. *If I only had an iron*, she thought as she held up her best dress, frowning at the wrinkles.

She finally joined Mr. Pipes and Drew and sat down to a leisurely Italian breakfast—the kind Drew liked best. When Drew had bolted one last pastry, Mr. Pipes read from Acts, Romans, and the Psalms. His eyes often strayed from the page as he read the psalm, but Annie and Drew loved how he continued reciting the words from memory. When he finished, they set out from their hotel for a day of adventure in Milan.

"That's a pretty big river for right downtown like this," said Drew, pausing a few moments later as they crossed a bridge. Men and women jostled past and cellular phones warbled as the crowds made their way to office buildings lining the river and piercing the sky in every direction.

"It is actually a canal," said Mr. Pipes, above the din of voices and clicking heels. "The Naviglio Grande is the central canal of an entire network of waterways, some built as early as the twelfth century."

Annie watched several bejeweled women crossing the bridge, their Como silk dresses shimmering in the sunlight. Men in Armani business suits swished past, the tassels on their alligator-skin pumps slapping haughtily as they strutted by.

"It's even worse here than at the train station," whispered Annie, her eyes wide as she looked shyly into the finely chiseled features of the next wave of these people from Milan, their black hair and olive skin lending an air of sophistication to the passing exhibition. Annie couldn't help noticing that hardly anyone had pale blond hair like hers—and no one had freckles.

"Pee-ew!" said Drew, waving his hand in front of his nose. "It smells like chemical warfare with all that perfume fighting away like that." He coughed and sputtered.

"*Drew,*" said Annie, "you are embarrassing us; they can hear, you know."

"As I say, Milanese folks are somewhat taken up by fashion," said Mr. Pipes. But even he smoothed his collar and checked the knot on his necktie as he spoke.

"It's got 'em by the throat," said Drew, gripping his own neck.

"It does make one feel somewhat, shall we say, below the bar." Mr. Pipes brushed a fleck of lint off the tweed of his jacket and adjusted his glasses.

"Yeah, it's making me kind of sick," said Drew, rolling his eyes and turning back toward the canal. As he turned, his knapsack clipped the silk-suited arm of a passing businessman. With cool dark eyes, the man looked down his pointed nose at Drew and slowly, deliberately dusted his sleeve.

"Sorry," mumbled Drew. He turned back to the canal and studied the rows of barges moored along its wall.

The man strode away.

"Though you did not intend to bump the gentleman," said Mr. Pipes, "one does want to be more careful. Wars have commenced for less."

"I am sorry," said Drew.

He counted the rows of wide, flat barges along the river. It was easy to lose count because they all looked pretty much the same. He halted in his count—*that one looks different*, he thought. Leaning farther out, he tried to see more clearly.

"Hey! Look at that," he cried, pointing toward the row of barges. "I think it's a sailboat."

"But it doesn't have a mast," said Annie, following her brother's gaze.

"It's shaped like a sailboat," said Drew, hesitantly.

"It certainly is a sailing vessel," said Mr. Pipes. "And a stout seaworthy craft, at that. Her mast is stowed on deck so that she can pass under the many bridges crossing over the canal."

"With the mast down, they can't sail her on the canal," said Drew.

"What's the good of having a sailboat if you can't go sailing?" asked Annie.

Mr. Pipes's eyes narrowed as he followed their gaze. He reached into his shoulder bag for his opera glasses and focused on the stern of the sailboat.

"Most extraordinary," he said, refocusing the little binoculars.

"What is it?" asked Annie and Drew together.

"She bears the name *St. Brendan*," said Mr. Pipes. "How extraordinary, indeed. She hails from Dublin. Here, have a go with the glasses."

Annie and Drew took turns looking more closely at the sailboat.

"Dublin's in Ireland, isn't it?" asked Drew.

"Indeed," said Mr. Pipes.

"Does that mean they sailed her all the way from Ireland?" asked Annie.

"Correction," said Drew. "If it's *St. Brendan*, we're talking 'him,' not 'her.'"

"Could you actually sail from Ireland all the way to Milan?" asked Annie, ignoring her brother.

"Certainly," replied Mr. Pipes. "If after leaving the Adriatic Sea you lowered your mast and motored up the Po River and thence into the system of inland canals—such they clearly have done. Must have been a wonderful voyage from Ireland," Mr. Pipes concluded, a faraway look in his eyes.

Drew looked intently at the sailboat through the binoculars. His imagination raced. Hauling, reefing, and steering into the foaming waves—he could just see himself on the decks of the little ship. What he wouldn't do to go to sea!

"So why did they build a canal right in the middle of the city in the first place?" asked Annie.

"This stretch of canal here where the *St. Brendan* lies," said Mr. Pipes, "opened in 1269 to aid in the construction of the great Duomo—the cathedral. Marble for her columns and façade was hauled on barges down the Naviglio Grande Canal over seven hundred years ago."

"Is it a pretty cathedral?" asked Annie.

"Most lovely, my dear," replied Mr. Pipes. "In fact, the Duomo is the largest, most complex and grand Gothic building in all Italy and the third-largest church in all the world."

"Do we get to see it?" asked Drew.

"Follow me," said Mr. Pipes, cheerily, as they dodged in and out of the crowds on the sidewalk.

They left the bridge behind and followed Mr. Pipes along the canal, eventually leaving it behind, zigzagging down small streets until they joined the Via Torino.

"We may very well be following the route to the cathedral site that oxen carts, loaded with marble from the barges on the canal, followed to the worksite," explained Mr. Pipes "If I have not miscalculated, she will come into view around the next corner."

Eagerly, they turned right onto the Via Dante Orefici, but a green-and-yellow bus blocked their view. After it passed and the air cleared from the diesel exhaust, the massive cathedral, bathed in sunlight, loomed against the deep blue sky above them.

Annie caught her breath. "It-it looks too delicate and beautiful to be real," she said, gazing at the pink-and-white Candoglia marble of the massive façade.

"I've never seen so many spires," said Drew.

"Though not as tall as some cathedrals," said Mr. Pipes, "the Duomo points to the heavens with no less than 135 spires, all delicately fashioned. It is a truly magnificent building."

"It looks like lace," said Annie, halting in the middle of the Piazza Del Duomo and staring at the richly ornamented stone building.

"Looks more like stone flames," said Drew, his hands stuffed into his pockets as he looked. "And the spires are just bigger flames leaping into the air—I'm not so sure why they would make it look like fire, though."

"All those lovely gables and pinnacles are the product of the flamboyant Gothic style," replied Mr. Pipes. "Stones, richly carved to look like flames of fire, creating an elaborately delicate trimming, all chiseled out of solid marble. Splendid, indeed."

"Hey, Mr. Pipes," said Drew, taking the old man by the arm and urging him toward the entrance to the Duomo. "Maybe they'll let you play the organ. Let's go inside. It does have an organ?"

"It does have a lovely organ, but let *me* play it?" said Mr. Pipes with a chuckle. "Not at all likely, my dears."

"It happened before," said Drew. "Remember Geneva?"

"And Strasbourg," added Annie.

"Playing an organ in such wonderful old churches is such an unlikely event," said Mr. Pipes, "the fact that it has already oc-curred suggests more rightly that it shall *never* occur again rather than that it shall. Though," he added a little wistfully, "it would be most gratifying."

"Well, at least we might get to hear someone else play it," said Drew.

"That wouldn't be as good," said Annie, smiling up at their old friend and looping her arm through his. "But let's go see."

Jostled by the crowds of tourists choking their way through the tall green doors, they entered the cathedral.

"An elephant could walk through these doors," said Drew, his eye estimating the massive opening. "Maybe two at a time."

Mr. Pipes frowned as the stone interior echoed with squeals and laughter from a large group of schoolchildren running and calling to their friends. The threesome worked their way through a line of people waiting to buy souvenirs from the cathedral shop positioned near the entrance. Cash registers blurped and warbled, coins jingled as heavily laden cash drawers opened and closed.

Straining to hear, groups of adults clustered around tour guides, who held little flags or colorful umbrellas aloft in an ef-fort to be more visible in the chaos of visitors. Annie and Drew heard a babble of different languages, one fading into the next as they snaked their way through the mob. If they had understood, they would have heard snatches of stories about hundreds of years of construction, the French and Germans that contributed to the Duomo's design, the importance of visual imagery in Roman Catholic churches, or the millions of dollars spent to build it. As the cacophony reechoed off the ancient walls, everyone seemed to speak louder and louder to be heard above all the rest; the noise was deafening.

"It almost sounds like elephants *did* come through those doors," said Annie, her hands pressed to her ears, "a whole herd of them."

"Yeah, and if someone did play the organ," said Drew, almost shouting to be heard above the piercing din, "we'd never hear it, not with all this racket."

"But then, we're adding to the noise ourselves," moaned Annie.

"It does seem a shame," said Mr. Pipes, "that such a grand place of worship has become so much a place filled with the babble of tourists that if God did speak, no one would be disposed to hear him. I wonder for how many centuries his voice has gone unheeded within these lovely walls."

Near the end of a row of massive marble pillars, they escaped from the crowds into a quiet corner without any statues or shrines to saints. With relief, they huddled against the dark stones, and Drew leaned against a little wooden door crisscrossed with iron strap hinges and with a Gothic arch no taller than a boy.

"Whew," said Drew, looking this way and that at the crowds as they rumbled by. "This is a little bit better."

"The floor's been so covered with feet," said Annie, gazing at the marble inlaid scallop and rose patterns at their feet, "I didn't notice until now how beautiful it is."

"They didn't spare much on this place, that's for sure," said Drew.

"I guess that's why everybody comes here," said Annie. "But it's too bad about all the noise."

"Yes, it is unfortunate," agreed Mr. Pipes. "But when people stop believing, they stop worshiping; and when they stop worshiping, they come to the house of God only to see what man has done." He shuddered. "It is so very noisy. I am reminded of what the prophet Habakkuk wrote long ago: 'The Lord is in his holy temple; let all the earth be silent before him.' Oh, that they would now. When we no longer come to his temple to render homage to him and to hear his voice, we then fill it with what we prefer—the chaos of our own voices."

The laughter and the gawking just seemed so out of place, thought Annie as she gazed upward at the beautiful columns, their capitals intricately decorated with marble statues.

"It doesn't seem like they've come to think about God and heavenly things," she said, looking back at the jostling crowd.

"Seems kind of irreverent," said Drew.

"We do, alas, so want to come before God on our own terms, my dears," agreed Mr. Pipes. "But Scripture demands that we come before him with trembling; even the angel hosts serving continually before him in heaven veil their faces in his presence. How much more ought we sinners."

"I wonder how the Christians in the early church came to worship?" asked Annie.

"That is a very good question," said Mr. Pipes. "And reminds me of a hymn written sometime during the fifth century. Listen to the words and see if it does not answer your question."

He pulled his hymnal out of his bag, adjusted his glasses further down his nose, and read:

Let all mortal flesh keep silence,
And with fear and trembling stand;
Ponder nothing earthly-minded,
For with blessing in his hand,
Christ our God to earth descendeth,
Our full homage to demand."

"Folks could use a good dose of those words here today," said Drew.

Mr. Pipes continued:

> King of kings, yet born of Mary,
> As of old on earth he stood,
> Lord of lords, in human vesture,
> In the body and the blood.
> He will give to all the faithful
> His own self for heav'nly food.

"Food," said Annie, "to eat?"

"Ah, my dear," said Mr. Pipes, "you've made the very error the medieval Catholic Church made regarding the Lord's Supper. Jesus is *spiritually* present in the bread and wine administered in the Lord's Supper, not physically present. Just as we feed on earthly food to sustain our earthly body, so we find our spiritual sustenance in the merits of Christ's sinless life and in his substitutionary atonement for our salvation."

"I see," said Annie. "Jesus is heavenly food, not earthly food."

"So when Catholics have the Lord's Supper," said Drew, wrinkling his nose, "they think they're actually eating Jesus?"

"I am afraid one of the Roman Church's errors is thinking something very much like that. But they did not come by such a notion, I assure you, from Scripture—or from this hymn."

"How does the rest of it go?" asked Annie.

Mr. Pipes read on:

> Rank on rank the host of heaven
> Spreads its vanguard on the way,
> As the Light of light descendeth
> From the realms of endless day,
> That the pow'rs of hell may vanish
> As the darkness clears away.

At his feet the six-winged seraph,
Cherubim, with sleepless eye,
Veil their faces to the presence,
As with ceaseless voice they cry,
Alleluia, alleluia,
Alleluia, Lord, Most High!

Mr. Pipes's voice rose as he read the last verse, and he lifted his eyes to the vaulted ceiling above and sang the alleluias with a passion that sent a shiver of pure longing throughout Annie's whole body. Drew blinked several times as he followed Mr. Pipes's gaze upward toward the ceiling.

"That tune is perfect," said Drew. "I just wish somebody in charge around here would come up right now and need a good organist. I'll bet you could crank the organ up and get everyone's attention with this hymn."

"'Tis a lovely melody," agreed Mr. Pipes. "And I would love to play Ralph Vaughan Williams's arrangement of it for you—on any organ." He rubbed his hands together as he spoke, and Annie thought the look in his eyes was how a man looks when he hasn't seen someone he loves for an awfully long time.

"'Ponder nothing earthly-minded,'" quoted Annie, checking the words in Mr. Pipes's hymnal before continuing, "'for with blessing in his hand, Christ our God to earth descendeth, our full homage to demand.'"

"Everybody here seems to be pretty much thinking about earthly stuff," said Drew, "that's for sure."

"As are we all far too much of the time, my boy," said Mr. Pipes.

"But this hymn sure glorifies God," said Annie. "It lifts us from ourselves to him. And it also calls Jesus the 'Light of light.' That'd be from the Nicene Creed, wouldn't it?"

"Indeed it would," agreed Mr. Pipes.

"Oh, I just wish all these people who seem so impressed with what men did building this church," said Annie. "I just wish they'd believe in him and worship him. It would be so much better to come to a place like this and sing hymns to God instead of making all this racket."

"We pray on, then," said Mr. Pipes, "'that the powers of hell may vanish as the darkness clears away.'"

Looking at the passing mob, and thinking about the hymn, Drew shifted his weight to his other foot. Suddenly the little door gave a groan and fell open with a bang. Drew vanished through the narrow opening.

"Drew?" called Annie and Mr. Pipes, poking their heads into the doorway.

Just inside the door, Drew sat in a heap, a winding staircase rising into the darkness above him.

"Are you hurt?" asked Mr. Pipes, reaching down to help Drew up.

"No, I'm fine," said Drew, looking eagerly at the narrow staircase. "Hey, where do you think this goes? To the organ loft?"

"I do not have the slightest idea," replied Mr. Pipes.

Annie looked back out the doorway at the noisy crowds clogging the aisles of the cathedral. She didn't particularly like the looks of the dark stairway, but rejoining the mob of noisy tourists didn't sound so good either.

"Let's find out where it goes," said Drew, jumping to his feet.

Mr. Pipes looked again at the door, stepped back into the cathedral, and studied all around the door frame before answering.

"There is no posted prohibition against our exploring in this passageway," he said, checking his watch. "However, we will most certainly need torches—with fresh batteries."

Drew rustled in his knapsack and produced his flashlight. Annie and Mr. Pipes snapped theirs on at the same time as Drew.

"I put fresh batteries in last night," said Drew, heading up the twisting stairs.

"Annie, you go next," said Mr. Pipes, leaving the door slightly ajar, "and I shall bring up the rear."

After several rising turns around the circular shaft of the staircase, the noise of the cathedral faded, leaving only the sound of their feet pad-padding on the smooth stones.

Annie gripped the thick rope that hung down the middle of the shaft and served as a handrail to steady them on the steep ascent. "We've b-been climbing quite a ways," said Annie, after several minutes, her voice echoing softly.

"Do you see any change ahead, Drew?" called Mr. Pipes, pausing and puffing slightly as he spoke.

"No, not yet," called Drew's voice above them. "Wait! Here's another door."

Drew gripped the iron ring where a doorknob should have been. He pushed, then he pulled, but nothing happened.

"It's just got this ring thing," he called, "no doorknob, and it won't budge."

"Try twisting the ring as you would a doorknob," Mr. Pipes said.

Annie held her breath.

With a creak and a metallic *thunk* the latch gave way, and Drew pushed the door inward. A rumble of noise from the crowds now far below them met their ears.

"It *is* the organ loft," said Drew excitedly. "And here's our big chance to stop all that racket down there. Okay, now how do we turn this puppy on?"

Annie and Mr. Pipes joined Drew at the organ console. Mr. Pipes blinked rapidly several times, his white eyebrows bouncing up and down as he blinked. Then, staring fixedly at the three-manual keyboard, he rubbed his hands together and flexed his fingers in anticipation.

Annie looked at their old friend. *Should he do it?* she wondered. *It would be so wonderful to hear the cathedral fill with Mr. Pipes's organ-playing. But is it right?*

"Give it to 'em," said Drew, smiling at Mr. Pipes. "Give 'em 'Let All Mortal Flesh Keep Silence'! That'll show 'em."

Mr. Pipes dropped his hands to his sides, and as if awakening from a dream, he took his glasses off and passed his hand

· across his forehead and over his eyes. With resolve, he fitted his glasses back on his nose.

"The Lord knows how delighted I would be to touch those keys and hear his sweet praises fill this place." He took a deep breath and held it for a moment before continuing. "But one never plays an organ without being invited to do so."

Drew's eyes grew wide. "But think how much good it would do all those people down there to hear 'Let All Mortal Flesh Keep Silence,' and then maybe lots of other hymns. It would be like witnessing to them, Mr. Pipes," urged Drew.

Mr. Pipes looked longingly at the organ, the rows of gilded pipes rising to the vaulting above. He shook his head.

Annie put her hand in Mr. Pipes's and smiled up at him.

"But there's no sign that says you can't," Drew urged on.

"Nor do automobiles have signs saying that no one else can drive them except their owners," replied Mr. Pipes. "Some things are manifestly obvious and need no signage."

"But you played the organs in Strasbourg and Geneva," said Drew, almost whining now.

"You will recall, I was specifically invited to do so," replied Mr. Pipes. "And here I have been given no such invitation. Therefore, I *must* not play"—he gazed at the ivory keys—"and, furthermore, I *will* not play this lovely instrument."

With that, he led them back into the narrow shaft of the winding stairway, and round and round with every step they rose higher in the old cathedral.

"Whew!" said Drew. "One hundred and fifty-eight steps; that's quite a hike."

"You counted them?" asked Annie.

"Yep, every one."

Annie gasped a moment later as they stepped out into the brilliant sunlight near the top of the cathedral.

"It's wonderful," she whispered, gazing at the flying buttresses so near overhead and the forest of lacy spires all carved in stone. "I've never seen anything so detailed and beautiful."

"Guys actually carved all this out of stone?" asked Drew, his eye following the flamelike cornicework on top of the buttresses, "and without power tools—a-and all the way up here?" He thought of the piles of rubble left in the backyard at home after he'd tried carving bricks with a hammer and chisel.

"And all the statues," said Annie, "they're all so perfect, except for those sort of ugly heads with their mouths open."

"In all, over three thousand statues, and every one carved by hand," said Mr. Pipes, clasping his hands behind his back as he admired the artwork on every side. "Oh, yes, and the ugly heads—gargoyles, ninety-seven of them; nasty-looking chaps they are. Mostly used as downspouts to help shed water from the roof. Now, follow me and we shall climb higher still to the roof above the nave."

"Look at all the spires!" said Annie moments later, her eyes wide as she took in the rows of stone tracery gables connecting more than a dozen spires, each rising fifty feet into the sky, all running along both edges of the roof like an enormously elaborate fence. "And we seem to have it all to ourselves."

"It must have taken forever to build this place," said Drew, following Mr. Pipes along the walkway at the crown of the roof. He felt a tightness in his stomach. His head began to spin. He tried to sound casual as he added, "Hope they did a g-good job," but his voice cracked and his attempt to cover with a laugh sounded more like someone winding up for a good scream.

"Her foundations, you will remember," said Mr. Pipes, pausing near the edge, "were laid in the thirteenth century—nearly 800 years ago. But they did not truly finish her until 1965. Perhaps one of the longest church building projects of all time."

"H-how many tons of rock do you think it took?" asked Drew, his knuckles turning white as he gripped the stone edges of one of the open gables and looked down over the plaza and streets far below. He pressed his forehead against the warm stone to steady himself.

Annie joined him.

"What a view!" she said calmly. "I like being up here above all the racket and hurry of those streets. And if somebody was trying to follow us, like Dr. Dudley's spy in Germany last summer," she laughed, "we'd spot him from up here, that's for sure."

"Dr. Dudley, dear man, assured me that he would send out no spies to keep us out of trouble this time," said Mr. Pipes, laughing at the memory of all they had gone through to try to lose the spy. "No, simply nothing to fear from anyone shadowing us this summer."

Drew's parched mouth hung open as he looked at the ant-sized people walking on the plaza far below. Frankly, he had thought the whole spy thing was a blast. But just now a fear, even greater than Annie's fear of the spy had been, gripped him with icy fingers. He tried to swallow. Almost without realizing what he was doing, he wrapped his arms around the stony head of a gargoyle. He stared back at the gargoyle's wide eyes, flaring nostrils, and gaping mouth, its tongue wagging in rigid horror; it seemed caught in a centuries-long scream. Drew felt the same way about heights. *But I am not going to scream*, Drew told himself; *I am not going to screa-eam! I am not going to—*

"—Screa-eam!" said Drew, not realizing that he had spoken out loud.

"What?" asked Annie.

"Ahem, ah, *seem*, not *scream*, ha, ha—I said *seem*—it seems a little high up here," stammered Drew. "D-do you think they did a good enough job on the foundation all the way back in the 1200s, you know, hee hee," his attempt at laughter now sounding more like an advanced stage of hysteria, "to hold up all these millions of tons of stone?"

"You are correct to ask about the foundation of such a place as this," replied Mr. Pipes, patting Drew comfortingly on the shoulder. "Without the most careful planning, the best materials, the finest craftsmen—"

"B-but did they have all that?" asked Drew. "If they didn't, w-we could be done for."

Annie looked at her brother and worried for the gargoyle. She detected fresh fingernail scratch marks crisscrossing its stone shoulders. Glancing back along the broad walkway at the peak of the roof, she spied a place to sit down well away from the edge.

"Mr. Pipes," she said, "wouldn't it be nice to go sit at the base of that tallest spire? It's quiet there, and we can relax in the shade while you tell us more about how well they built this place."

Drew looked gratefully at his sister.

"Lovely idea," said Mr. Pipes, looking at Drew's pale face.

After prying Drew's fingers off the gargoyle, Annie and Mr. Pipes led Drew along the walkway to a low wall topped with Gothic arches. When they had all sat down in the shade, Annie pulled a bottle of mineral water and some chocolates out of her knapsack and offered them to her brother.

From where they sat, Drew couldn't see anything but sky above the many spires. He took a deep breath and looked at his sister. She was always doing nice things like this for him—he took a big bite of chocolate—and she never wanted credit for any of it. She could have made fun of him for being scared of heights; she never did.

"So tell us all about how *well* they built this church," said Annie, winking at Mr. Pipes.

He smiled.

"Clearly, they were brilliant engineers in those days," said Mr. Pipes distractedly, "and I am certain they built her foundation to last." He furrowed his brow in thought. With a frantic beating of wings, a flock of pigeons circled and landed nearby along a row of stone fleurs-de-lis. At the far end of the cathedral appeared several tourists, who must have ascended the main staircase to the roof. Frowning, Mr. Pipes stared at them for a moment.

Then, slapping his knee as if an idea had just occurred to him, he said, "I know a hymn—an ancient hymn—about the foundation of the church. Shall I teach it to you?"

"Oh, do," said Annie.

"About the foundation of *this* church?" asked Drew, looking puzzled. "They sing about stuff like that?"

"Remember, Drew, Mr. Pipes taught us about figurative language," said Annie, looking up from her sketchbook open on her lap. "I'm sure it's not a hymn about rocks and gravel."

"No, indeed," said Mr. Pipes, laughing. "It is a hymn that finds its inspiration in the biblical metaphor of Christ the cornerstone or foundation upon which the church—the elect throughout the ages, not a mere building—is forever securely founded."

"'The church's one foundation is Jesus Christ her Lord,'" quoted Annie. "You taught us that hymn that first summer in Olney."

"Stone," said Drew, his mouth full of chocolate.

"What?" said Annie.

"Stone; Mr. Samuel Stone wrote that one," he explained. "You know, the guy with the big muscles who punched the lights out of that bully—" Drew was feeling more himself, and smashed his fist into his palm with a crack that echoed down the row of spires.

"Yes, yes, Drew," laughed Mr. Pipes. "The things you remember about these hymn-writers! I do wonder."

"Hey, you know that Bible reading schedule you gave us?" Drew went on. "I just read in Zechariah the other day about the cornerstone."

"So did I," said Annie.

"Ah, and as did I," said Mr. Pipes. "Now, there is a source of inspiration for your poetry, Drew," continued Mr. Pipes. "Return to your passage in Zechariah, and rise to the heights—er, ah, rather, fill your poetry with gems from those pages of Holy Scripture."

"Gems?" said Drew. "You know, there's something about gems—or is it jewels?—in that Zechariah passage, I'm sure of it."

"I liked that part," said Annie, closing her eyes as she tried to remember. "It said something about his flock sparkling in the land like jewels in a crown."

"That was it," said Drew.

"Well, the metaphor of Christ the cornerstone of the church appears frequently throughout Scripture." Mr. Pipes opened his hymnal. "But this hymn likely found its source in Isaiah 28:16: 'See, I lay a stone in Zion, a tested stone, a precious cornerstone for a sure foundation.'"

"Who turned it into poetry?" asked Annie.

"No one knows," said Mr. Pipes.

"Too bad," said Annie. "When did she write it?"

"Wait a sec," said Drew. "We don't know if a 'she' wrote it."

"We don't know that a 'she' didn't write it, either," said Annie.

"More likely a man," said Drew.

"Well, whoever wrote it, the text appeared in the A.D. 600s," said Mr. Pipes. "Ironically, it was written in a time, alas, when many were attempting to throw their shoulder against Christ the foundation of the church and replace him with the crumbling stones of a sacramental religion—a religion where man in vain attempts to try to please God through all kinds of rituals. You build a cathedral like this on that kind of rubbish of a foundation"—Mr. Pipes's eyebrows bristled and a glint of indignation snapped in his eyes—"and down she comes in a heap of rubble." He brought one hand down on the other with a loud slap.

Drew swallowed hard, remembering how far below the plaza had looked.

"H-how's the hymn go?" he asked, hoping to steer Mr. Pipes back.

Annie and Drew looked over Mr. Pipes's shoulder as he read aloud:

Christ is made the sure foundation,
Christ the head and cornerstone,

Chosen of the Lord and precious,
Binding all the church in one;
Holy Zion's help forever,
And her confidence alone.

"Notice here, once again, my dears," said Mr. Pipes, his long index finger pointing to the words of the second verse, "the importance of singing hymns forever. Do read the next lines for us, Drew."

Drew read:

All that dedicated city,
Dearly loved of God on high,
In exultant jubilation
Pours perpetual melody;
God the One in Three adoring
In glad hymns eternally.

"There's the Trinity," said Annie.

"Yes, an essential priority of early Christian hymnody," said Mr. Pipes.

"What does 'perpetual' mean?" asked Drew.

"Without end," said Mr. Pipes.

"From age to age," said Annie.

Mr. Pipes read the next two verses, prayers for God to come and hear his people who one day will reign with him forever.

"It concludes in lines filled with the most grand and enduring praise," said Mr. Pipes. "Listen—forgive me, but I simply must sing them."

His voice rose above the highest pinnacle of the ancient cathedral, and an anthem of praise filled Annie and Drew's ears and souls as they listened.

Laud and honor to the Father,
Laud and honor to the Son,

Laud and honor to the Spirit,
Ever Three and ever One,
One in might, and One in glory,
While unending ages run.

Mr. Pipes's singing caught the attention of the tourists, who stared from the other end of the cathedral roof.

"Oh, Mr. Pipes," said Annie, "you sang that melody so beautifully!"

"You are too kind, my dear," said Mr. Pipes, smiling. "Credit, however, must go to the beautiful melody itself."

"I'd sure like to hear it on an organ," said Drew. "Who wrote it?"

"Henry Purcell, the fine English composer whose life overlaps the more famous J. S. Bach," replied Mr. Pipes. "'Tis a grand tune called *Westminster Abbey*, and suits this text to near heavenly perfection."

"Can we sing the whole hymn with you?" asked Annie.

"We shall," said Mr. Pipes.

To the accompaniment of cooing pigeons, and helped by the many spires pointing to the sky from the roof of the cathedral, they lifted their voices to heaven.

6
Mr. Pipes in Tights!

Christian, Dost Thou See Them?
(St. Andrew of Crete)

When I was a kid, did I like singing about,
"We Are but Little Children, Weak"?
or "Jesus, Meek and Gentle?" Not on your life!
I liked "Christian, Dost Thou [See] Them"?
—especially the bit about "prowl and prowl
   around."

DOROTHY SAYERS

"What is the meaning of this!" cried Mr. Pipes that same evening as they stood at the open door of their hotel room.

"Looks like someone's bedroom I could name," said Annie, her eyes wide as she stared at the chairs turned over and the bedsheets strewn about the room. "What a mess!"

It took Drew a moment longer to realize that something was amiss. "We didn't leave it like this, did we?" he asked.

102

Mr. Pipes looked back down the hallway and then reentered the room and closed the door.

"Of course we did not, Drew," he said. "We've been robbed!"

"Robbed?" said Drew, his cheeks flushed with excitement. "Robbed for real?"

"What do you think they were after?" asked Annie, winding a strand of hair around her finger and chewing nervously on her lower lip.

Mr. Pipes looked at the children, his eyes narrowed. Suddenly he slapped his leg.

"Passports! Do check for your passports," he said, opening his shoulder bag, "and your money. You didn't leave any valuables in the hotel, I trust?"

Annie and Drew opened their knapsacks and showed Mr. Pipes their passports, money, Bibles, cameras, and notebooks.

"Just like you taught us," said Drew, looking eagerly around the room, "travel light and keep important things on your person at all times. We got 'em this time. The only thing they could have stolen of mine would be my spare shoes and extra clothes—and they were dirty."

After several minutes of sorting through their spare luggage and tidying up, the three had returned the hotel room back to normal.

"They didn't take anything," said Annie. With a shudder, she added, "Though I don't like the idea of their prowling around our rooms and pawing through our stuff any better."

"Wasn't much to take in the first place," said Drew.

Mr. Pipes paced back and forth, stroking his chin in thought. He paused at the window and looked down on the narrow street, searching the faces of the passersby below.

"Hmm-mm," he said at last, running his long fingers through his white hair.

"Mr. Pipes," said Annie slowly, "why do you think they even tried finding anything of value in our rooms?" She laughed. "I mean, do we look like rich tourists?"

"Good point, Annie," said her brother. "It doesn't add up. This is an inexpensive hotel; rich people don't stay in inexpensive hotels. Now, if I were going to rob somebody, you can bet your bottom dollar—or lire—I'd make good and sure they had lots to rob, wouldn't you, Mr. Pipes?"

"*Drew*, how can you say that?" said Annie.

"I say, it takes considerable imagining, praise be to God," replied Mr. Pipes, with a wry smile, "to delve into the dark recesses of the criminal mind. But, my boy, you are correct to assume that no skilled thief would attempt a robbery of the likes of us."

"Yeah, the risk's just too high," said Drew. "I've read that in Italy they dump you in jail for next to nothing and throw away the key. I've also heard that the jails are the worst: hungry rats, big as cats; stale bread and bad water; and even torture—"

"Yes, yes, Drew, my boy," said Mr. Pipes, cutting him short. "Jails in Italy, no doubt, fall somewhat short of the country-club amenities you sport in American prisons. But we needn't dwell upon the baser details."

"So why did they do it?" asked Annie slowly. "Try to rob *us*, I mean."

Mr. Pipes removed his eyeglasses, breathed on them, and wiped them deliberately before replying. "We can only hope it was all a—a mistake," he said, but without conviction.

Drew looked at Mr. Pipes. "Mistake? No way! With all these rich Italians strutting around everywhere you turn, why bother with us? No, I think someone's after us again." He clapped his hands together and rubbed them briskly. "But we're ready for 'em this time! Okay, what's the plan? Tell you what, I'll start tying bedsheets together so we can escape out the window. Annie, you go get a couple of bottles of catsup off one of the tables in the dining room—we'll make it look like somebody got—"

"Drew, Drew!" said Mr. Pipes, gripping him firmly by the shoulders. "This is not a game. Of that much I am certain. I do not pretend to know why thieves broke into our hotel room but stole nothing. Dr. Dudley, however, has given me his solemn word, assured me with the most virulent language. No, I am most certain he has not sent along his nephew to watch over us."

"Th-that makes this the real thing," said Annie, biting her lower lip again.

"You mean," said Drew, his eyes dancing and a smile creeping across his face. "Let me get this straight, Mr. Pipes. You actually think someone's after us—for real? Oh, this is too good to be true!"

Mr. Pipes did not answer immediately. Again he walked over to the edge of the window and peered cautiously into the street.

"Mr. Pipes?" said Annie, joining him at the window. "Do you really think someone's a-after us?"

Mr. Pipes put his arm around Annie's shoulder and patted her reassuringly.

"I do, my dear," he said, looking at her with worried eyes. "I only wish I could whisk both of you away from this place to somewhere safe."

"But why are they following us?" asked Annie.

"That I do not know," he replied, peering again out the window.

"Do you see them out there?" asked Drew.

"Careful, Drew," said Mr. Pipes, grabbing him by the arm and pulling him to the edge of the window. "Try not to be seen. If you look carefully between the curtain and edge of the window you will see a man and a woman—see them, just there—sitting cross-legged on the pavement, leaning against the base of that fountain. Do you see them?"

"Sure," said Drew.

Annie bit her lip and frowned.

"We'd call them granolas—you know, hippies or greeners," said Drew. "*That's* who's following us?" He sounded disappointed.

"I know, Drew," replied Mr. Pipes. "You were hoping for something a bit more sinister—"

"I was hoping they'd be wearing camouflage," he said. "You know, with AK47s slung over their shoulders—like Partisans, or something."

"Of course, that would never do; concealment is of the utmost importance," replied Mr. Pipes.

"So you think they do have g-guns?" asked Annie, steadying her voice as best she could.

"I have no idea," said Mr. Pipes. "We must assume they do not, and though they are following us—I have observed them on at least three occasions now, but said nothing for fear of worrying you—I am most convinced that it is still very much a mistake. They mean to be following someone, but for some inexplicable reason have attached themselves to us instead."

"They were on the cathedral today," said Drew. "I'm sure of it."

"Indeed they were," said Mr. Pipes.

"I-I think I saw them along the canal this morning," said Annie.

"Perhaps you did," said Mr. Pipes. "I first saw them back in Rome. But that is all by the bye. I for one do not plan to remain here the passive object of their surveillance. Gather your things. I shall ring for a cab."

He picked up the phone and began to dial.

"Stop!" said Drew. "What if they've tapped the phone?"

"Jolly good thinking, my boy," said Mr. Pipes, returning the receiver gently. "We shall check out of the hotel and find a phone somewhere else. But we must make haste."

Annie stayed close to Mr. Pipes as they left their room and crept softly down toward the lobby. Drew flopped onto his belly in the hall and signaled them to low-crawl like the Marines, but to Annie's relief, Mr. Pipes said it was most unnecessary.

"All right, my dears," said Mr. Pipes under his breath. "We must not exit by way of the main door; they are certain to see us. Follow me down this hallway. Ah, yes, here is a back exit."

Mr. Pipes turned the doorknob.

Clang! clang! clang! A noisy bell rang throughout the hallway and rattled off the brick walls lining the back street of the hotel. Several heads poked out of windows. Shouts joined the clanging.

"It's an alarm!" squealed Annie. "We're done for."

"Oh, no, we are not," said Mr. Pipes, grabbing their hands. "We shall duck into that narrow alleyway just there! Now, run for it!"

The next few moments were a blur to Annie. Later that evening she tried writing down in her journal all that had happened. They zigzagged through narrow alleys, climbed over a brick wall, and even found themselves nearly tangled in laundry strung across the pavement of a side street. They darted past the wall of a back garden and heard the full-throated operatic singing of an Italian soprano—they later discussed at length whether it had been a real person or just the radio. For a whole block a ferocious little pug-nosed dog nipped menacingly at their heels. Finally, they came out on a busy street and quickly joined the crowd.

"Taxi!" called Mr. Pipes.

Within fifteen minutes they found themselves at the Milan train station, where Mr. Pipes bought tickets for passage on the next train leaving the station. "For anywhere," he told the ticket clerk. Five minutes later, they sat down on the hard wooden seats of a train bound for Genoa. As the train squeaked and grumbled over the rails, Mr. Pipes tried to reassure the children.

"I was not planning to take you to Genoa," he said, sighing heavily and wiping his face with his handkerchief. "Ah, and I had so hoped to show you, while in Milan, Leonardo da Vinci's great painting of The Last Supper. It cannot be helped; under the circumstances, it is actually safer to alter our plans in an apparently random direction. We are so very much harder to follow when we ourselves hardly know where we are bound." He smiled and, taking both Annie's hands in his, gave them a reassuring squeeze. "Ah, yes, we should be most safe now," though his eyes searched down the aisle of the train as he said it.

Annie hoped he was right.

"I don't see how anyone could find us," she said, smiling up at him.

"Unless they're really good," said Drew, hopefully.

Late that night they fell exhausted into lumpy beds in a hotel near the train station in Genoa. Though Annie was worried, weariness was greater than her worry, and she soon fell fast asleep. Drew sat up with his flashlight for some time writing in his notebook. Mr. Pipes lay awake, hands clasped behind his white head and occasionally emitting a heavy sigh. He tried desperately to come up with a plan of escape from whoever was following them.

They awoke the next morning to blaring engines, tooting horns, people greeting one another with "Buon giorno," and the deep, mournful blast of a foghorn drifting over the city from the sea.

Mr. Pipes crept to the window and peered cautiously out over the street far below. Annie and Drew joined him.

"Do you see them?" whispered Annie.

"Not a trace," said Mr. Pipes, triumphantly.

"Are you sure?" asked Drew, squeezing closer to the window for a look himself. "That was too easy."

"Oh, be sure of it," said Mr. Pipes, "I do not intend to take any chances. We shall proceed only with the greatest caution."

Just then a long blast of the foghorn rose above the din.

"It's sunny here," said Drew. "But I can just make out a low bank of fog with some cranelike things sticking up through it."

"And that looks like a row of masts," said Annie, pointing toward the harbor, "and some kind of enormous lighthouse—it all seems to be growing out of a field of cotton candy."

"That is, of course, the sea covered at the moment in morning mist," said Mr. Pipes. "Strategically situated as she is on the Mediterranean Sea, Genoa has been an important port city for centuries where ships from all over the world came to trade and where one of the world's greatest seamen began learning his craft."

"Who was that?" asked Drew.

"Perhaps the greatest navigator of all time was born in Genoa," said Mr. Pipes. "You Americans should know who he is."

"'In fourteen hundred ninety-two, Columbus sailed the ocean blue!'" said Annie.

"Precisely," laughed Mr. Pipes. "Genoa was his hometown."

He walked over to the door, put his ear up close to it, and listened for a moment. Then he opened the door just enough to look both ways down the hall.

"No one in sight; that is good," he said. "Aha, what have we here—the morning paper, and in English."

"I'm starving," said Drew. "Maybe we can go out and find some food and see some Columbus sights?"

"But what about the robbers?" asked Annie. "They'll see us if we leave the hotel."

"But we can't stay here forever," said Drew. "I say we go face them like men and have it out in the streets once and for all." He brandished an imaginary sword and cornered an invisible enemy against the wall. "Take that, garlic breath."

"Hmm-mm," said Mr. Pipes, as he sat reading the front page of the newspaper. "What a happy providence this is."

"What is?" Annie perched on the arm of his chair and looked at the paper.

"This entire week is a festival week in Genoa," he explained. "Some kind of maritime festival where the whole town dresses in medieval costume and parades about the streets. It should be quite a show. Look, they've printed photographs of last year's celebration; isn't it lovely?"

"She is very pretty," said Annie, admiring a smiling young woman wearing a yellow-and-green silk gown with billowing split sleeves. "Oh, it looks so festive. I'd love to see everyone all dressed like in the olden days."

"Nice sword," said Drew, pointing to a man in tights and doublet, the goldwork of his sword flashing proudly at his hip.

"But do we dare go out?" asked Annie again.

Mr. Pipes refolded the newspaper thoughtfully; then, looking at Annie and Drew, he slapped it into his hand.

"I have got it!" he said with a laugh.

"Got what?" asked Annie and Drew.

"The solution to our being followed by those brigands."

"So we can go out and see the sights?" said Annie.

"And have some breakfast?" added Drew.

"And spend the day going wherever we please," said Mr. Pipes. "How would you like to dress up *yourselves* and join all Genoa in her festival as a fine lord and lady?"

"Oh, Mr. Pipes, and you will, too!" said Annie, squealing with delight at the thought. "Let's see, you could be a wise old wool merchant."

"In t-tights?" said Drew, sounding a little uncertain.

"With a sword at your belt, Drew," said Annie, spinning around and curtsying.

Mr. Pipes rang the front desk and requested the address of the nearest costume shop. Then he had Annie and Drew lie down on newspapers spread out on the floor, and he carefully traced the outline of each of them.

"You both must stay here while I go select your costumes," he said, tucking the newspapers under his arm. "I shall get fitted myself and return as another man from another time." He laughed. "We will hardly recognize each other. More importantly, the ne'er-do-goods tailing us will lose our scent for certain."

"Please try to get me something . . . well, something . . . pretty," said Annie, as Mr. Pipes turned up his collar and opened the door.

"Don't forget the sword," said Drew. "I think I can wear anything as long as I have a sword."

After an anxious hour, a series of light taps came at the door. Annie and Drew froze.

"Who goes there?" barked Drew, trying to sound tough.

"It is I," Mr. Pipes's familiar voice called in a hoarse whisper from the other side of the door.

Drew flung open the door. They stared in amazement.

An elderly gentleman stood awkwardly at the door; his head seemed to be perched on a round ruffle collar that looked like a large cake—in this case, a cake with a head protruding through it. He wore a green silk cape tied with a cord over a lighter green doublet striped with shiny gold chevrons. Instead of pants, he wore striped shorts that flared out and seemed to tuck back under, and though he wore an all-business looking sword at his waist, Drew could not take his eyes off the tights—shimmering gold tights.

Drew was first to find his voice. "No necktie," he said, wonder in his voice.

"Is it really you?" asked Annie, her eyes and mouth wide at the sight of him.

"Indeed it is," replied Mr. Pipes, setting down two large boxes. Wringing his hands, he asked, "Do I look so very silly? I certainly feel so. Perhaps it was all a very bad idea."

Drew was silent.

"Oh, no," Annie squealed with delight. "You look wonderful—even dignified."

Her brother stared at her.

"And I can't wait to see what you got for Drew and me," she went on. "Oh, the robbers will never recognize us wearing clothes like that."

"I can believe that," said Drew, still staring at Mr. Pipes's tights.

Annie and Drew took their boxes into their rooms, and after several minutes Annie came out wearing a green silk dress split at the waist with a full-length skirt in gold underneath. Her long striped sleeves were fitted to the elbow, then flared wide and gathered in three billows to her shoulders. Fine embroidery trimmed the edges of the neckline and hem. She had left her hair down and braided only two small strands from her forehead and gathered the braids at the back in a silk ribbon.

"You look absolutely charming, my dear," said Mr. Pipes, bowing low. "And your hair collected by those two lovely little braids looks for all the world like a golden crown built right in, never to come off."

Beaming with pleasure, Annie spun around in a circle, and curtsied.

"Thank you, Mr. Pipes," she said, "for picking something so pretty."

"Let us hope your brother finds his costume as much to his liking. I fear he may not. Drew, do come out," he called.

Drew's door opened slowly. He wore an outfit much like that of Mr. Pipes—including tights. He kept pulling down on the puffy shorts, and his face was very red.

"Couldn't I wear jeans with it?" asked Drew.

"It looks . . . well, dashing," said Annie. "Oh, what fun this is."

"Never fear, Drew," said Mr. Pipes. "I thought you might prefer covering most of your outfit with the knight's tabard of St. George the Dragon Slayer, patron saint of Genoa—and of merry England, I might add."

He held up a long white shirt with no sleeves and a bold red cross covering the front.

Drew pulled it over his head, and Mr. Pipes helped him buckle a wide leather belt around his waist.

"And of course, Sir Andrew," said Mr. Pipes, "your sword."

Drew's eyes grew wide, and a smile crept over his face as he gripped the sword and admired the twisted gold of the basket hilt.

"I'm thinking this was not a bad idea, after all," said Drew, grinning from ear to ear as he admired himself in the mirror. "And you know something? With this sword at my belt," he snorted and waggled his head confidently in the mirror, "I hope I do meet our robbers; I'd take 'em on."

Annie and Mr. Pipes burst into laughter.

"Ah, yes, Drew; well," said Mr. Pipes, "we have time for a quick bite of breakfast, which I have brought back for us.

Then I have a plan for our certain escape from our shadowing brigands. Our worry from that quarter shall soon be past."

During breakfast, Mr. Pipes spread a map of Genoa on the table, showed the children where they were, and pointed out the church of Santo Stefano only a few blocks away. When they had collected their luggage, Mr. Pipes explained:

"It is far better if each of us leaves alone. Those following us are used to seeing three people together. Even if they have managed to track us, they shall see us only one at a time and, dressed as we are, shall never figure out that we are the ones that they, for whatever reason, are chasing. I shall go first to be certain we are not watched. Then, after waiting but ten minutes, you, Annie, will follow—remember, two left turns, pass through the Porta dell'Olivella, then right down the narrow street ending at the old church. Drew, you will bring up the rear and make certain we are not followed. Ready?"

Ten minutes later Annie stepped into the street and turned left. Everyone she saw looked like they had stepped out of a fairy tale, and she saw no sign at all of the robbers. She passed down narrow cobbled streets no wider than sidewalks. The buildings on either side, connected by electric wires and clotheslines, seemed almost to bump into each other far above, and only occasionally did a shaft of sunlight make its way to glow off the worn cobblestones.

There's the gate, she said to herself. *And it looks like a real castle fortress gate*, she thought, admiring the round towers and narrow entrance between them as she passed under the ancient gateway. To her right she caught sight of a broad stone wall with rounded arches but only a few small windows. *This must be Santo Stefano*, she thought as she came into the sunlight and mounted the stairs.

"Oh, there you are, my dear," Mr. Pipes's voice came out of the darkness as she entered the church.

Annie blinked, trying to see him in the gloomy interior. She reminded herself that he now looked like someone who had lived hundreds of years ago.

"You took longer than I thought you would, and I was beginning to worry," said Mr. Pipes.

"I'm sorry," said Annie. "But all those narrow streets and the city gate were so old and lovely. Oh, and almost everyone is dressed just like we are; it was like stepping back in time."

"Did you see anything of the robbers?" asked Mr. Pipes.

"No."

"Good. Now we wait for Drew."

Moments later the door flew open and Drew stood in the doorway, his legs spread wide and his hand on his sword hilt. Sunlight glowed from behind him and cast his shadow nearly all the way across the smooth stone floor of the narthex.

"My, my, what have we here?" said Mr. Pipes. "He looks for all the world like the Dragon Slayer himself."

Drew swaggered toward them.

"Good, we are all together again," said Mr. Pipes, sighing with relief.

"Yeah, but it's kind of a bummer," said Drew. "I didn't see anyone who looked even remotely like our robbers." He crossed his arms and flopped against a column, his sword clanging against the stone floor and echoing throughout the old church. "I was ready for 'em."

Mr. Pipes laughed and, putting his arm comfortingly around Drew's shoulders, led them around the dark interior of the church.

"It's kind of gloomy," said Annie.

"Romanesque churches were often like that," said Mr. Pipes.

"What's so special about this church?" asked Drew.

"Ah, your Christopher Columbus was born very near here," replied Mr. Pipes. "Perhaps the house once stood on one of those narrow cobbled streets through which we have just passed. But this church, historians all agree, was the church wherein Columbus was baptized."

"How do you know all this stuff?" asked Drew. "You weren't even planning to bring us here."

"Ah, it's books, my boy," replied Mr. Pipes with a chuckle. "I find it all in books."

"But Columbus didn't write a hymn, did he?" asked Annie.

"Certainly not that I have any knowledge of. I fear that whatever commitment Columbus claimed to Christ was soon overshadowed by his lust for gold and personal glory, not fit ambitions from which one writes hymns."

"So where were you going to take us?" asked Drew. "Before we got robbed, that is."

"Crete," said Mr. Pipes. "I had planned for us to catch a flight to the island of Crete."

"Hey, when you read from Acts at breakfast the other day," said Drew, "wasn't there something about Crete?"

"Yes, there was," replied Mr. Pipes.

"When the apostles preached on the day of Pentecost," said Annie, looking up at the barrel-vaulted ceiling in thought, "Cretans—that must be people from Crete—along with lots of other people, heard the gospel in their own language."

"That is correct," said Mr. Pipes. "And throughout the first few centuries after Christ's ascension, the gospel continued to spread in Crete. Meanwhile, in A.D. 660, a boy was born in Damascus who would eventually grow up to be the archbishop of the church in Crete. You, Drew, will like his name; it was Andrew of Crete."

"Does have a nice ring to it," agreed Drew.

"Tell us about him?" asked Annie.

"The story goes," continued Mr. Pipes, "that he was born mute, that is, he could not speak a word. But when he turned seven he partook for the first time of the Lord's Supper and soon thereafter began speaking."

"Is that really true?" asked Annie.

"That is the story; I do not know if it is true or not. But in any case, Andrew grew up with a great love of the singing of the human voice."

"If at first he couldn't even talk," said Drew, "that probably made him appreciate singing all the more."

"He must have written hymns, then," said Annie.

"Yes, he wrote a great deal of poetry for singing in church, but most of it was far too long for our worship today. One of his canons, written for Lent to be sung just before Holy Week, has over 250 stanzas and requires some three hours of continuous singing to complete!"

"Wow!" said Drew. "That's not going to be in your hymnal."

"But he must have written one we can learn," said Annie.

"Oh, indeed he did," said Mr. Pipes, turning the pages of his hymnal. "This is a worthy favorite for any young Christian serious about making war with the powers of evil and gaining victory over sin waging battle against his soul. It is set to an unusual two-part melody, the first part almost chanted in a minor key, then resolving with a tune full of triumph and gladness."

He hummed the first lines, and Annie thought the sinister-sounding strains worked well in that gloomy church.

"Now, then, I shall try and sing it through for you once, and then you must join me.

> Christian, dost thou see them
> On the holy ground,
> How the pow'rs of darkness
> Rage thy steps around?

"Listen carefully, now, to the dramatic change in this next part of the verse," said Mr. Pipes.

> Christian, up and smite them,
> Counting gain but loss,

116

In the strength that cometh
By the holy cross.

"That sounds great, and I've got an idea!" said Drew. "How about, Mr. Pipes, if you stand on this side of the church and Annie and I stand across from you a little ways. Then you sing the first part—you know, the warning part—and we'll sing the 'up and smite them' part. I like that part," he added, drawing his sword and taking a swipe at the air.

"Hey, watch it with that thing," said Annie, ducking behind a pew.

"Yes, a wonderful idea, but do be careful, my boy," said Mr. Pipes, taking his place across the aisle from the children.

Mr. Pipes began the second verse:

Christian, dost thou feel them,
How they work within,
Striving, tempting, luring,
Goading into sin?

And Annie and Drew replied:

Christian, never tremble;
Never be downcast;
Gird thee for the battle,
Watch and pray and fast.

Christian, dost thou hear them,
How they speak thee fair?
"Always fast and vigil?
Always watch and prayer?"

Christian, answer boldly,
"While I breathe I pray!"
Peace shall follow battle,
Night shall end in day.

Hear the words of Jesus:
"O my servant true;
Thou art very weary—
I was weary too—"

Mr. Pipes continued singing with Annie and Drew to the end, and the dark church resounded brightly with Jesus' comforting promise:

But that toil shall make thee
Some day all mine own,
And the end of sorrow
Shall be near my throne.

When the last echo had died away and Mr. Pipes had shown them the baptismal font where, in 1451, Columbus had been baptized, he said, "We must make the most of this providential change in plans. There is much to see in Genoa, and I have taken the liberty of booking the most extraordinary accommodation for tonight. If we have not wholly lost our robbers already, which of course I believe we have, where we slumber tonight is so unconventional, so out of the ordinary and unplanned, that it is sure to finally throw them off our course!"

"Oh, tell us!" begged Annie and Drew.

"It will remain my surprise whilst we tour the city."

"How about lunch first?" suggested Drew.

"We shall dine on *pesce azzurro alla griglia*, for those who like grilled fish from the sea. And for you, Annie, anything you would like."

"Show me the way," said Drew, heading for the door of the church.

"And after lunch," continued Mr. Pipes, "we shall walk all about the narrow streets of the city. During which time we must see what many folks in Genoa consider to be the Holy Grail—the cup used at the Last Supper. Furthermore, I think it is high time we ring up your parents and Dr. Dudley, to let them know we are alive and in one piece. I suggest we not worry them with the little matter of the robbers. And after dinner we shall conclude the day by climbing the thirteenth-century Lanterna, the lighthouse symbol of Genoa, to the very top, all 383 feet of it. I hear from there the views of the city, the ships, and the Mediterranean Sea are magnificent."

*

As that very full day came to a close, Drew explained to Mr. Pipes and Annie that because he had some pressing things to write in his journal that just couldn't wait, he insisted they climb the lighthouse without him. Though it was all a pretext to avoid looking down on the city from 383 precarious feet, Drew did reread those verses in Zechariah chapters 9 and 10, and he did continue working on a poem:

He makes his children mighty men,
    They bend the battle bow;
So in God's strength, against the proud,
    His foes they . . .

Annie and Mr. Pipes were gone for well over an hour, but that seemed to be all he could think of for the moment. He'd work on it some more later.

When they returned, both Annie and Mr. Pipes were flushed from the exercise and from the exhilaration of the magnificent view from the top of the lighthouse. Annie wanted to tell Drew all about it, but not wanting to make him feel bad because of his trouble with heights, she said little. Mr. Pipes led them along the nearby pier to a place where several wooden schooners lay moored. Wearing their fifteenth-century costumes, they blended right in with the crowds gathered along the waterfront for the maritime festival.

"We saw these ships from the lighthouse," said Annie. "Aren't they beautiful?"

"And which one do you think is the most beautiful?" asked Mr. Pipes, pausing at the stern of a vessel bearing the name *Euroclydon* on her wineglass transom. "Aha, fancy that; this one hails from Boston," he added, reading the smaller letters under the name.

"That's in America," said Drew.

"Well, then, this one's the one for us, I guess," said Annie.

"Gather your things," said Mr. Pipes, a twinkle in his eye. "And prepare to board her."

"You mean to actually go on board?" asked Drew.

"And see down below?" added Annie.

"Oh, yes, you shall see down below," said Mr. Pipes, laughing. "And in every nook and cranny if you wish. Everything is arranged; though oddly the chap on the telephone this morning spoke very little English and that poorly enough, I booked three berths on her. We are spending the night on board! Ahoy, *Euroclydon!*" he called.

No answer.

"I say, Ahoy, *Euroclydon!*" he cupped his hands around his mouth and tried again. "Ahoy there!"

He checked his watch and frowned at a booking form he'd pulled from his shoulder bag.

"This must be the vessel," he said, his eyes searching the deck. "I say, Ahoy, the ship!"

Suddenly, from somewhere belowdecks came the distant reply: "Avast, mateys—bilge breath, bilge breath—welcome aboard, welcome aboard!"

"Ah . . . there we are," said Mr. Pipes, a slight frown still wrinkling his brow. "Not what one might consider a proper welcome, but her plank is out. Perhaps most of the crew is on shore enjoying the festivities. We shall go aboard, stow our things, and wait about for the captain. Follow me, my hearties." And he led them up the plank at the stern of the vessel and onto the meticulous deck of the schooner.

Annie paused near the polished brass compass binnacle and laughed as she caught sight of their reflection wearing their medieval finery, now all twisted and distorted by the curve of the brass.

"So it's just for the one night," said Drew, gazing up at the rope-ladder ratlines, the masts and spars, and the sails neatly stowed but ready for unfurling at a moment's notice. "And we're not going to sea on her?"

"Oh, Drew, my boy," said Mr. Pipes, "don't be ridiculous. Of course we cannot actually go to sea on her—lovely if we could, but it is simply out of the question, I am sure. Let us go below and stow our things and enjoy the view of the harbor from her excellent decks—she is so very shipshape, yes, yes, a wonderful seagoing vessel, indeed she is."

He paused just aft of the forward mast. "Now, where is that chap who welcomed us on board?"

"Welcome Aboard!"

All Glory, Laud, and Honor
(Theodulph of Orleans)

To thee before thy passion,

They sang their hymns of praise;

To thee, now high exalted,

Our melody we raise.

We simply cannot proceed one step further," said Mr. Pipes, pausing at the companionway before descending the steep stairs leading belowdecks. "I must have your confirmation, children, before we go belowdecks: Did you or did you not hear, most distinctly, a voice on board this vessel inviting us to board? I must have your answer."

"Sure, we both heard him," said Drew.

" 'Welcome aboard.' He said it twice," said Annie.

"Just as I remembered it myself," said Mr. Pipes. "But, you understand, I had to be sure. And now that I am, we shall make ourselves welcome, and hope the captain arrives before nightfall. Now, let us see where we are to stow our things." He led them down the steep companionway.

"Oh, now, this is a real ship," said Drew, breathing in the strong aroma of well-oiled hardwood, sail canvas, and spare rope. "It even smells like one."

"Everything's so scrubbed and tidy," said Annie. "And I love all the brass—must take lots of rubbing to keep it so shiny."

"Ahoy there," called Mr. Pipes down the narrow passage they entered at the foot of the companionway. He cupped his hands around his mouth and tried again. "We are a Mr. Pipes and two booked for the night on board your lovely schooner. Hello there! Ahoy!"

He held up his hand for silence, cocking his head to one side while he strained to hear a reply.

"They've abandoned her," said Drew, eagerly. "And we can claim salvage—she's ours! Let's see, Mr. Pipes will be captain; I'll be first mate; and Annie, you can be the cook and do all the swabbing and stuff—while we sail the ship."

"No ship this meticulously fitted—she's absolutely ready for sea, right down to the last knot," said Mr. Pipes. "I say, no ship cared for as this ship is cared for has been abandoned; be sure of it. Her crew must simply be enjoying the festivities and will soon return. Aha, here is a cabin marked 'guests quarters.' That would be us."

He opened the narrow teak door, and they entered a cabin no longer than a grown man was tall. Two built-in berths lined either side of the compartment, and a narrow folding table made of solid teak and polished to a brilliant shine extended halfway between the berths. Amber light from the setting sun shone through a thick round porthole secured with massive wing nuts and positioned between the berths above the table.

"We get to stay here tonight?" squealed Annie. "Oh, and each berth has its own little brass reading lantern, and curtains that'll make things so cozy. This is a wonderful surprise, Mr. Pipes. Thank you."

"Can I have a top bunk?" asked Drew.

"You may," said Mr. Pipes, unloading his luggage on one of the lower berths and sliding in and sitting on the edge of the berth at the table. Annie took the berth opposite Mr. Pipes and immediately set to work arranging it to her liking.

"As soon as you have settled your things," said Mr. Pipes, "we must go back on deck for what looks like a lovely sunset. Perhaps we shall meet our host. Drew, I believe we both would do well to leave our swords belowdecks; I'd hate for us to accidentally damage the fine woodwork in one of these narrow passageways."

"But what if pirates try to board?" asked Drew. "Night's the best time for a surprise attack from pirates; I think we should be ready for them."

"Nevertheless, we shall leave our swords below, my boy," said Mr. Pipes.

"Oh, I'd love to see the sunset," said Annie, "but I can't wait to cuddle up in my berth and read. Whoever designed these berths must have loved reading before going to sleep, just like I do."

"Does look like a good deal," said Drew, reluctantly unbuckling his sword. "And this way, we don't use up our flashlight batteries."

"And with the curtain pulled, like this," said Annie, pulling her curtain closed, "you don't have to read under the covers. Oh, it's all just perfect."

"Indeed," said Mr. Pipes. "However, I would feel ever so much better about it all if we could meet the captain."

Back on deck they lounged on the roof of the main cabin, admiring the schooner and the evening. Then a noise in the water caught Drew's attention.

"Did you hear it?" he asked, holding up his hand for silence.

"Hear what?" said Annie and Mr. Pipes.

"Fish," hissed Drew. "Big one." He jumped up and headed toward the companionway. "Got to get my pole."

"Drew, your light fishing gear, I fear, would be of little use with saltwater quarry," said Mr. Pipes. "Perhaps our host will have some stout sea gear with which you might fish in the morning. Do sit with us, my boy, and enjoy the sunset."

Drew reluctantly sat back down. Together they watched the lights of the city twinkling on shore and the rhythmic pulse of the great light atop the Lanterna lighthouse near the entrance to the harbor.

"There it goes," said Annie dreamily, as she watched through the ratlines of the schooner the orange ball of the sun touch the horizon and steadily flatten out as it sank in the west. "It seems to go down so fast. Is it moving that fast during the day, too? Of course I know it is."

"Going, going, gone," said Drew, as the last of the sun disappeared below the horizon. "Wait! I'll bet I can see it again."

With that, jumping up and grabbing the rope rungs of the ratlines, Drew took several cautious steps upward. "There it is again!" he called down excitedly. Then, looking down, he caught his breath. With clenched teeth he fumbled for the lower rungs with his feet, finally heaving a sigh of relief when he felt the solid bulwark and then the deck under him.

Mr. Pipes looked at Drew in the dim light but said nothing.

"I wish these moments would last forever," said Annie, leaning against the main mast; she smoothed the silk of her skirts and pulled her knees up under her chin.

Mr. Pipes clasped his hands around his knee and looked tenderly at the children. He understood something of Annie's longing. The adventures enjoyed with these children over the last few years were one of the great pleasures of his long life, and seeing them brought to a living faith in God and singing praises to him was the crowning pleasure of all. But he and his late wife had so wanted children of their very own. He loved Annie and Drew as if they were his own—which they were not. In any case, sooner than he cared to admit, moments like this enjoyed with these dear ones would come to an end—forever. With bushy eyebrows lowered, he sat pensive for several moments.

And then he slapped his knee, shook himself, looked heavenward, and broke out laughing.

"What are you laughing at, Mr. Pipes?" asked Annie.

"Myself," he said. "Humph. Old fool that I am sometimes. It is precisely this that *will* last forever, my dears." He laughed again.

Drew turned toward the horizon where the sun had disappeared; puzzled, he looked back at Mr. Pipes.

"No, no, that sunset is gone," said Mr. Pipes, waving his hand as if giving it permission to go. "But every true pleasure we enjoy in this life—and that includes all the adventures we have shared, my dears—I say, every sunset, every good meal, Drew (temperately consumed, I might add), is only a foretaste of the eternal pleasures to be enjoyed by God's children forever in his glorious presence. And with the wonder we feel when we witness the heavens declaring the glory of God—as they just have in that sunset—if we will think rightly about what we see and experience in this life, we are to turn all such wonder, all such pleasure, to the glory of God."

Annie looked up at the first stars twinkling faintly in the east. "So heaven will be something like a sunset that doesn't end, but just gets prettier and prettier."

"Hey, will you look at that!" said Drew.

He pointed at the afterglow of brilliant color from the fading light. The wisps of cloud fanning out along the horizon glowed like fire, and the clear sky shone in deepening shades of violet.

"Oh, isn't it lovely," said Annie.

"Most lovely, indeed," said Mr. Pipes, smiling at the beauty all around them. "Oh, but heaven will be glorious beyond expression. And one of the ways we now may taste of heavenly things is when we give to God the glory, the praise, and the honor that are due him. Therefore, we are closest to heaven in this life when we are offering God prayers and praises suitable to his majesty."

"Well, maybe we should sing a hymn right now," suggested Annie.

"I cannot think of a better idea," said Mr. Pipes, opening his hymnal and holding it toward the light from a lamp on the pier. "Oh, how I miss my little Binns," he said, referring to his organ back in the parish church at Olney. "We shall do our best without it."

The children looked over his shoulder as he read out the words and then hummed the tune. And while revelers passed nearby on the pier, the threesome sang:

All glory, laud, and honor
To thee, Redeemer, King,
To whom the lips of children
Made sweet hosannas ring!
Thou art the King of Israel,
Thou David's royal Son,
Who in the Lord's name comest,
The King and blessed One!

The people of the Hebrews
With palms before thee went;
Our praise and prayer and anthem
Before thee we present:
To thee, before thy passion,
They sang their hymns of praise;
To thee, now high exalted,
Our melody we raise.

Thou didst accept their praises;
Accept the prayers we bring,
Who in all good delightest,
Thou good and gracious King!
All glory, laud, and honor
To thee, Redeemer, King,
To whom the lips of children
Made sweet hosannas ring!

"Oh, it is another beautiful hymn," said Annie, when they finished singing. "I especially like the part about children."

"That part I, too, find most agreeable," said Mr. Pipes, smiling at them.

"Maybe the guy who wrote it liked kids," suggested Drew.

"Do you know who wrote this one?" asked Annie.

"Ah, this time, we do," said Mr. Pipes. "Originally from Spain, like Prudentius, the pastor, and later bishop, Theodulph of Orleans lived in the eighth century during the time of the great French king Charlemagne. You will, no doubt, remember from studying history that Charlemagne had ancestors with the rather unfortunate names Big Foot Bertha and Pepin the Short."

"But he just called them Mom and Dad, I hope," said Annie. They laughed together.

"The fact is," continued Mr. Pipes, "Theodulph's poetic genius came to the attention of Charlemagne, who called him to court as his personal scholar and poet. Eventually, the king appointed Theodulph Bishop of Orleans, where he attempted to reform the church and established Christian schools throughout his diocese, including free schools for the children of poor families."

"See, he did like children," said Annie.

"Ah, yes, he did indeed," said Mr. Pipes. "And any wise Christian who reads his Bible will love children. Remember the account recorded in Luke's gospel when parents brought their nursing infants to Jesus?"

"Didn't the disciples tell them to get lost?" asked Drew.

"Well, yes, in so many words. But Jesus said, 'Suffer little children, and forbid them not to come unto me, for of such is the Kingdom of Heaven.' He goes on to explain that every believer must come to Christ like these babies who were carried to him in their parents' arms. We come to Christ not on our own two feet, but carried like little ones who must have everything done for them and can do nothing."

"That sounds like Clement of Alexandria's hymn," said Drew. "It went something like, 'Here we our children bring to shout your praise.'"

"Precisely. And make no mistake, my dears," said Mr. Pipes, "the Psalter and the great hymns are for children; nothing less is needed."

After a moment of silence Annie put her hand on Mr. Pipes's sleeve and said, "Mr. Pipes, you did for us what those parents did for their children when they brought them to Jesus."

"How do you mean?"

"Well, you've been like—" she paused, searching for words. "Our parents don't yet know the Lord, but you—well, you brought us to Jesus, showed us the way, and carried us to him. And I don't know how I can ever thank you enough."

For a moment Mr. Pipes could not speak, nor could he help being somewhat grateful for the darkness that may or may not have entirely hidden the tears of joy gathering in his eyes. He patted Annie's hand tenderly.

"Thank you, my dear," he said. "In that glad duty I have found the greatest delight. You must give to God 'all glory, laud, and honor.'" He squeezed her hand again. "It is, however, an honor to know that I am thought of by you in such ways."

"What happened to Theodulph in the end?" asked Drew.

"After the death of Charlemagne," continued Mr. Pipes, "he was wrongfully accused of complicity in a plot to assassinate a royal successor and was thrown in prison."

"A dungeon, no doubt, full of huge rats with sharp yellow teeth," said Drew, champing his teeth and making scurrying noises in the dark by running his fingers along the roof of the cabin.

"*Drew,* stop it!" said Annie with a shudder.

"What a raw deal, though," said Drew. "He didn't even deserve it."

"Unjust, indeed," said Mr. Pipes. "But it was while suffering in prison that he wrote this lovely hymn."

"And though he sat in a prison for something he didn't do," said Annie, "he still wrote and sang such praises to God."

"How could he do it?" asked Drew.

"Faith," said Mr. Pipes, simply. "God has ordained that trials strengthen true faith, my dears."

"Did he ever get out of prison?" asked Drew.

"No, not in the manner you might hope," said Mr. Pipes. "His was to be an ultimate trial. He died somewhat mysteriously in prison; some historians believe he was poisoned to death. But not prison, nor even death, could hold him; he sings unwearied praises around the throne of God in heaven. And someday, so shall you and I."

He rose to his feet. "Now, then, it grows late; I for one am feeling weary from our tramp all over Genoa. Captain or no captain, I propose that we go below and settle in for the night."

Annie wriggled with delight as she curled up in her berth. The pulled curtain made it seem like her own private stateroom, and the warm glow of the kerosene lantern shimmering on the polished teak played with her imagination. The soft creaking of the rigging and the rhythmic rocking of the big vessel made her feel as though they had actually gone to sea on a real ship. Whether from the swaying of the ship or her own weariness, she soon fell into a deep, contented sleep.

Above in his berth, Drew wedged his shoulders in between two curved timbers and leaned against the stout planking of the inside of the hull. His leather sketchbook open on his knees, he frowned at the first part of his hymn. Glancing down at his Bible open to Zechariah, he positioned his tongue in the corner of his mouth as he did when casting his fishing rod, and after rereading what he had written, he added to it:

The Lord alone, the Cornerstone,
   His wandering sheep will bring,
Through distant lands and deep blue seas,
   To sing before their King!

Clement used "shout," he said to himself, scratching out the word "sing" in the last line and replacing it with "shout." *And "shout" is in Zechariah, so it's got to be the best word. And now there's all this about the deceitful shepherds here in the text.* He bit the end of his pencil and then wrote again:

Deceitful shepherds, false and vain,
  In anger the Lord burns;

That's good stuff—the part about trampling down enemies, he mused, before continuing with:

His enemies he tramples down,
  And, joyful, Judah turns!

Very soon, the rocking of the ship did its work; a squiggle trailed down the page after the word "turns," and Drew's pencil fell onto his blanket. Mr. Pipes stole out of his berth and snuffed out both Annie's and Drew's lanterns. After tucking their blankets in around them, he placed a gentle kiss on each of their foreheads. In moments, only steady breathing came from the three berths as Mr. Pipes, Annie, and Drew settled into that delicious soundness of sleep available only on board a boat gently rocking in a quiet harbor.

8
Pirate and Parrot

Jesus, Thou Joy of Loving Hearts
(Bernard of Clairvaux)

Our restless spirits yearn for thee,
Where'er our changeful lot is cast;
Glad when thy gracious smile we see,
Blest when our faith can hold thee fast.

(TRANSLATED BY RAY PALMER)

The peaceful sleep Drew enjoyed throughout the night drifted into what must have been a dream—a dream, predictably for Drew, about actually sailing on the ocean. Combine sleeping on board a real sailing ship for the very first time with Drew's imagination and his longing to go to sea, and a dream about real sailing was inevitable.

His dream went like this: the almost imperceptible motion of the schooner gently rocking him to sleep last night gradually increased until it became more of a steady rolling; before long, the rolling became a pitching side to side, then a sustained heeling to one side with an occasional lurch and plunge. The sounds in this dream seemed so real, too: water swishing and hissing against the hull, the creaking of spars and rigging, the whistling of the wind, the rustling and snapping of the sails. It was all very satisfying, and Drew smiled broadly in his sleep.

Then as the ship seemed to plunge deeply into the trough of a wave, and at the same time heel more steeply than it had yet heeled, he felt himself skidding in his berth. The next thing Drew knew, he felt as though he'd been shot out of a catapult. A weightless sensation came over him. And for an instant he felt as though he were actually flying through the air.

And then his eyes popped open and with a sharp intake of breath he realized: this was no dream! He *was* flying through the air! Groping for something solid to grab hold of, his arms and legs flailing wildly, he looked like a baby albatross out for its first flying lesson. Finally, with a thud, he landed on the floor between the two bunks.

At almost the same instant, disturbed by the noise of Drew plunking onto the floor, Mr. Pipes and Annie woke up. They both pulled their curtains aside and stared at Drew lying in a heap on the floor between their berths.

His face a picture of complete bewilderment, Drew looked from Annie to Mr. Pipes. Blinking rapidly and rubbing his elbow, he murmured, "Guess I fell out of bed." He then cocked his head to one side and seemed to hear the noise and feel the motion of the sea all at once.

Before he could say anything, Annie stammered, "Wh-why is it moving?"

"I am, myself, most anxious to know the answer to that question," said Mr. Pipes, the spidery hairs of his white eyebrows more active than usual. "What on earth are we doing on a schooner that seems for all the world to be very much at sea?" He passed his hand over his face and fumbled for his glasses. Then, jumping from his berth and staggering for a moment as the narrow floor fell beneath his feet, he said, "Everyone get dressed; we must discover whatever in the world is going on."

"Did you say 'at sea'?" asked Drew, his eyes wide, a smile slowly spreading across his face.

Just then, the schooner plunged forward with a shudder. Annie looked at Mr. Pipes, her eyes wide with terror.

"I've got it!" said Drew, his head popping out of a sweatshirt as he pulled it on over his pajamas. "Pirates did come!" He staggered to the porthole and plastered his face against the glass. "Yippee! We *are* at sea! Here's what must have happened: real pirates boarded in the night—I'll bet it was the same guys who broke into our hotel! Yahoo! We've been kidnapped by real pirates! Oh, Mr. Pipes, you come up with the best adventures! You had me going about spending a night on this ship tied up at the dock," he snorted. "That was a good one. Now repelling the rotten pirates up there," he tossed a defiant look upward at the deck, "we'll get to use the swords for sure." His face shone with excitement as he grabbed his sword.

Mr. Pipes looked at Drew in wonder. "Annie, my dear," he said, patting Annie's hand comfortingly, "did you understand anything your brother just said?"

Not trusting herself to speak, Annie looked up at Mr. Pipes and could only shake her head. *Surely Drew couldn't be right about pirates*, she told herself. The ship shuddered as it fell into another trough. *Is it a storm?* she wondered, biting her lip and gripping the edge of her berth. *What* was *going on?*

"There, there, now, Annie," said Mr. Pipes reassuringly. "We shall go on deck and get it all sorted out. From the sounds of things out there," he added, looking out the porthole, "we are most emphatically not tied securely to the pier in Genoa."

"I-is this a s-storm?" stammered Annie.

"Have no fear, Annie," replied Mr. Pipes, "we are on good terms with the God who makes it his business to calm storms—if this is one. Steady yourselves, now, and follow me."

He opened their stateroom door and looked cautiously down the narrow corridor. Then, bouncing off the walls of the hallway and clutching for handholds wherever they found them, they passed the galley. Pans, hung on large hooks, clanged in time with the surging of the vessel.

"Welcome aboard! Welcome aboard!" a voice suddenly called at them.

"Ah, here, finally," said Mr. Pipes, looking this way and that, "we meet our host. I say, thank you ever so much, sir. However, there does seem to be some—"

"Bilge breath! Bilge breath!" the voice cut him off.

"I beg your pardon?" said Mr. Pipes. "I say, show yourself; where are you—sir?"

Just then Annie spotted a cage partially hidden around the end of a row of cupboards; it swung wildly from a crossbeam. Indifferent to the motion and preening its feathers casually, a large green-and-red parrot perched inside the cage lifted its head and stared haughtily down its beak at them.

"It's a parrot!" she said. "He must have been locked in one of the crew's cabins last night."

"That makes him the fellow who welcomed us aboard," said Drew.

"Which very well means," said Mr. Pipes, leaning heavily against the counter for support, "whoever is up there sailing this vessel may have not the slightest idea that we are even on board. It could prove most embarrassing—if not worse. But there is no help for it now. We must carry ourselves on deck, with a stiff upper lip and a stout heart, and tell all to whomever we find there. It could prove most inconvenient."

"Where do you think they're taking us?" asked Annie, with a backward glance at the colorful parrot as she followed Mr. Pipes up the companionway.

"Probably an Algerian pirate prison," said Drew, nodding his head knowingly. "That'd be after they've sent the ransom notes home to Mom and Dad."

"I do not have the slightest idea," Mr. Pipes called down to Annie. "But you must hold on and exercise the greatest care on the listing deck of a vessel at sea under full sail."

Not only were the stairs leading on deck very steep, but due to the heel of the vessel, they tilted precariously to starboard. Halfway up the companionway steps, Annie looked down at the striped teak and holly floor and gripped the handrail more firmly.

Once on deck, Mr. Pipes's white hair spun in circles and fluttered back and forth in the breeze. The sky shone an intense blue, and morning sunlight sparkled on the whitecaps. He breathed in the scent of salt air and, gripping a cable of the standing rigging, reached out his hand to steady Annie on the slanting deck. His eyes wide with curiosity, Drew appeared in the companionway and, looking up at the white billowing canvas and the ratlines disappearing upward in the maze of rigging, nearly lost his footing.

"Steady, my boy," said Mr. Pipes. "Stay low, and remember: one hand for the ship; one hand for yourself." Then, gazing out over the sea, he added, "What a perfect day for sailing!"

Most people when stepping onto the deck of a vessel driving forward through the sea, sails trimmed and pulling powerfully, feel a compulsion to look up at the magnificent sails and then to gaze forward in the direction the ship is sailing. In the first moments on deck, though wondering profoundly about their circumstances, Mr. Pipes and Annie and Drew—their eyes drawn by the heel of the boat, the angle of the spars, and the bulging curve of the sails—without a glance astern gazed upward and forward.

"It's alive!" yelled Drew, over the thrumming of the breeze in the rigging and the hissing of the vessel through the blue water.

Annie felt her worries give way to a rising thrill at the sheer beauty of the big sailboat rising confidently with each new wave.

"She does seem alive," she yelled, "and more beautiful than anything!"

Mr. Pipes smiled, but before he could reply, from behind them came: "I sure am glad to see you lot."

They spun around and stared at the speaker. He stood at the helm, one hand firmly on the wheel, the other thrust casually in the pocket of a pair of paint-splattered walking shorts. Annie stared at the bright red handkerchief tied around his head and knotted at the side. With legs spread wide and bare feet comfortably gripping the teak decks, he stared back at them looking rather wild and, Annie decided, very much like a pirate.

Mr. Pipes found his voice first. "Of course, you will want to hear an explanation of our presence." He cleared his throat awkwardly. "And I am prepared to offer that explanation. We had no intention—"

"Save it," the young man at the helm said, with a shrug of his shoulder, his eyes moving in a rhythmic cycle from masthead, to horizon, to compass, and back to Mr. Pipes.

"I beg your pardon?" said Mr. Pipes inquiringly.

"Doesn't much matter why you're stowed away on my boat, now, does it? Here we are, then, aren't we? Besides, I need crew."

"You need crew?" Mr. Pipes repeated, his eyebrows rising and falling as he worked at making out what the man meant.

"If you need crew," said Drew, "that must make you the skipper."

The young man pulled his hand out of his pocket, his other hand steady on the helm all the while. Twirling his free hand dramatically, he feigned a bow.

"Admiral Christopher Columbus at your service," he said, thrusting his hand back into his pocket. "You can call me Abdul." Then he added, "I used to like the name Christopher Columbus better, but I think it's already taken, and Abdul fits my chosen path better."

They all wondered what his chosen path might be. Abdul seemed like an odd name for someone who sounded most of the time like an American. Annie wanted to ask what his real name was, but she thought it might be rude. Instead, she said, "Are you really sailing this huge sailboat by yourself—without any crew?"

He looked at Annie as though she'd asked a very silly question.

"Alone? I'd never try sailing a boat this size on my own," he said. Then, winking, as if letting them in on a secret, he added, "I've got my first mate, Virgil. Naw, I'm not alone. Only crazy people sail alone."

The stowaways looked at each other and back at their host.

"Where is Virgil?" asked Annie.

"Below." The skipper nodded toward the companionway.

"Resting for the next watch, I presume," said Mr. Pipes.

"Naw, he's probably gnawing on an apple core," he laughed.

"What?" all three said together.

"In his cage," he said, laughing harder.

"The parrot?" said Mr. Pipes. "He is all the crew you have on board?"

"Saves on provisions, and we do make a good team of it," said the skipper. "Though I have to fill in for him more often than not—and what with the sleep deprivation, I get to feeling a little odd now and then. Anyhow, I like blaming it on the sleep deprivation."

"May I inquire what happened to your—to the *rest* of your crew?" asked Mr. Pipes.

The skipper's face clouded. "Jail," he said with a shrug. "Picked 'em up months ago in the Suez. They got it for drunken and disorderly conduct last night at the doings. Hard to get good crew, you know. It's good riddance, as far as I'm concerned. But since my boat was their home address, I decided that a quiet nighttime departure with the ebb tide might be in order. Could have used your help last night, I could. Anyway, here we are. And now the gods send me new crew—you lot. We make the most of it, I say."

He extended his hand, and they shook hands all around as Mr. Pipes made introductions.

"Two kids and—pardon me for saying so—an old man," said Abdul with a shrug, his eyes continuing their watchful cycle. "New combination for me. Have you done any sailing?"

"Lots!" said Drew, eyeing the ratlines.

"A little," said Annie at the same time.

"Absolutely none on a vessel of this proportion," said Mr. Pipes. "Though the children and I have sailed my little vessel, *Toplady*, on The Great Ouse in England."

"And in *Minstrel* on Lake Geneva," said Drew.

"Nevertheless, you must consider us inexperienced," said Mr. Pipes. "However, what am I saying? We are not meant to be here. That is to say, we were meant only to sleep on board for one night, perhaps two, not to sail away like this."

"But here we are," said Drew hopefully.

"Looks to me like you were meant to be here," said Abdul. "You know, whatever will be will be. If you'll forgive me for saying so, that's just the problem with old people: everything's got to be in its place. You need to learn to just hang loose and go with the flow. You know, do your own thing; let your hair down; kick off the shackles, old man."

Mr. Pipes smiled at Abdul and then looked around the meticulously cared-for deck of the schooner.

"We must all be most grateful, however," said Mr. Pipes, fixing his gaze on Abdul, "that you have not taken that devil-may-care approach to the upkeep of your fine vessel. For the sake of our personal safety, we thank you for your selective application of your philosophy."

Abdul looked at the polished teak cap rail, the carefully knotted rigging, the scrubbed and polished decks. He stared dumbly back at Mr. Pipes for a moment before replying.

"But that's—well, that's different," he blurted defensively.

"Nevertheless," said Mr. Pipes, "if we are to sail to the next port with you, we feel much safer in a vessel whose skipper has not 'kicked off the shackles,' as you say." As if to emphasize his point, Mr. Pipes patted the oaken cheek of a block held securely in place by a well-oiled bronze shackle.

Drew raised his eyebrows at Annie and, smiling, motioned a triumphant thumbs-up. He whispered in his sister's ear, "Round one goes to Mr. Pipes. And did you hear what he said about sailing to the next port?"

"However," continued Mr. Pipes, "I must be so bold, Abdul, as to ask what is the next port at which you plan to make landfall—Marseilles? Or Corsica, perhaps?"

Abdul, glad to change the subject, snorted. "None of those. No, I'm off to the old country."

"That sounds rather nostalgic," observed Mr. Pipes. "May I be so bold as to deduce that you are American? I believe I am correct. What, then, is the 'old country' for you?"

"Ireland," said Abdul, digging his hand deeper into his pocket, his gaze lingering on the horizon longer than usual.

"Abdul's an Irish name?" blurted Drew.

Annie dug her elbow into Drew's ribs. But Abdul didn't seem to have heard him.

"Ireland?" said Mr. Pipes. "You don't plan to make landfall before Ireland? How long will it take to sail to Ireland?"

"Months, I hope," said Drew. "Maybe we'll even miss school in the fall."

"Two weeks, if all goes well," said Abdul.

"Two weeks!" said Mr. Pipes. "How shall I explain to your parents, children? And to Dr. Dudley? This, of course, will confirm his worst fears."

"If the wind holds like this," said Abdul, "we'll make it in a week." He looked down at the knot meter, breathed deeply, and smiled. "She's clipping along at fourteen knots. Can't expect it to last the whole passage, though."

"She is galloping along brilliantly," agreed Mr. Pipes. "But she must be a great deal to handle alone; how do you trim sail and steer all at the same time?"

"It's not easy," said Abdul. "And just now I'd like to add more sail forward. She'd make another knot and a half if we hoisted the flying jib. Can you steer?" he asked, looking sideways at Mr. Pipes.

"What's your course?" asked Mr. Pipes, stepping up to the helm and gripping the spokes. He planted his feet wide, looked aloft, and smiled.

"South by sou'east," said Abdul. "Now, follow me, Drew. We'll hoist on some more power."

Drew followed Abdul forward along the windward side of the heeling decks. He felt his heart racing with the excitement of it all.

"Annie, come sit here behind me on the aft cabin roof," said Mr. Pipes. "You'll feel secure here, and I can teach you a thing or two about steering this magnificent little ship."

Annie watched Mr. Pipes from behind as he gazed from horizon to compass to sails, the wheel turning slightly as he corrected for a gust of stronger wind or to get the most out of the downward side of a swell. He made it look easy.

Meanwhile, on the foredeck, Abdul tossed the end of a line to Drew and told him to tie off with a bowline.

"You'll need that so we don't lose you overboard," called Abdul above the hissing of the waves.

"The rabbit comes up out of the hole," said Drew to himself, trying to remember how to tie a bowline. "Then runs around the tree and back down the hole. That's it." He pulled the knot tight.

"Good," said Abdul, checking the knot. "Now follow me out onto the bowsprit and we'll hank on the flying jib."

Drew swallowed. The bowsprit stuck out eight or ten feet forward of the bow. As the schooner drove through the seas, it dipped and plunged so near the waves that salt water soaked the protective netting under the sprit.

Dragging the sail bag behind him, Abdul stepped out onto the bowsprit. While the ship rose and fell with the sea, like a cat, he covered the distance in a few quick steps and stood at the fore stay, motioning for Drew to follow.

"Straddle it like a horse," he yelled. "Then just keep your feet on the netting. Nothing to it. You'll love it. Great view out here."

White foam hissed only inches below Drew's feet when the schooner plunged into the trough of a wave. He crept forward, hugging the bowsprit with his knees and arms. At one point his foot slipped off the netting below, but after his heart started again, he made his way inch by inch to where Abdul worked.

"I-it is a nice v-view," said Drew, trying to steady his voice. Drew sighted up the forestay until he lost it aloft in the rigging. Against the deep blue of the Mediterranean sky, the taut sails shone a brilliant white in the sunshine. He looked back at Mr. Pipes and Annie at the helm. They seemed far away. And sticking out over the sea so far forward on the boat, Drew felt almost as though he weren't on board anymore. Abdul shackled the lowest corner of the sail to the bowsprit and then showed Drew how to open the bronze hanks fitted along the leading edge of the sail. "We call this part of the sail the luff," he called. With a solid click, he latched each hank around the forestay, Drew helping, and finally shackled the halyard to the head of the sail.

"Back we go," he called to Drew, motioning to the foredeck.

Minutes later at the base of the forward mast, Drew and Abdul, pulling arm over arm, hoisted the flying jib. It rattled and snapped irritably the farther they raised it.

Back near the helm, pulling with all their might, Abdul showed Drew how to sheet in the jib. Then wrapping the line around a large bronze winch, they eased it in and out, Abdul scowling critically at the wrinkles in the sail until it bulged just right.

"That's it," he said, nodding in a self-satisfied manner. "Cleat her off there."

"Trimming sails is a precise business," observed Mr. Pipes, when they rejoined Annie and Mr. Pipes at the helm.

"You bet," agreed Abdul. "With sail trim it's got to be just right for things to work. How's our speed?"

"Fifteen-point-five," said Mr. Pipes, glancing at the knot meter. "Just as you predicted. I say, well done up there, Drew. A good view, was it?"

"I can't believe we're actually at sea," replied Drew, wonderingly. "Two weeks of this from here to Ireland, did you say?"

"I can only guess," said Abdul. "With sailing anything can happen, so it's best not to have too much of a schedule. But something around two weeks; that's my guess."

Mr. Pipes's smile faded. "I can hear most distinctly what our dear Dr. Dudley would be saying at this moment," he mumbled under his breath.

"But like you say," said Drew, "it can't be helped; so we'd better make the most of it. We can explain everything to him when we get back to England."

"We shall," said Mr. Pipes, a hint of dread in his voice.

"He'd never have let us come," said Drew, gripping the ratlines.

"Where are we now?" asked Annie. She thought she might feel better about this change of events if she could see where they were on the map—and where they were going.

Abdul spread a chart on the cabin roof, consulted his logbook, and said, "Here."

"And that's France," said Annie, pointing to the land north of the position that Abdul had marked on the chart. She looked off to starboard. "You can see it, a little bit."

"Yep, that's France," said Abdul.

Drew, looking from the chart to a faint hint of land off the port side of the schooner, said, "Then that must be Corsica, where Napoleon was born."

"And still part of France," said Mr. Pipes from the helm.

"Oh, this is so great!" said Drew. "We're actually at sea! It doesn't get any better than this!"

"Now you're talking," said Abdul. "I came to realize long ago that there really is nothing as great as the salt air in your teeth, the wind in your sails, and a seaworthy sailboat under your feet.

If you think of the sea as sort of the lifeblood of the earth, then sailing becomes for you an organic return to man's primal oneness with nature—a sort of voyage on the arteries of the earth."

Annie frowned.

"Huh?" said Drew, looking sideways at the skipper and scratching his head.

"I normally lash the helm at times like these, but if you don't mind carrying on for a while," said Abdul to Mr. Pipes, "it's time for my morning meditation."

Annie raised her eyebrows and looked at Abdul.

"Meditation?" she said.

"Yoga," he said.

Mr. Pipes glanced over his shoulder.

Annie and Drew stared in amazement as Abdul closed his eyes and put a little pillow down on the heeling deck of the schooner. Then, squatting before it and with a quick motion of his feet, he flipped over into a ball curled up on his head, his arms steadying him. His legs now slowly unfolded, until they extended straight up into the air. He remained upside down, eyes closed, and apparently in some kind of trance.

As he did all this at the very stern of the vessel, Mr. Pipes snatched only occasional glimpses over his shoulder of Abdul in this odd posture. Annie and Drew stared, dumbfounded. Finally Drew said, "Look at the way he sways with the ship. I don't know how he does it."

"I should think he has had considerable practice at this yoga of his," said Mr. Pipes.

"Do you think he can hear us?" whispered Annie.

"I am not certain," said Mr. Pipes. "However, we have been befriended by a generous man (though something on the eccentric side of the ward) who is to be commended for his longing."

"His longing?" said Annie. "What do you mean?"

"His search for the true meaning of things," replied Mr. Pipes.

"Does that make this yoga stuff good?" asked Drew.

"If you mean whether it is truth," said Mr. Pipes, "I am constrained to say no. It is not God's way. However, insofar as it is the expression of someone's longing after truth, someone's acknowledgment of there being something real that we cannot see—" He sighed and steered the schooner silently for a moment before continuing.

"If he could hear—" Mr. Pipes broke off and then began again. "That is to say, if while in this trancelike state he could understand a reasoned argument, I would begin perhaps as Paul did to the people of Athens recorded in Acts 17. After seeing all the shrines built to their pagan gods, he came across the shrine to the unknown god—evidence of the Athenians' hedging their theological bets, as it were. I would say to Abdul—if he could hear me—Abdul, the God after whom you long with your yoga can be known and worshiped and loved, because he made us in his image to know him, to worship him, to love him."

Annie and Drew studied the silent, upside-down features of Abdul to see if there were any signs that he heard Mr. Pipes. There were none.

"But then I would be quick to say," continued Mr. Pipes, "Abdul, you and I have terribly wronged God, have sinned against his divine law, have mocked his holiness, and he is justly angry—very angry with us. We have preferred our will to God's will. Furthermore, we have even set ourselves up as our own god. Undeserving, proud, arrogant, self-serving wretches though each and every one of us is, God in his mercy has sent his beloved Son, Jesus Christ, to redeem sinners, to pay the debt we owe to God and wash us clean in his blood, to satisfy God's justice, and to assuage our thirst and fill our every longing after God with himself. I would continue, if I thought he listened, and say, Abdul, yes, sailing on the deep blue sea on a day like this is . . . is bliss. I readily admit it. However, if sailing is all there is, you would not be on your head doing yoga. No, no, you must draw right conclusions from your longings."

Drew thought he detected a twitch developing in Abdul's left cheek.

"I'll bet he's got an itch," whispered Drew. "Anytime I try to hold still and be quiet, I start itching in more than a bazillion different places all at once. Do you think he's listening?"

"Shh-hh," said Annie. "Not with you talking. Let Mr. Pipes go on."

Mr. Pipes smiled at them over his shoulder and winked. "I am reminded of the words of the poet—Abdul, if you can hear me, you surely appreciate the otherworldly interests of poets who in every age make it their business to express their yearning, their longing, after the ideal in poetic verse. The poet who comes to mind as we sail off the coast of France is the great Bernard of Clairvaux."

"Sure sounds like a French name," said Drew.

"It is," said Mr. Pipes. "Bernard was born in 1090 near a French village called Dijon."

"Like the mustard?" asked Drew, suddenly aware of a gnawing sensation in his stomach. He moaned; they hadn't eaten anything for breakfast. He moaned again.

"Precisely," said Mr. Pipes. "Blond-haired Bernard grew up under the influence of his father, a valiant knight, and under the influence of his mother, a saintly woman remembered most for her goodness. Bernard was a distinguished student, especially known for his eloquence of speech and tenderness toward the things of God. Alas, his mother died when he was twenty-two, and for a time his interest, like his father's, moved more toward worldly fame and military exploits.

"Until one day when riding on his war horse, eager to join his brothers in the siege of a castle, a vision of his pious mother sprang into his mind. She had taught him not to love the things of this world but to seek after eternal pleasure rather than earthly delights. A church spire came into view, and he reined in his horse and entered the church to pray. God worked in his soul, and hereafter Bernard was never the same. He called his

146

brothers, his uncle, and other knights to join him by devoting their lives to the service of Christ. Soon thereafter they joined the Order of the Cistercians, a monastic order devoted to the strict observance of the Rule of St. Benedict, and to manual labor and farming, the proceeds from which they used to relieve the needs of the poor. Within three years, in 1115, the abbot recognized Bernard as a true lover of Christ; they appointed him abbot of a new monastery deep in the robber-infested Wormwood Valley."

"That's a good one," said Drew. "How would you like to have to say, 'Yeah, I live just over the way in Wormwood.'"

"Undaunted by the dark reputation of their destination," continued Mr. Pipes, "Bernard and his few followers sang hymns to the Lord as they entered the benighted valley. But as Bernard and his followers proclaimed the Light of the World in that dark place, the original inhabitants of the valley renamed it Clara or Clear Valley—in French, Clairvaux. One visitor described the peaceful silence of the place broken only by the scraping of the hoe and the singing of hymns."

"So that's how he got his name," said Annie. "A valley named after Clara," she added, a faraway look in her eye as she thought of their friends back in Olney. "Oh, I miss her so much. Do you think we'll see Clara and Bentley when we get back to England?"

"Perhaps we shall," said Mr. Pipes.

"Did you say 'robber-infested'?" said Drew. "I'll bet Bernard used his sword on them." He brandished an imaginary sword and almost lost his balance on the heeling deck as he made a thrusting lunge.

"No, indeed," said Mr. Pipes. "He left that up to others. Though, one day, walking along the road, Bernard came across a robber being dragged away to the gallows led by a noose already cinched around his neck."

"Bernard must have been glad that there'd at least be one less robber," said Drew.

"That is where you are wrong, Drew. Bernard took pity on the condemned man and begged his life for the church. After instructing the poor man in the Christian faith, he welcomed him into the service of the monastery."

"What became of him?" asked Annie, gazing across the sea at the coast of France. Listening to the story, she'd almost forgotten about Abdul.

"By all accounts the robber was rescued from the gallows to live a useful life in the service of God," replied Mr. Pipes. "Bernard's concern for the affairs of the mighty as well as the low, his leadership, and his eloquence eventually brought him before kings and bishops, putting him in position to negotiate the outcome of wars, and even to settle the differences between rival popes. In defense of true faith, he boldly debated with scholastic thinkers who he feared made human understanding more important than faith and piety. Because preaching played such a central role in Bernard's ministry, the pope called on him to preach a crusade against the Muslims, calling all Europe to drive the infidels out of Jerusalem. Though many things about Bernard's doctrine were not as true to God's Word as they ought to have been, he did spend long hours reading his Bible and praying when he prepared his sermons. And out of that meditation on the Bible came a deep love of Jesus, which he eventually expressed in his 'Jubilus Rhythmicus de Nomine Jesu.'"

"His what?" asked Drew.

"That is the name of his 192-line poem, 'Joyful Rhythm on the Name of Jesus.'"

"Is it a hymn?" asked Annie. "I mean, can we sing it?"

"We may sing parts of it," replied Mr. Pipes, steering the schooner to gain the most from the lift of a following wave. "Annie, open my shoulder bag and turn to the hymn 'Jesus, Thou Joy of Loving Hearts.' Several other hymn-writers translated parts of this poem by Bernard, but I am inclined to think our American friend Ray Palmer did the finest job of it in this hymn. Annie, read it out for us, would you, please? And do observe how Palmer—I mean Bernard—contrasts the meager pleasures derived from earthly pursuits with the eternal satisfaction found only in Jesus." He glanced over his shoulder at Abdul, then added, "Nice and loud so that we can hear it over the noise of the sea."

Annie read:

> Jesus, thou joy of loving hearts,
> Thou Fount of life, thou Light of men;
> From the best bliss that earth imparts,
> We turn unfilled to thee again.
>
> Thy truth unchanged hath ever stood;
> Thou savest those that on thee call:
> To them that seek thee thou art good,
> To them that find thee, all in all.
>
> We taste thee, O thou living Bread,
> And long to feast upon thee still;
> We drink of thee, the Fountainhead,
> And thirst our souls from thee to fill.

"If Abdul could hear you, Annie," interjected Mr. Pipes over his shoulder, "I would pause here and ask him to listen especially to this next verse. I would urge him to realize that his restless longing is fulfilled only through faith in Jesus Christ. Read on, my dear, loudly; remember the sea."

> Our restless spirits yearn for thee,
> Where'er our changeful lot is cast;
> Glad when thy gracious smile we see,
> Blest when our faith can hold thee fast.
>
> O Jesus, ever with us stay;
> Make all our moments calm and bright;
> Chase the dark night of sin away;
> Shed o'er the world thy holy light.

"Ah, for a sturdier faith that holds fast to Christ alone," said Mr. Pipes. Then, looking at Annie, he added, "My dear, would you read that first verse again?" Annie did.

"'The best bliss that earth imparts,'" said Mr. Pipes. "That includes sailing, fishing, eating, you name it—for some, even yoga; from the most enjoyable earthly pleasures we always return unfilled if we are not satisfying ourselves in Christ the living Bread, the Fountainhead. In him alone our thirsting souls are filled."

Abdul suddenly rolled into a ball and sprang to his feet in a sort of reverse somersault.

"Did you have a satisfying meditation?" asked Mr. Pipes.

With an effort Abdul put a languid expression on his face. Drew thought he looked as though he had just swallowed a whole pickle without chewing.

"Meditation is always good for the soul," said Abdul, a little defensively.

"Oh, I most assuredly agree," said Mr. Pipes, "when the object of that meditation is the living and true God."

Abdul made no reply; he just looked critically at the sails and glanced over Mr. Pipes's shoulder at the compass. Studying the chart, with occasional glances at the narrow strip of land visible on the distant shore, Abdul glanced at the sun and then at his watch.

"It's almost noon," he said.

"Oh, don't I know it," said Drew, groaning loudly, his eyes rolling back in his head.

"I think I'll try for a noon sighting with the sextant," said Abdul, "just to get a good fix on our position."

Drew moaned.

"Abdul," said Annie, drumming up her courage, "as a crew member, how about if it be my job to fix meals. I could have lunch put together in no time."

"You don't cook and eat animals do you?" he asked, looking narrowly at her.

"Not if you don't have any to cook," replied Annie.

"I never eat," said Abdul, inhaling deeply, his eyelids at half-mast, "my fellow creatures."

Drew rolled his eyes and gave a long sustained moan.

"Mr. Pipes, carrying on at the helm," said Abdul, "I'll just pop below and set out some tasty things to eat. Poor Virgil'll be lonesome down below by himself all this time."

Meanwhile back on deck Mr. Pipes glanced over his shoulder at Drew who had squatted down, bracing himself against the cabin, his face buried in his hands.

"I'm starving," he moaned. "And this guy doesn't have any meat to eat—no bacon, no ham sandwiches, no sausage, no hamburgers, no tuna fish . . ." His voice trailed into a whimper.

"Now, now, Drew," said Mr. Pipes. "It simply can't be as bad as all that. I grant you, Abdul has some rather unusual ideas, this notion about not eating meat prominent among them, no doubt. Nevertheless, things could be much worse." He paused looking out over the expanse of blue sea surrounding them. "Drew, my boy. Chin up! We are completely surrounded by water, water teaming with life!"

"With life?" said Drew. "I'm about to die of starvation—" clutching his stomach, he groaned loudly, "—and you're talking about life?"

"Oh brother," said Annie.

"Fish, my boy," replied Mr. Pipes with a laugh. "Fishing! You are surrounded by the very opportunity for which you have so long awaited." He was about to add "so patiently," but decided against it. "What with Abdul's notions about vegetarianism, if we are to keep our protein intake up on this voyage, my boy, it falls to you to catch as many fish as you can. That is of course if Abdul does not object to our eating fish."

Just then Abdul came back on deck, Virgil perched on his shoulder, nibbling at his ear and making him look more than ever like a pirate, though Drew had never thought of pirates as anything like vegetarians.

"Annie," said Abdul, "I've set out tofu, dried seaweed and soy bean paste." Virgil screeched loudly. "If you'd be so kind as to put things together for lunch. We'll have something to eat in a few minutes."

A wave of nausea swept over Drew. He steadied himself against the mainmast before summoning up courage to speak.

Annie made her way below to the galley. She took one look at Abdul's fare. *That may be fine for Abdul,* she thought, *but I've got to find something else to serve Mr. Pipes and Drew—especially Drew.*

She began rummaging around the lockers. *What's this?* She said, opening the last one. *It's certainly not anything Abdul eats.* There were a few cans of chili, curried beef, a package of cured ham—thinly sliced, a small tub of honey, a jar of peanut butter, one box of crackers, one bag of chocolate chip cookies, a tin of tea, five apples and one not-too-stale loaf of bread. She decided it was the food locker of Abdul's former crew. It wouldn't last long, but it was something. She went to work.

Meanwhile, back on deck, Drew gathered his nerve.

"Say, Abdul," he said as casually as he could. "You wouldn't happen to have some deep-sea fishing line and maybe some hooks on board?"

9
On the High Seas

Jerusalem the Golden (Bernard of Cluny)
All Creatures of Our God and King
(St. Francis of Assisi)

Thou rushing wind that art so strong,
Ye clouds that sail in heaven along,
O praise him, Alleluia!

After eating, as discretely as they could, the bowls of chili, sandwiches, and cookies Annie had prepared, and washing it all down with cups of tea, they spent the afternoon exploring and getting more familiar with the schooner. Annie worked at drawing the billowing sails while juggling her sketchbook on her lap. It wasn't easy drawing a moving schooner from lurching decks with everything all around you rising and falling with the waves.

Later, Mr. Pipes showed Annie how to steer to the compass course and the trim of the sails. Both hands gripping the spokes of the great helm, her blond hair sparkling as it blew sideways in the breeze, she thought the schooner felt alive and that she was somehow a part of it. When Mr. Pipes went below to rest up for his turn during the night, she gave the helm to Abdul who took the bulk of the afternoon watch, and returned to her sketchbook and journal. There was so much to write about.

Meanwhile, Drew spent a good deal of the afternoon down below, his head buried in one after the other of the myriad of nooks and crannies and seemingly endless lockers and compartments. Earlier, when Drew asked about fishing tackle Abdul just shrugged, scowled disapprovingly and said there might be some hooks somewhere. So Drew, determined to find fishing tackle that would work on the huge fish he just knew he was going to catch in these waters, rummaged everywhere. He found miles of old rope, cans of paint, old rags, a flare gun—(hmm, that looked interesting), spare life jackets, tools, even a hammock—(that looked interesting too). But by dinnertime he'd found no fishing tackle.

Discouraged, Drew went on deck.

"Aha, there you are," said Abdul, as Drew's smudged and frowning face appeared in the companionway. "Take the helm while I go below and fix us some dinner. I'll show you what *real* food is."

He left Virgil perched on the helm. The parrot tilted his head doubtfully and seemed to narrow his eyes at Drew as he took the helm. Drew made a face at Virgil and gripped the wheel with determination.

"I'm not looking forward to his kind of real food," said Drew to his sister.

"Can't be all that bad," said Annie.

Drew tried keeping his eyes moving as he steered, but he began imagining that he was a pirate plying the seas for unsuspecting merchant ships loaded with gold—and fishing tackle. He looked at the expanse of water on every side. All those fish just waiting for him to catch them, and no hooks.

"Uh, Drew," said Annie from behind him. "Something's wrong with the sails."

"You're right!" he said, snapping out of his reverie. "Now, let me see: Mr. Pipes said that when the sails luff like that . . . ah . . ." Virgil screeched mockingly.

"It's just like sailing *Toplady*," said Annie.

"Only a bazillion times bigger," said Drew.

"Bilge breath! Bilge breath!" called the parrot. It spread its wings and pecked at the wheel.

"Yeah, go ahead," said Drew to the parrot, "fly away, you overindulged buzzard."

"He's just trying to help, aren't you, Virgil?" crooned Annie.

"Avast, mateys! Avast!" screeched the parrot.

"He's a know-it-all," said Drew.

"But sailing's sailing," said Annie, still thinking of what Mr. Pipes had taught them while sailing *Toplady*. "And wind's wind."

"That's it!" cried Drew. "They're luffing because I've let her turn up into the wind, so . . ."

"—fall off the wind!" they both said together.

Virgil screeched and nodded his head vigorously.

Drew turned the helm to starboard; he felt the wind hitting his left cheek; the sails filled with what Drew thought sounded like a scolding snap, and the schooner heeled and pranced forward into the waves.

Looking refreshed from his nap, Mr. Pipes joined Annie and Drew on deck a few moments later.

"You two—that is to say, you three—seem to be managing things rather well," he said, nodding his white head politely at Virgil. From its perch on the wheel the parrot spread one wing wide, waggled its head, and gave what looked like a prolonged bow.

"Yeah, yeah, take all the credit," said Drew, giving the wheel a quick jerk. Virgil screeched and flapped his wings to keep his balance. He gave Drew a hard stare.

"Abdul wants you two down below for dinner," said Mr. Pipes almost apologetically. "I fear your courtesy might be somewhat tested; do beware."

Moments later, Drew stared in horror at the plates that Abdul set in front of them.

"You don't cook your food either?" Drew asked Abdul as he sat down with them around the wedge-shaped table in the fore-castle of the schooner.

Annie swallowed and stared hard at the mound of soaked, raw seaweed on her plate. A slimy green trickle of liquid oozed from the seaweed and swirled around the pale jellylike squares of tofu. This was almost worse than eating . . . fish.

"My fellow creatures don't cook their meals," replied Abdul, chewing a mouthful of seaweed, "and neither do I." Annie watched in revulsion as he actually swallowed it. "You've got to understand, cooking is a human invention designed to elevate humans over other creatures," continued Abdul. "Why should I think cooked food is better when every other animal—including birds and fish—eats his or her food uncooked?"

Drew decided that finding fishing tackle was no longer an option but a matter of survival.

*

Exhausted from his night watch, Mr. Pipes lay fast asleep in his berth when Annie and Drew awoke the next morning. They dressed quietly and tiptoed out of their quarters so as not to disturb him and went on deck. Abdul, though tired from steering the ship through the dark, sleepy morning hours after midnight, seemed very pleased.

"If the wind holds like this," he said, yawning, "we'll make it to British waters in record time."

Drew didn't say it out loud, but he decided that if they had to eat Abdul's food, even record time would not be fast enough.

"Drew, it's your watch," Abdul said. "Oh, I'll bring Virgil up," he added, yawning again. "He hates being cooped up in his cage during the day, and he'll keep you company through the morning watch."

"He really is a pretty clever parrot," said Annie. Drew scowled at his sister.

"I'm off to the sack," said Abdul. "Call me if anything goes wrong."

"Abdul," Annie called after him.

"That was quick," he said, as his head poked back up through the companionway hatch.

"I thought I'd inventory our food supply, you know, see if there's enough to last the voyage. You don't mind, do you?"

"Go ahead," he said, and then disappeared below.

"And while you're at it," said Drew, gripping the helm and admiring the deep blue of the sea with the morning sun rising behind them, "chuck all the seaweed and tofu overboard—poor fish—and any of that other rotten stuff he calls food."

"I couldn't do that," said Annie, but without much conviction in her voice. "I'll just try to find things we all like—you know, rice, oatmeal, flour, things like that. I could bake bread and we could have rice with our meals."

"Cooked rice," said Drew.

"Good morning, my dears," Mr. Pipes's voice came from the companionway. Abdul had given him Virgil, who looked perfectly comfortably perched on Mr. Pipes's fist.

"Good morning!" they greeted him together.

"Avast! Avast!" screeched Virgil.

"We tried not to disturb you," said Annie, stroking the parrot's green head. "You must be really tired after steering the ship half the night."

"Oh, but with the stars sparkling above and shimmering on the sea," said Mr. Pipes, looking heavenward, "nighttime at sea feels as if God had flung all the windows of the cosmos open. There is nothing quite like a night at sea in these conditions for a long conversation with the One who rules the minutest detail in earth and sky and sea."

"It is so beautiful on the sea," agreed Annie. "Sort of lonely-feeling, but at the same time you do feel more immediately in

God's hands." A stronger gust of wind whipped Annie's hair across her face. "Just think, he sent us this wind."

"I'd sure like it if he sent us more real food," said Drew from the helm.

"Ah, he has," said Mr. Pipes, opening his shoulder bag. He opened a package of oatmeal biscuits and tore open a bag of dried apricots.

"Where did that come from?" asked Annie.

"Oh, I took in provisions yesterday, thinking we might want a snack sometime or other," said Mr. Pipes. "But we are clearly going to need to do something about the food."

As they ate, Annie told Mr. Pipes that she had gotten Abdul's permission to inventory all the food. "I just hope I can find some more good things to eat," she said.

"Well, I'm going to keep looking for fishing tackle," said Drew. "My little pole won't do much good out here in the real ocean, but there's just got to be heavy-duty fishing gear somewhere on this boat."

"I can probably find all the food we'll need in the crew's lockers," said Annie.

"But we've got to have protein," said Drew. "Right, Mr. Pipes?"

"A well-balanced diet would demand a judicious amount of protein," agreed Mr. Pipes, looking carefully at Annie, who he knew hated fish. "But I say, how about this to top off our little breakfast?"

He pulled a large chocolate bar from the pocket of his tweed jacket.

"Now you're talking," said Drew, looking over his shoulder, the sails snapping as the schooner came a bit too close into the wind.

Virgil squawked loudly and stared at the bright-red package as Mr. Pipes tore it open.

"Perugina Chocolate," said Mr. Pipes, "made in Italy. And there's more where that came from—but not an endless supply, so we must conserve."

"Virgil looks like he'd really like some, too," said Annie.

"Oh, all right, you poor thing," said Mr. Pipes, giving a small piece to the parrot. "I'll bet he's none too keen on Abdul's excuse for food, either."

They munched in silence for several moments.

"Mr. Pipes," said Annie, "do you think Abdul listened when he was standing on his head yesterday?"

"The guy's a nut," said Drew over his shoulder.

"And if it were not for the electing grace of God," said Mr. Pipes to Drew, "we would all be nuts, as you say." Then, leaning back comfortably on the cabin roof, he continued, "I do, however, believe he was listening."

"I just don't understand how he can see how big and how beautiful the ocean is and not believe in Jesus," said Annie. She looked up at the billowing sails and watched a wisp of cloud scudding across the deep blue of the sky. "And the sky—and everything. Like you were telling us, it all shows God's handiwork. Why doesn't he believe?"

"He, like most everyone, believes only in what he can see," replied Mr. Pipes, "but in nothing beyond what he can see. You may be sure, my dears, that Abdul is longing for something true and real. His heart is restless and will forever remain so until he finds his rest in God. Created in the image of God as all men are, we spend our lives seeking for what is beyond us, but most men choose to invest their time and energy in all that is fleeting, preferring idols that we set up in place of the living and true God. Only in heaven will we finally see him in all his splendor and worship him and love him as we ought."

"And all the good things of this life are only foretastes of heaven," said Annie. "Isn't that what you said?"

"It is," said Mr. Pipes. "Which reminds me of the words of a twelfth-century hymn by another Bernard, Bernard of Cluny, who may even have been from England; no one knows for sure. His hymn "Jerusalem the Golden" includes a prayer of eager longing for the eternal pleasures that God promises his children at his right hand forevermore. It goes like this:

> O sweet and blessed country,
> The home of God's elect!
> O sweet and blessed country
> That eager hearts expect!
> Jesus, in mercy bring us
> To that dear land of rest;
> Who are, with God the Father
> And Spirit, ever blest.

"As faith grows and with it a clearer sight of heaven," continued Mr. Pipes, "we value the world less and less. In fact, it might be rightly said that true faith has a certain scorn for the world. These lines are taken from Bernard of Cluny's lengthy poem *De Contemptu Mundi*, extending to some three thousand lines in very complex meter and rhyme."

"What does that Mundi stuff mean?" asked Drew.

"That is Latin for 'Of Scorning the World,'" replied Mr. Pipes. "And it is from those many lines that John Mason Neale, in 1851, translated the words of the hymn."

Drew squinted at the compass as he thought about Mr. Pipes's words—and about what he loved and what he scorned.

"So is it fair to say," said Drew, his eyes on the horizon, "that we always love some things and we always scorn some things?"

"It would be fair, I believe, to say that," said Mr. Pipes. "Do go on, my boy," he urged.

"Well, I was just thinking that if we don't scorn the world," said Drew, furrowing his brow in thought, "then we—that is to say, I—scorn heaven . . . and the Lord." He paused, the breeze steady on his left cheek, but he barely felt it. It seemed to be easier to talk to Mr. Pipes and his sister about these things with his back to them. "Which would mean that the extent to which I love the world . . . then I'm not loving the Lord Jesus."

160

"True, indeed, Drew," said Mr. Pipes, joining Drew at the helm and putting his arm around him, "and well put. The solution, of course, is to make full use of all the means of grace to know and love Christ more each day. In your worship, both public and private, Cluny's hymn can help build up your faith so that you can see and long more eagerly for heaven."

*

Annie nearly gave up in despair after opening every cupboard and inspecting every drawer in the galley. It looked as though Abdul had stocked the schooner with bags of dried seaweed, jar after jar of wheat germ, and odd-looking vegetables that Annie did not have the least idea how to prepare. She did find a sack of what looked like rice and another of turnips—at least she guessed they were turnips—and a small bag of garlic cloves.

Then, while rummaging in a hanging locker just aft of the galley, she came across what must have been a former crew member's duffel. Annie deliberated with herself for some time before finally deciding that just opening it was not the same as playing an organ without an invitation or driving someone's car without permission. Inside she found a gold mine of canned goods: green beans, applesauce, corned beef, tomato sauce. She even found a bag of pasta noodles. But it was what she found in a box at the bottom of the duffel that posed a problem. It was a tackle box filled with fishhooks, spools of heavy line, weights, and everything else her brother would need to bring slimy, stinking fish on board—probably lots of them. What would the galley smell like if Drew pressured her into cooking the rotten stuff for him? Maybe she could just bury the tackle box and everything in it deep in the locker. Drew would never know.

While Abdul slept, she made spaghetti—cooked spaghetti—vegetables, and applesauce, and took steaming plates of it up to Mr. Pipes and Drew.

"Lunchtime!" she announced proudly as she arranged the tin plates so that they wouldn't slide across the deck. "Here, let me take a turn at the helm while you eat, Drew."

"Your hunting through the food inventory," said Mr. Pipes, balancing his plate on his knees, "has proven most successful."

Smiling, she handed Virgil a peanut. She watched her brother as he gave up the helm and looked hungrily at the lunch she had prepared. Yes, her hunt had proved more successful than they knew; what would she do if Drew asked her about the fishing gear? Planting her feet on the deck, she gripped the wheel and did her best to keep the schooner on course. The wind seemed to be letting up; at least her hair didn't swirl around as much as it had earlier.

A few minutes later, Mr. Pipes took the helm and Annie ate lunch. When everyone finished eating and Annie came back on deck after tidying up the galley, Abdul came bounding up the companionway. His long red hair waved in the breeze until he finished wrapping his handkerchief around his head, pirate-fashion.

"Wind's let up a bit," he said, sniffing the air and looking critically at the sails.

"Yeah, slow enough now that I could go fishing," said Drew. "If I could only find some fishing gear."

Abdul frowned.

"Why you would want to kill fish," said Abdul, "is beyond me. I think I should tell you that I am a member of the well-known international organization Caring, Respecting, Everything, Everywhere, Protection Society. Instead of slaughtering and eating them, we take care of animals and treat them as common creatures."

"Say that name again," said Drew.

"Caring, Respecting, Everything, Everywhere, Protection Society," said Abdul again.

Drew leaned over and whispered in his sister's ear, "First letters spell CREEPS!" He rather unsuccessfully stifled a laugh. "Get it, Annie?"

"And when I was in Genoa," continued Abdul, "I met with the Italian chapter of Caring—we just shorten it to Caring. Those Italians can get pretty upset about animal-rights violations. They were all talking about the declining population of indigenous Italian lizards."

"There were tons—" began Drew, but Annie cut him short with an elbow in his ribs.

"It's a real shame," continued Abdul, "poor things are so friendly that the uncaring—that's what we call those who aren't part of Caring—exploit and oppress lizards all the time." He paused. "Fact is, some of them were on a rescue mission trying to save the lives of several lizards"—he paused again—"several lizards that had been kidnapped by"—he looked from Mr. Pipes to the children—"by tourists . . . three tourists from America or England; they weren't quite sure which." His voice grew slower as he related the story.

Mr. Pipes seemed to be listening intently to Abdul.

"Fascinating," said Mr. Pipes, breaking the uncomfortable silence. "I say, do you have topsails we might set to get a touch more speed out of the wind?"

Abdul shot a glance up at the triangular area between the top of the gaff and the top of the sail. "Good idea," he said.

Annie took the helm while Mr. Pipes and Drew helped Abdul set the triangular fisherman sails, first on the foremast and then high on the mainmast. For a time they gained speed, but the wind continued to lessen. And by midafternoon the schooner was making her way lazily, lifting as if in slow-motion through the gentle swell, her decks nearly flat.

Later in the afternoon, Abdul grabbed up four spare belaying pins from the standing rigging. While Annie and Drew looked on, he began juggling two of them, eventually adding the other two until he had all four spinning in a circle, his tongue poised in concentration, his eyes darting in circles with the wooden belaying pins.

"Bravo!" said Annie, clapping.

"Show me how you do that," said Drew.

Belaying pins clattered to the decks for the next half hour as Drew fumbled through his first juggling lesson. He caught one on his nose and nearly gave himself a black eye with another.

Laughing, Mr. Pipes said, "You must stop for today, Drew, or you shall be black and blue all over." He laughed again. "I am reminded of what St. Francis of Assisi said about juggling."

"I have heard of St. Francis," said Abdul. "But what could he have possibly said about juggling?"

"He called himself and his followers 'God's jugglers.'"

"Well, if he was a juggler, then that's probably the only thing I have in common with any Christian," said Abdul.

"To my knowledge," said Mr. Pipes, "St. Francis did not literally juggle with balls or belaying pins. But he did say, 'The servants of God are like jugglers, intended to revive the hearts of men and lead them into spiritual joy.'"

"Humph," grunted Abdul, knocking two belaying pins together.

"And it is spiritual joy after which you are seeking, Abdul," said Mr. Pipes.

"Is it?" said Abdul, almost mockingly.

Annie watched Abdul closely; frowning, he fidgeted with a coil of line.

"St. Francis grew up in the home of a wealthy cloth merchant in the Italian hills around Assisi. Loved by everyone in Assisi for his witty poetry and good humor, he spent his carefree youth singing and playing with a gang of young roughs, who, due to his fun-loving ways, dubbed him the 'King of Feasts.' Along with his friends, he longed for adventure, for military glory, for riches, but most of all for fun. His chance came when in his twentieth year he rode proudly off to fight with the nearby town of Perugia."

"Perugia? Wait a second," said Drew, digging in his pocket and pulling out a bright-red chocolate wrapper. "Perugina Chocolate! It's got to be made in the same place!" he said. "A place like that's got to be sort of like heaven." He sniffed the wrapper, and his eyes rolled back in his head.

Mr. Pipes and Annie laughed. Abdul looked completely absorbed in splicing and tying some kind of knot.

"Do you think they made chocolate there in Francis's day?" he asked. "Hey, maybe that's what the whole fight was about: Assisi wanted the chocolate factory, and Francis was gonna help 'em get it." Drew paused, a philosophical look on his face. "You know, so many wars were fought over such unimportant things—oh, but not this one. No, sir. This one's worth a good fight, and you can bet I'd have joined up."

Abdul looked up at Drew, rolled his eyes, and shook his head.

So he is listening, thought Annie.

"You've entirely befuddled me, Drew. Now, then, where was I?" asked Mr. Pipes, looking over his glasses at Drew's grinning face.

"Francis rode off to fight with . . ." prompted Annie, scowling at her brother and not wanting to repeat the name for fear he might start off again about chocolate.

"Ah, yes," said Mr. Pipes. "Though hopeful of military glory, things went badly for Francis."

"They didn't capture the chocolate factory?" asked Drew.

"Perugia took Francis prisoner," continued Mr. Pipes, ignoring Drew, "and threw him in chains in a dungeon, where he stayed for over a year until his father raised a sufficient ransom for his release. For several long months after returning home, he lay shivering and sweating in his bed, gravely ill from his long imprisonment. Thoughts of death and judgment gripped him and held him fast. He no longer felt invincible; he was afraid of dying. As fame and wealth and earthly pleasure seemed to be forever slipping from his grasp, his hold on them slowly began weakening as well.

"Gradually, his health improved, but his friends noticed a change in him. Frivolous songs and feasting no longer captured his attention, and he seemed subdued and thoughtful. One day, while riding alone on his horse in open country near Assisi, a beggar appeared on the path ahead. As Francis reined in his horse, he stared in revulsion at the man's disfigured hand stretching toward him and clutching for alms. Death-white sores oozed infection from his skin. Francis grimaced; the man was a leper. This was no fit company for Francis; on impulse he began to yank on the reins and turn his horse away from the disgusting spectacle. But then he looked again at the poor man. Suddenly a wave of pity overcame him, and leaping from his horse, he embraced the leper. Then, holding the man's decaying hand in his, he kissed it. Francis then pressed into the poor man's hand his purse filled with money. Mounting his horse, he rode away, rejoicing and singing praises to the Lord. Some accounts of the story add that Francis then stopped his horse to look back at the leper, but search though he may, to his astonishment not a living soul could be seen anywhere."

"No way," said Drew. "What happened to the guy? Who was he?"

"I really do not know," said Mr. Pipes.

Abdul's lip curled derisively; he tossed the coil of line onto the deck with a thump.

"No reasonable person could believe that," he said. In disgust, he plopped his little pillow onto the deck, flipped upside down, and stood on his head.

"Wait a second!" Drew said, staring at Abdul's upside-down face. "You call *that* reasonable?"

Annie scowled at Drew.

Mr. Pipes looked sadly over his shoulder at Abdul before continuing.

"Many legends developed from the overworked imaginations of medieval mystics," he said. "But the fact that distortions of the truth exist in no way means that no truth at all exists. In fact, the distortions are something of a confirmation of truth. In any case, after this experience, Francis's friends

166

saw even more dramatic changes in their old friend, the 'King of Feasts.'

"Trying to figure out the change, one friend asked, 'What is the matter with you?' Another friend replied, taunting Francis, 'He is in love; he is thinking of taking a wife.' To which Francis smiled and said, 'That is it; I am thinking of taking a wife more beautiful, more rich, more pure than you could ever imagine.'"

"Oh, who was she?" asked Annie, from where she sat at the base of the compass binnacle looking eagerly up at Mr. Pipes as he steered the schooner.

"Let him tell the story," said Drew.

"Of course, Annie, Francis's friends asked the same question," continued Mr. Pipes. "To which Francis replied that he would wed 'Lady Poverty.' Thereafter, he renounced all wealth, committed himself to serving God and the poor, and went about in monk's habit, singing and preaching, and caring for the needs of all he met. All Assisi and especially his father mocked him. They threw clods of dirt at him and called him 'fool.' Hoping to force his son to give up this new way of life, Francis's father even chained him up in the basement, but his mother released him when his father was away. Enraged, his father publicly disinherited him.Whereupon, Francis sadly acknowledged that 'henceforth I desire to say nothing else than our Father who art in heaven.'

"After giving up all his wealth, he went to live among poor lepers, preaching, singing, and ministering to the needs of the despised and dying. Everywhere he traveled, his message of repentance and joy in the Lord Jesus animated his witness. The prayer of his life became:

> Lord, make me an instrument of thy peace.
> Where there is hatred, let me sow love;
> Where there is injury, pardon;
> Where there is doubt, faith;
> Where there is despair, hope;

Where there is darkness, light;
Where there is sadness, joy.

"Eventually, when Francis returned to Assisi and preached in the open air, many who had mocked him turned from their sins and love of wealth and became followers of Christ. Francis warned these new converts of the cost of true discipleship with Christ's words in Matthew 16:24, 'If anyone would come after me, he must deny himself and take up his cross and follow me.' Nevertheless, his followers swelled to thousands, and in 1210 the church recognized Francis as head of the monastic order of the Franciscans."

Mr. Pipes eyed Abdul's upside-down figure from over his shoulder before continuing.

"Drew, you no doubt remember the kestrel and the coots that make their homes along the banks of my little river," he said.

"Oh, I sure do," said Drew, looking up from the knot at the end of the coil of line that Abdul had abandoned. "There's all kinds of good birds around Olney."

"Well, Francis also loved our feathered friends," said Mr. Pipes, squinting up at the relaxing canvas of the sails as the wind lessened still further. "So much so that he earned the reputation of preaching to the birds for his tender appreciation of their singing that he loved so much. One day as he came upon a noisy flock of birds, he stopped and said, 'Oh, birds, my brothers, you have a great obligation to praise your Creator, who clothed you in feathers and gave you wings with which to fly, and cares for you.'"

"Pretty Virgil!" screeched the parrot, sunlight shimmering on the green feathers of his extended wings.

Only Abdul didn't join in the laughter.

"I almost think you can really understand," said Annie to the parrot.

Mr. Pipes offered the parrot a peanut and continued. "Francis, who liked calling himself and his followers 'Lesser Brothers,' traveled on numerous missionary journeys, and everywhere he went he taught the people to sing psalms and hymns of praise to God. His followers spread out to Northern Africa—off our port side, though too far away for us to see—and to Spain—coming up soon off our starboard side—and even to England."

"Coming up . . . dead ahead, off our bow," said Drew, eyeing the horizon.

"But not for some time yet," said Mr. Pipes, wiping perspiration from his brow and scowling upward at a white speck circling high over the schooner.

"When still a young man," Mr. Pipes went on, "in only his mid-forties, Francis's eyesight grew dim, and eventually he became completely blind."

"Mid-forties is young?" asked Drew, stepping onto the ratlines. He felt the rope against his bare feet and gazed cautiously up at the converging lines of the shrouds on which the weblike network of the ratlines was laced—*good and strong and just right for climbing*, he thought, *if I could only do it.*

"When compared with my years," said Mr. Pipes with a chuckle, "mid-forties is quite young, indeed. But it matters not; young or old, we all will one day face death."

Drew had taken several steps up the ratlines as Mr. Pipes spoke; he looked at the sea drifting slowly past the hull of the schooner, gulped, and scrambled down, landing with a thud on the teak deck.

Mr. Pipes snatched another glance at Abdul.

"Francis faced death unafraid, for he said to the followers gathered around him,

It is in giving that we receive;
It is in pardoning that we are pardoned;
It is in dying that we awaken to eternal life.

"During his last days on earth, those attending him often heard faint songs of joy coming from his little hut. One day near

169

the end he composed 'The Canticle of the Sun.' Rather than write it in Latin, he wrote it in the tongue of the common people—early Italian. Since then, many have translated it. Annie, if you would be so kind as to dig through my shoulder bag and open my hymnal, I shall teach it to you. If only Abdul could hear it; I am most certain he would like Francis's love of nature and all creatures of our God and King."

Annie and Drew gathered near Mr. Pipes and the helm of the schooner and sang the ancient poem:

> All creatures of our God and King,
> Lift up your voice and with us sing
>   Alleluia, alleluia!
> Thou burning sun with golden beam,
> Thou silver moon with softer gleam,
>   O praise him, O praise him,
>   Alleluia, alleluia . . .
>
> Thou rushing wind that art so strong,
> Ye clouds that sail in heav'n along,
>   O praise him, alleluia!
> Thou rising morn, in praise rejoice,
> Ye lights of evening, find a voice,
>   O praise him . . .
>
> Thou flowing water, pure and clear,
> Make music for thy Lord to hear,
>   Alleluia, alleluia!
> Thou fire so masterful and bright,
> That giveth man both warmth and light,
>   O praise him . . .
>
> And all ye men of tender heart,
> Forgiving others, take your part,
>   O sing ye, alleluia!

Ye who long pain and sorrow bear,
Praise God and on him cast your care,
    O praise him . . .

Let all things their Creator bless,
And worship him in humbleness,
    O praise him, alleluia!
Praise, praise the Father, praise the Son,
And praise the Spirit, three in one,
    O praise him . . .

When they had finished, all three of them stole a glance back at Abdul.

"Francis died," continued Mr. Pipes, "singing—perhaps singing these very words."

"Francis understood that everything in all the world was made by God," said Annie, stroking the parrot. "And that means that we're doing what we were made to do when we sing our praise and thanks back to him."

"That's true even of birds—lizards too, right?" asked Drew. He narrowed his eyes at what had at first looked only like a white speck, but now he thought it looked like some kind of bird hovering closer to view above the mainmast.

"So then . . . is that where some people get the idea of not eating any creatures?" asked Annie slowly.

Abdul flipped onto his feet behind them on the quarterdeck.

"Welcome back, Abdul," greeted Mr. Pipes. "Annie just asked—"

"I heard," said Abdul, nodding encouragingly to Annie. "Sounded like a good question to me."

Annie's face reddened. She'd forgotten that Abdul might actually be listening, and she didn't like the idea of Abdul's thinking that she was on his side of the question instead of Mr. Pipes's. She bit her lip.

"Ah, if what Psalm 84 records about the sparrows' finding a nest for their young in the very sanctuary of God were all Scripture had to say about birds," said Mr. Pipes, "then we might all be compelled to come to the same dietary conclusions as you have, Abdul. However, one must never take the smorgasbord approach to the Bible, sampling a little of this and a little of that, but leaving anything that one doesn't like behind. One must reject many passages of Scripture if not eating meat is to be made a tenet of faith.

"St. Francis is to be highly commended for his self-sacrifice on behalf of the poor and outcast sick. Yet he, too, made the errors of his day, embracing unbiblical practices and beliefs, such as praying to Mary and the saints, transubstantiation—believing that Jesus' body is physically present in the Lord's Supper—purgatory, and others.

"But in his great hymn he captures perfectly the universal praise that all creatures owe to God the Creator of all things. A day is coming when every knee will bow and confess that Jesus Christ is Lord—even you, like it or not, Abdul, will bow before him. But alas, for those who reject and scorn him in this life, their confession of what is true about God will be . . . too late."

Abdul suddenly became very interested in the precise trim of the jib sheet.

Mr. Pipes and Drew looked at the bird gliding with long, narrow wings above the sails. Annie followed their gaze.

"It is a bird," said Drew. "And a whopping big one."

"And it has been slowly descending for some time," said Mr. Pipes.

"Maybe it's hungry," said Annie.

"He won't find anything worth eating on this ship," snorted Drew, before Annie could stop him.

"H-he means, birds eat different things from people," stammered Annie, not wanting to offend Abdul.

"Maybe he wants to go fishing, too," said Drew. "Say, Annie, you didn't happen to come across any gear when you were down in the galley, did you?"

"Avast, matey!" squawked Virgil, flapping his wings menacingly at the drifting white form above them.

"Nothing to fear, Virgil; it is only an albatross," said Mr. Pipes, before Annie could reply to Drew.

Abdul frowned.

"So what's he after?" asked Drew. "Fish, I'll bet."

With a chuckle, Mr. Pipes recited:

It is the Hermit good!
He singeth loud his godly hymns
That he makes in the wood.
He'll shrieve my soul, he'll wash away
The Albatross's blood.

"What's that from?" asked Annie with a shiver.

"The poet Coleridge," said Mr. Pipes. "Thanks to him, the albatross has long been considered the bird of ill omen." He laughed again. "Only by those, of course, who've entrusted their souls to omens and other such superstitions."

Abdul scowled up at the albatross and back at Mr. Pipes. He then tapped impatiently on the barometer mounted near the compass.

"Drat it all," he said, looking angrily at the sky. "The barometric pressure has plunged in just the last few hours." Yanking off his red handkerchief, he mopped his brow.

"What's that mean?" asked Annie.

Abdul looked at Annie for a moment before replying. "We could be in for a biggie."

10
The Albatross Was Right

Fierce Was the Wild Billow (Anatolius)

> Fierce was the wild billow,
> Dark was the night;
> Oars labored heavily,
> Foam glimmered white . . .

(TRANSLATED BY JOHN MASON NEALE)

Turning her freckled face, Annie looked up at Mr. Pipes inquiringly. "A biggie?" her eyes seemed to say.

One hand resting on the schooner's helm, Mr. Pipes drew Annie close and gave her shoulders a reassuring squeeze.

"The sea may kick up her heels a trifle," said Mr. Pipes. He scanned the blue expanse all around them. "A blow could follow a calm such as this." Clear eyes twinkling, he smiled down at Annie. "However, no sense our worrying over the future; we are in God's hands, my dear, not some storm's."

She returned his smile. "'The changes that are sure to come,'" she recited with studied determination, "'I do not fear to see.'"

"Precisely, my dear," said Mr. Pipes, smiling and patting her shoulder.

Nearly becalmed, the schooner *Euroclydon* ghosted through the glassy sea, slowly carrying her unlikely crew toward England. The sails hung limp. Now and then a slight movement of the heavy air set a wooden pulley from the rigging tapping ominously against the bulwark of the ship. Still overhead the albatross flew.

"Drew, open your Bible to where we left off in our morning reading," said Mr. Pipes.

Abdul rolled his eyes and disappeared below.

"Acts 27:13," Drew began. " 'When a gentle south wind began to blow, they thought they had obtained what they wanted; so they weighed anchor and sailed along the coast of Crete.' Hey, that's where Andrew of Crete wrote 'Christian, Dost Thou See Them,' right?"

"Right you are, my boy," said Mr. Pipes, one hand resting lightly on the helm.

" 'Before very long, a wind of hurricane force,' " continued Drew, " 'called the "Northeaster," swept down from the island. The ship was caught by—' "

"Do forgive me for interrupting," said Mr. Pipes, glancing at Annie as Drew read. "But may I suggest we read our text in the gospels first?"

Drew looked puzzled. "But—"

"That would be the gospel according to John chapter 6, about verse 18, I believe," said Mr. Pipes, firmly.

Drew shrugged, turned to the text, and began reading again: " 'A strong wind was blowing and the waters grew rough. When they had rowed three or three and a half miles, they saw Jesus approaching the boat, walking on the water; and they were terrified. But he said to them, "It is I; don't be afraid." ' "

As Drew continued reading, Mr. Pipes looked at Annie and smiled.

When he finished reading, Annie curled up on a sail bag in the shade of the mainsail, pulled out a postcard from Genoa, and began writing to her friend Clara Howard. But if you had looked over her shoulder at this moment, you would not have understood a word she wrote. The friends had long ago worked out an elaborate code using dancing dolls to make the letters and words of their frequent correspondence. Annie wished there were some way to send postcards from the schooner.

She paused, biting her pencil and gazing at the horizon in thought. Then from under the boom she caught sight of Drew swinging his leg over the bulwark. *Uh-oh*, she thought, *he's going to try it again.*

Drew gripped the ratlines, took a deep breath, and began to climb. Within moments he felt as though some really fat guy were jumping up and down on his chest—and then the guy wasn't jumping *up* anymore, just bearing down heavier and heavier; Drew felt as though he couldn't breathe. Blood pounded in his temples. Perspiration trickled into his wide eyes. His hands felt wet and slippery.

If I just go a few rungs higher each time, he reasoned with himself, *pretty soon I'll make it; I know I will.*

"Well done, Drew," called Mr. Pipes's calm voice, from just below on the ratlines. Drew looked down; he flushed as he saw Abdul grinning up at him from the helm. They must have switched, he thought.

Mr. Pipes continued. "That is perhaps far enough for right now; this afternoon we shall try it together on the starboard lines—in the shade. So much easier to keep a good grip in the shade."

The big fat guy on Drew's chest seemed not to weigh quite so much; Drew could breathe again. Relieved, he stepped carefully down the ratlines. Once again on deck, Mr. Pipes disappeared down the companionway, only to reappear moments later carrying four bottles of ginger beer, cold from the icebox.

"Fwisht, fwisht, fwisht, fwisht," went the four bottles. Then for a moment all was silent.

"Ah, we are, in many respects," said Mr. Pipes, "far better off than the ancient mariner in Coleridge's famous poem. He was becalmed"—he took another long pull on his bottle of ginger beer—"but without any such refreshment for his thirst."

"How does it go?" asked Annie.

"Famous lines, they are," said Mr. Pipes, clearing his throat:

Water, water, every where,
And all the boards did shrink;
Water, water, every where,
Nor any drop to drink.

"Yeah, we've got plenty to drink," said Drew. "But does the poem say anything about what they had to *eat?*" Abdul scowled.

"Look at me," said Drew, holding out his arms and doing his best to look gaunt. "I'm dying from lack of protein. On my tombstone they'll put: 'Water, water, everywhere, but not a fish to eat!'" He ended with a groan.

Mr. Pipes and Annie laughed; then Annie abruptly grew sober. She felt a twinge of remorse about concealing the fishing gear.

Later, Mr. Pipes climbing alongside, Drew made it just beyond the halfway point up the ratlines. He wasn't sure if it was because they climbed mostly in the shade of the limp sail or because Mr. Pipes climbed, slow, steady, and calm, next to him, but for whatever reason, his hands didn't sweat nearly as much.

There's nothing to this, he told himself, his chest swelling as he gazed out over the calm sea to the thin line of land on the horizon. A smug grin creased his face; he imagined himself a stouthearted Genoese mariner on the lookout for pirates. Leaning away from the ratlines, he even let go with one hand. *Yeah*, he told himself, *I could fight off pirates and climb these ratlines all at the same time.* Swiping viciously with a make-believe cutlass, he sneered down at imaginary foes. *Rats, if only I had my real sword.*

His grin froze. The deck suddenly seemed too small and very far below, as though he were looking at it through the wrong end of a spyglass; then the schooner started spinning in dizzying circles. Wider and wider the circles grew. Drew's head felt light, and his stomach convulsed into a twitching knot. His face now pale, he lunged back at the ratlines with his free hand, clutching the lines until his knuckles shone bone-white.

"I am inclined to think," Mr. Pipes's voice broke in on Drew's growing panic, "that you would do well, just now, to look to the heavens, my boy. Divert your eyes from what is below, divert your thoughts from unpleasant potentialities, and for goodness' sake, hold tight to the lines."

Inch by inch, with Mr. Pipes's encouragement, Drew pried his hands loose and made his way to the deck.

*

"Bilge breath!" squawked Virgil later that afternoon.

Drew looked up and scowled at the parrot. *He'll scare any fish away for sure*, Drew thought to himself as he dangled a length of his own lightweight fishing line and a trout fly over the bulwarks. He hoped Mr. Pipes was wrong about his fishing gear being too light and small for sea fishing. Water lapped lazily at the hull as he looked over the side. Anyway, he had to try fishing; now it was no longer just a matter of fun. He needed meat; Abdul's diet and Drew's appetite had nothing in common.

Meanwhile, Abdul gave Mr. Pipes and Annie a small, stiff jib sail and told them to check it carefully for any weak points or broken stitching. It rustled as they laid it out.

"What kind of sail is this little one?" asked Annie, stitching a frayed spot near the clew of the sail. "Seems awfully small for a boat as big as *Euroclydon*."

"Storm jib," said Abdul simply.

"S-storm?" said Annie, looking up at the huge sails hanging limp above her and then back at the scanty sail. "But even in a storm"—she laughed louder than she meant to—"this wouldn't be enough to sail her, would it?"

"If it blows hard," said Abdul, pointing with his knife at the sail, "that could even be too much sail."

Annie winced as the needle slipped and pierced her finger. A red drop stained the corner of the sail.

"Avast, mateys! Avast!" squawked Virgil.

"It must be difficult to teach a parrot to talk," observed Mr. Pipes, smiling at the parrot. Then he asked, "Do you have plans to add new vocabulary to Virgil's stock and store?"

Before answering, Abdul finished lashing the helm, freeing anyone from needing to steer in the calm. Virgil perched proudly on the helm and strutted from spoke to spoke, preening his feathers as if he were actually steering the ship all by himself.

"I'm trying to teach him a new word," said Abdul, sitting down cross-legged on the cabin roof. He took up the end of a heap of coiled line next to him, and began inspecting every inch of it, his bare toes serving as a guide for the line as he played it out from the coil.

"What's the word?" asked Annie.

" 'Freedom,' " said Abdul.

"A fine word," said Mr. Pipes, adjusting his glasses and looking up at Abdul.

"I think so," said Abdul.

"Why teach him the word 'freedom'?" asked Annie.

"Life's not worth living without it," said Abdul. With his rigging knife he sliced off a chafed section of line and added, "No freedom, no life."

Mr. Pipes paused at the frayed stitching around a brass cringle in the sail.

"You take freedom quite seriously, then," said Mr. Pipes. "In fact, I would venture to suggest that you take freedom as seriously as many take their religion."

Abdul paused, the line suspended in his hands for a moment.

"If I have any religion," he said, " 'freedom' is the best word to describe it."

"Well, then, my dear captain," said Mr. Pipes, "we have a most important religious doctrine in common."

"We do?" said Abdul, doubtfully.

"Indeed," said Mr. Pipes, a smile playing at the corners of his mouth. "True Christianity, though many misunderstand this, is precisely the same as true freedom."

"No way," said Abdul, with a sneer.

"Allow me to explain myself," said Mr. Pipes. "But first we must define our terms," he said, winking at Annie. "What do you mean, Abdul, when you say 'freedom'?"

"What?" snorted Abdul. "Everyone knows what 'freedom' is: 'master of my fate, captain of my soul'—some poet put it something like that."

"High-sounding sentiment," said Mr. Pipes, "but is it true?"

"If I want it to be, it is," said Abdul, with a nod of his head.

Drew couldn't help overhearing.

"Freedom," Abdul continued, "is doing whatever I want, when I want, how I want—you know, *freedom*."

"So 'freedom' means," said Mr. Pipes, "ruling your world for yourself. Is that it?"

"You got it," said Abdul. "After all, why should I let anyone else rule it for me?"

Annie looked at Abdul's face. *He really believes this*, she thought.

"Hold on," said Drew, from where he sat on the bulwark. "So this freedom—does everybody get to be the captain of their fate, or whatever it was you said?"

"Sure, why not?" said Abdul.

"I've never heard anything more—" Drew began.

"What I think he means," cut in Annie, staring hard at her brother, "is that it's impossible for everybody to do what they want without affecting everybody else's ability to do anything they want. I think that's what he was going to say," she said, doubtfully.

"Indeed," said Mr. Pipes, cutting a length of coarse thread and closing his knife with a snap. "The desire for freedom is a noble one, Abdul. In that respect your theory is correct, and I commend you for such a lofty religion. But I must also point out, with due respect, that you fail to grasp certain critical assumptions—foundations, if you will—without which the rest of one's religion cannot hold water."

"Why not?" asked Abdul, almost defiantly. "I can believe whatever I want."

"So I have heard," said Mr. Pipes. "You would not, however, have wanted the one who built your schooner to make so free with what he believed about shipbuilding, now, would you? No, he built this vessel according to the rules, according to what is true about ships and about the sea. If he built it according to your religion, she would have rested at the bottom of the sea long ago. So it is with all things, and thus with religion; a false religion, one that is not true, can never deliver what it promises—freedom. Allow me to explain."

Drew looked at Mr. Pipes; he'd seen that same eager sparkle in Mr. Pipes's eye before.

"You would, no doubt," continued Mr. Pipes, "feel that your freedom was taken from you if someone stole your fine schooner, or your parrot."

"I sure would," said Abdul.

"But what of that man's freedom to be captain of his soul," continued Mr. Pipes, "by making himself captain of your ship? Who are you to take this freedom from him?"

"Well, I—" stammered Abdul. "Okay, okay," he said, nodding his head. "So maybe I exaggerated a bit. Some things are just not good, and people shouldn't be allowed to do them."

"Agreed," said Mr. Pipes. "But who decides what is good?"

"That's got to be up to me," said Abdul. "I decide what's good for me."

"As did the man who stole your schooner," said Mr. Pipes, looking over his glasses at Abdul. "You simply cannot have it both ways. You say you are free, yet you must sail this vessel according to all kinds of boundaries. You follow charts to avoid hitting real rocks and foundering; you can do nothing to change the wind direction or stir up wind when we have none; you caulk and paint, and polish and scrub. Is that real freedom? Your religion depends so heavily on exceptions to your own rule; it is very like a patchwork sail, made of a little of this and a little of that. You would never want to depend on such a sail in a storm, nor must you depend on such a religion in the storms of real life."

Annie looked at the sail they had been repairing; then she looked at the rigging and the schooner. If a storm was coming, she hoped Mr. Pipes was right about the sail and the ship.

"If you seek freedom, Abdul," continued Mr. Pipes, "you must also seek truth. Jesus said, 'You shall know the truth and the truth shall make you free.' We must swallow our pride and admit that we are sinners, rebels against God who made us, who alone rules the wind and the waves, and all things; and that he is just to be angry with us and to damn each of us to hell."

Abdul's eyes narrowed.

Mr. Pipes continued, "You see, Abdul, man is not free when he thinks he can do whatever he wants; he is free when he *wants* to do, and *can* do what he *ought* to do, what he was made to do—to glorify and enjoy God. That is freedom. But before you can ever have it, you must acknowledge that you don't have it, that you are enslaved to sin—that you, dear man, are not free."

Abdul's eyes flitted from side to side. But he said nothing.

"Seek freedom, Abdul," continued Mr. Pipes, "but seek it from the only one who can give it. Christ is the way, the truth, and the life; if you want true freedom, your search is over."

For a moment, Annie thought Abdul looked as though he were about to drop the line he was inspecting and stand on his head. Then he glanced up at the gliding albatross and resumed checking line. In the silence that followed, Annie watched Abdul turn the same length of line over and over, as if he were not really seeing it.

"Hey! I've got one!" Drew cried, breaking the stillness. "It's huge," he said, clutching at his fly pole. He pulled. The pole bent almost instantly into a near circle.

Then, with a splintering snap, the pole broke off at the reel and disappeared into the water. What remained of the line curled like Christmas ribbon and hung limp from Drew's hand.

Annie bit her lip as she looked at her brother's face. Mouth hanging open in astonishment and with hollow eyes, he searched the surface of the water for some sign of the fish.

"It was so big," he said weakly, his voice nearly cracking.

Annie watched his shoulders sag. He slumped onto his knees on the deck, shaking his head, a faraway look in his eyes.

Even Abdul looked mildly sympathetic.

"And my pole's gone," he moaned softly. "That fish"—his voice grew louder. "No, that was no *fish*"—his voice grew even louder. "That *sea monster* wrecked my pole!" he shouted, shaking his fist at the still water.

For a moment Annie feared that Drew might jump overboard and go after the fish.

Mr. Pipes patted Drew on the shoulder, but said nothing.

Suddenly, Annie knew what she had to do. She raced down the companionway, Virgil squawking as she passed, her head reappearing only seconds later. Lugging the tackle box and a large spool of line that looked like small rope behind her, she brought them to Drew.

"I'm s-sorry about your pole," she stammered. "And about the big fish. It's all my fault. I found all this—this *stuff* the other day, but I knew you'd catch something if I showed it to you." Tears glistened in her eyes. "And I didn't want to have to cook any fish. Oh, it was so selfish of me. Please, Drew, will you forgive me?"

Drew opened the tackle box and stared at the compartments, each filled with shiny hooks, some as big as his hand. And the spool was huge; *there's hundreds of feet of it*, Drew thought.

183

"Ahem, Drew," said Mr. Pipes, nodding at Annie's pleading face.

"Oh, sure," Drew said to his sister. "I forgive you, no problem, and thanks a lot."

"I'll even try some of the fish you catch," said Annie, with an effort.

"Okay, but how's this spool deal work?" asked Drew.

Abdul, now at the helm, absently answered over his shoulder, "Goes in the yoke at the stern."

Drew looked at Mr. Pipes and Annie and raised his eyebrows.

"Thanks, Abdul," said Drew.

Mr. Pipes and Drew locked the axle of the spool into the yoke, and Drew quickly figured out how to work the staggered handles extending from the axle. After tying on a large hook, Drew watched eagerly as the shiny metal of the lure glittered below the surface of the water.

"Oh, this'll do it for sure!" he said as he let out more line. "Come on, you sea monster, bite my hook!"

Mr. Pipes and Annie laughed with Drew as he tied off the line.

Meanwhile, Abdul, with Virgil perched on his shoulder, stood silently at the helm, frowning at the horizon, frowning at the rigging, frowning at the albatross.

Mr. Pipes looked at his wristwatch. "I'll take my go at the helm now, Abdul, if you please."

Abdul looked down at the barometer and frowned again. "I'm okay," he said shortly.

Mr. Pipes looked puzzled and held his watch up to his ear. *So many days at sea following the same routine, and now this?* wondered the old man. For a fleeting moment it came to his mind what Dr. Dudley and the children's parents must be thinking at this moment. *It's best that they don't know all,* he concluded with a wry smile. He looked at Abdul again; he always stood on his head in meditation at this time of day, and Mr. Pipes and the rest of the crew had come to accept it as a matter of course.

"Ah, I say," Mr. Pipes tried again. "Perhaps our captain, in the press of duty, has mistaken the time. I believe it is your hour for . . . well, for your . . ."

Abdul did not meet Mr. Pipes's eye. He just repeated, "I'm okay."

"Fine, then," replied Mr. Pipes, remaining companionably at Abdul's side and following his gaze at the barometer.

"You know it's coming?" said Abdul, guardedly.

"Yes," said Mr. Pipes, glancing over his shoulder at the children. "How serious will it be?"

"I don't know," said Abdul, running his hand through his long red hair. "But I've never seen the barometer drop so fast." He nodded astern at the northeast horizon. "You've seen the clouds gathering, I'm sure."

"Of course, it has been quite gradual, but yes, I have," said Mr. Pipes, sniffing the air, a strand of his white hair swirling and tangling briefly in his left eyebrow.

"It could be upon us . . . sort of suddenly," said Abdul, looking over his shoulder at Annie and Drew, talking together at the stern.

Tap, tap, tap, went a wooden block against the bulwark. Mr. Pipes looked up at the sails. The tapping grew to a steady knocking. From all sides, the air was charged with tension.

"We await your orders, captain," said Mr. Pipes calmly. "Drew, Annie, prepare to lend a hand. Be sure your fishing line is secure."

Drew hesitated for a moment: should he reel it in? No, he'd leave it out; what if he reeled in the line just before the fish, or whale, or whatever it was, bit the hook?

"Lower the topsails," called Abdul.

"Aye, aye, sir," called the crew.

Releasing the halyards, Mr. Pipes and Annie and Drew lowered the triangular topsails from both masts, folded them, and stowed them below.

"Drew, you go forward," yelled Abdul, "and douse both jib and flying jib. Don't forget to tie off—use your bowline, but be quick about it! Stow 'em down the forward hatch."

"Yahoo! We're getting some wind," hollered Drew as he scrambled forward.

"Down with the foresail!" Abdul ordered Mr. Pipes and Annie. "Reef the mainsail—to the smallest reef point. Stir your stumps, and be quick about it!"

A flush of excitement shone on Annie's cheeks while at the same time fear shone in her eyes. But, reassured by Mr. Pipes's smile, she wondered whether anyone had ever ordered their old friend to "stir his stumps" before.

"Lash the boom!" yelled Abdul, after they had finished folding and tying the sail along the horizontal spar.

A proud grin on his face, and with a salute, Drew reported back to Abdul at the helm.

"Awaiting further orders, sir!" he shouted over the sound of the wind in the rigging.

"Hank the storm jib on the inner stay," said Abdul. "Inner stay; on the double!"

"Aye, aye, sir!" called Drew, grinning at Mr. Pipes and his sister as he grabbed up the storm jib and headed forward.

Sweat trickled down Annie's back as she and Mr. Pipes gathered armloads of the mainsail and tied each reef point under the loglike boom. Mr. Pipes's white hair swirled around his head as he, looking up the mast, winched the halyard tightly. The schooner rose and fell with the gathering seas. Mr. Pipes took Annie by the arm. Holding tight to the grab lines, they made their way back to Abdul and the helm. Out of breath, Drew joined them moments later.

"Reefed main," said Abdul, a set to his chin, his eyes running over the rigging, "and storm jib forward—we should be in good shape." Annie thought he was trying to reassure himself as much as the crew. "Behind me," he went on, "in the stern locker," he gestured with his head, "are the harnesses. Everybody wears one—now! Nobody is to be on deck without clipping into the jack lines—these safety lines running fore and aft. I don't want to lose my crew overboard," he added.

"How is our course, captain?" yelled Mr. Pipes above the storm.

"On course for Gibraltar," Abdul yelled back, his feet braced as he strained at the helm. "Winds on our starboard quarter." He stopped as a powerful gust tried wrestling the helm from his grip. "Good point of sail to make up for lost time—but we've got to watch these following seas! Slam us down on the mat if we're not careful."

"Whee! Haw! That was a biggie!" Drew hollered, as the schooner rose and then plunged into the trough of the next wave. "Ride 'em, cowboy!" he whooped as another relentless wave approached.

"Hold on, my boy," called Mr. Pipes; then he recited:

Courage is the golden mean
Recklessness and fear between.

Annie scrunched her brow in thought. "Coleridge?" she asked, cupping her hands to the old man's ear.

"Pipes," shouted Mr. Pipes with a quick wink.

"Mr. Pipes!" yelled Abdul. "I've got to get Virgil below—and check the bilge; I need to make sure of our position before it gets too dark. Can you steer in these seas?"

"I shall do my best," said Mr. Pipes, taking the helm and bracing his feet.

Abdul and Virgil disappeared below.

Annie wondered how the sea, so calm only moments ago, could change so violently: angry chop had quickly grown into mountainlike ridges with white foam hissing irritably as the winds ripped the tops off the waves. Clouds darkened the sky. The decks grew steep as *Euroclydon* heeled under the fierce press of the wind; Annie adjusted her harness and checked to see that she was securely clipped to the jack line.

Drew, on the other hand, holding both hands in the air and trying to balance on the pitching decks, let loose another whoop and holler.

For an instant, Annie looked at her brother and wondered how he could be so afraid of heights one minute and so crazy about the motion of the ship in a storm the next. "Boys," she said, scowling. "I'll never understand them."

Then, as the schooner plunged down the lee of a treacherously steep wave, she gasped in horror. Drew's feet splayed out on the slippery decks. Rolling as he fell, he looked back up at Annie. There was nothing she could do. His eyes now wide with terror, he clutched frantically at the deck planking with his fingers. Annie dug her own fingers into Mr. Pipes's arm and did what any sister ought to do upon seeing her brother about to be swept overboard into a raging sea: she screamed, loud and long.

Drew's legs and arms flailed as he skidded just above the clutching waves. Everything was so slippery! He couldn't hold on.

Suddenly, *twang!* the jack line went taut; Drew squealed like a kicked pig as his harness gripped him, wrenching the breath from his lungs. The pitch of the schooner eased, and Drew, shaking, his face a pasty white, scurried back to his sister and Mr. Pipes near the helm.

"Drew," called Annie, fiercely, "I thought you were gone!" She threw her arms around her brother. Eyes wide with shock, he patted her on the back.

"'Peace, it is I,'" shouted Mr. Pipes so that they both could hear above the howl of the sea. He smiled comfortingly into Annie's face.

Though her stomach felt as angry as the sea, she smiled back at Mr. Pipes.

"Remember, Jesus said much the same," continued Mr. Pipes, salt spray dripping from his chin and nose, "when a fierce storm, much like this one, threatened his terrified disciples." Saltwater droplets clung to his bushy eyebrows. Drew moved closer to the old man.

Annie watched Mr. Pipes's wet hair stream forward around his head. A calm smile spread across his face, and his eyes sparkled even as he blinked back the salt spray showering them while the bow buried itself in the next wave. *He's enjoying this,* she thought to herself in wonder. *But what would Dr. Dudley say if he could see Mr. Pipes now?* The thought almost brought a smile to her face in spite of her fears.

"Now, if you'll both stay near me," shouted Mr. Pipes, "we shall wonder and worship the Lord together. I say, where does one go to find such a gloriously concentrated display of the power of God? We are, indeed, most privileged."

Annie and Drew felt many things at that moment, but "privileged" was not among them.

Dripping with salt spray, the children huddled near Mr. Pipes, comforted by his occasional comments: "Ah, now, that is a fine specimen of a wave, a fine one indeed." Or: "Ah, if not a hair falls from our head without our Father's will, watch him hold us in his hand on this wave top." All the while his hands calm and steady on the helm.

Drew looked up at their old friend's face. *Here we are in a wham-o of a storm, and he looks as calm as if he were home in his cottage on the Ouse, rocking chair creaking away, sipping tea and stroking his cat, Lord Underfoot, before a crackling fire.*

"Now, then, my dears," shouted Mr. Pipes, smiling broadly, "I can think of no better circumstances in which—nor no better ship on which—to teach you an ancient hymn about the One who rules the wind and the sea."

Stealing a glance at Annie, he added, "Greek chap named Anatolius wrote the poetry, about A.D. 810. Beyond that, we know almost nothing about him." Then, eyebrows billowing in a fierce scowl, he began lustily singing above the storm:

Fierce was the wild billow,
Dark was the night;
Oars labored heavily,

189

Foam glimmered white;
Trembled the mariners,
Peril was nigh—

Here he nodded reassuringly at them. Annie almost felt that Mr. Pipes's voice, as he continued, grew stronger—stronger even than the storm.

Then said the God of God,
"Peace! It is I."

Ridge of the mountain-wave,
Lower thy crest!

Annie and Drew looked at each other: maybe if only for a moment . . . but they both felt sure that there was a lull . . . the next wave seemed tame compared to the one before it.

Wail of Euroclydon,
Be thou at rest!

"Wait a second," said Drew. "Did you add that part?" he asked, accusingly. "*Euroclydon*'s the name of Abdul's schooner—Mr. Pipes, you added that bit about *Euroclydon.*"

"Drew, he's singing. You're interrupting," said Annie. "Oh, please finish, Mr. Pipes."

"Very good," he said, smiling.

Sorrow can never be,
Darkness must fly,
Where saith the Light of Light,
"Peace! It is I."

Mr. Pipes and Annie and Drew didn't see Abdul as he came up out of the companionway. He stopped and listened.

Jesus, Deliverer,
Come thou to me;
Soothe thou my voyaging
Over life's sea:
Thou, when the storm of death
Roars—

Here, Mr. Pipes furrowed his brow fiercely, raised his fist, and roared—his voice louder than ever above the wind and seas.

Roars, sweeping by,
Whisper, O Truth of Truth,
"Peace! It is I."

"Now sing it with me," said Mr. Pipes; then, looking out over the stormy seas, he roared again: "Blow, there, till you burst! You might kill us—surely you might—but you cannot hurt us!" With a chuckle he turned back to Annie and Drew. "There, now, we'll have this storm in its proper place in no time. Sing it with me, to the God whom even wind and waves must obey!"

11
Drew's Monster Fish

St. Patrick's Breastplate
Be Thou My Vision

Be thou my battle shield, sword for my fight;
Be thou my dignity, thou my delight,
Thou my soul's shelter, thou my high tow'r:
Raise thou me heav'nward, O Pow'r of my
pow'r.

The storm howled on relentlessly.

"At this rate," yelled Abdul, "she'll shoot us out of the Med like a cannonball; we'll be in the Celtic Sea in no time!" He paused. "That is, if nothing breaks."

Abdul finally ordered Annie and Drew below for some sleep. Throughout the night Mr. Pipes and Abdul took turns battling the storm, one catching a few minutes of well-earned sleep while the other steered. As *Euroclydon* passed through the narrow Strait of Gibraltar in the early hours of the morning, Annie and Drew, exhausted from the storm, slept on.

"Mr. Pipes," said Abdul, wearily taking the mug of hot tea that Mr. Pipes offered him, "it's over."

The first hint of dawn shone on the horizon at their stern as Mr. Pipes replied, "She is a fine ship"—he extended his hand—"and you have commanded her well."

"Without you and my crew," said Abdul, taking a sip of the tea, "I couldn't have done it. I—I really couldn't have done it."

"You have done your part well," said Mr. Pipes, untying the reef points on the mainsail, "but, God be praised, he has brought us safely through."

Abdul took another swallow of tea.

After shaking out the reef in the mainsail and raising the halyard on the foresail, Mr. Pipes rejoined Abdul at the helm.

"May I suggest that you make your way below for some well-deserved sleep," said Mr. Pipes. "Dawn approaches, and a gloriously beautiful morning it promises to be; I shall be invigorated by it all and can thus carry on for a while longer."

While Abdul and the children slept, with Portugal now off the starboard beam, Mr. Pipes lashed the helm and added more forward sail. He hoped to make the most of the steady breeze and favorable seas.

After a quick check of the compass, he narrowed his eyes toward the northwest. *How long before Land's End comes into view*, he wondered, *or will Mizen Head, the southern point of Ireland, come into view first? If this wind holds and all goes well, we could be near England and home soon.* Just how he would go about explaining all this to Dr. Dudley and the children's parents he had no idea.

"'The best laid schemes,' and all that," he mused aloud, "'gang aft agley.' Can't be helped," he said, chuckling to himself. "And who would desire to change what God has clearly ordered?" Alone at the helm after an exhausting night in the storm, he found that talking aloud kept his own weariness at bay. "An experience of the most extraordinary kind, and one that I and my dear ones, my children—durst I call them mine?" he interrupted himself with a frown. "Perhaps in all the ways that truly matter," he persisted, "God has given them to me to nurture in faith, and they in turn to succeed me, to be my spiritual heirs, wanting as I do physical ones." He carried on for a while in this vein, sometimes frowning deeply, that wistful, faraway expression clouding his eyes. Then, chiding himself, his speech full of admonitions, exhortations, and assurances from the Book he loved above all books, a settled smile returned to his face.

Sometime later, yawning and blinking at the bright sunlight sparkling on the Atlantic, Drew staggered out of the companionway and stretched.

"Top of the morning to you, my boy!" called Mr. Pipes.

"Will you look at this; that storm's gone as fast as it came!" said Drew. "And we're sailing along just right—like the first day we left Genoa! Seems like ages ago."

Suddenly Drew slapped his forehead "What about my fishing line?" He bolted to the stern."Oh, no! I left it in the water through the whole storm! I completely forgot about it!"

Drew looked at the spool lolling in the yoke, line trailing loosely in the water behind the schooner. With very little drag, the line bunched up around the spool as he grabbed the handles and frantically reeled it in. It didn't take long. He held the frayed end in his hands and frowned.

"What have you found?" asked Mr. Pipes from his place at the helm.

"Nothing," said Drew. "I even lost the hook." Then, remembering where he had stowed the fishing tackle just before the storm, he opened the stern locker and rummaged in the tackle box.

"But I'm going to tie on another one of these monster hooks," he said, making a clean slice at the end of the line with his pocket knife. "Are you hungry, Mr. Pipes? I mean for some really great-tasting fish?"

"I must confess," said Mr. Pipes, awake through much of the storm without eating a proper meal the whole time, his stomach growling in protest at the situation, "I would most enjoy a fine breakfast, lunch, or dinner that included fish freshly caught by you. Indeed, I would."

"Of any kind?" said Drew.

"Well, perhaps not any kind," said Mr. Pipes.

"Well, I am going to catch you a monster fish for breakfast," said Drew, cinching the knot on a new lure with his teeth. He crimped on several lead weights to help the line sink deeper and tossed it astern. The lure flashed through the water as he played the line out in the schooner's wake.

"Good morning, Mr. Pipes," said Annie with a yawn as she came on deck. "What a gorgeous day!"

" 'Tis a lovely day," agreed Mr. Pipes, smiling at Annie.

"And the storm's gone," she said, with a sigh that sounded as though she had been holding her breath through the entire ordeal. Then she asked, "Where's Abdul?"

"Resting below," said Mr. Pipes. "Partaking blissfully of much-needed sleep, I trust."

"Wow, did you ever give him the stuff," said Drew, checking the tension of his line.

" 'The stuff'?" repeated Mr. Pipes.

"You know, all that about freedom," said Drew.

"I think Abdul was listening to you," said Annie. "I don't know who wouldn't be convinced of the truth by your arguments. I just wish I could put it like you do when I'm talking with Mom or Dad."

"Yeah," agreed Drew. "You beat him at his own game."

"Remember, Drew," said Mr. Pipes, "my goal is not to beat him, but to demolish his false arguments and confront him with the truth. And, Annie, we must also remember that reasoned argument alone will lead no one to Christ; we must persuade, but we must pray, depending completely on God's sovereign mercy to open the eyes of his understanding. After all is said, salvation is entirely of the Lord."

"You will say more to him, won't you?" asked Annie, hopefully.

"'Course he will," said Drew from the stern. "I've seen it in your face, Mr. Pipes; you love talking about the things of God with unbelievers—with anyone!"

"I endeavor, by God's grace," said Mr. Pipes, "in word and deed, to take every thought captive."

"Whoa!" hissed Drew, checking the tension on his line. "I felt something." Unblinking, his eyes searched the foamy water.

"Drew's going to catch us breakfast," said Mr. Pipes, nodding toward her brother.

Annie swallowed hard. "Oh," she said. "Where are we?" she added, trying to change the subject.

"That is Portugal to our starboard," said Mr. Pipes, his hand sweeping toward the land on their right.

Annie strained her eyes forward. "When will we see Ireland?"

"Perhaps by this afternoon—if the wind holds," replied Mr. Pipes, sighting along the bowsprit thrusting ahead of the schooner to the north.

"Yowza!" yelled Drew.

Annie joined her brother at the stern. His mouth hung open in astonishment. "Did you see him?"

"See who?" asked Annie, following his gaze.

"*Whom*, Annie; see *whom*," corrected Mr. Pipes. "Nevertheless, a good question. What have you hooked, Drew?"

"There it is again!" screamed Drew.

This time Annie did see the silvery flash as a fish broke the surface. Whirring like a steam turbine, the reel spun wildly.

"He's a monster!" yelled Drew. "But I can't grab the handles." His voice sounded desperate. "He'll get away!"

"Patience, Drew," Mr. Pipes called from the helm. "Allow him to play out line until he grows weary; you want him weary, Drew."

"But he just keeps going," said Drew, looking worried.

"If you could stop the reel at this moment," said Mr. Pipes, "you'd be certain to lose your fish—not to mention a finger or two. Wait until he gives up hope; then, when he thinks all is lost, and he can no longer resist, reel him in with all your might."

Annie looked at Mr. Pipes. It almost sounded like he was talking about something else.

The reel continued spinning as Drew watched, occasionally groaning in dismay.

"Hey, I think he's slowing down—a little," he said after several minutes.

"As soon as the handles stop spinning," said Mr. Pipes, "grab them firmly—but see to it that you don't force him in too fast. Big fellow will snap even that stout line of yours if you don't play him till he entirely gives up struggling."

For a quarter of an hour they waited.

"Look, Drew," said Annie at last, her brows arched in pity. "He's slowing way down—oh, the poor thing looks exhausted."

With a determined set to his jaw, Drew grabbed hold of the handles on the big reel and narrowed his eyes toward the fish.

"I'm not going to let him get away," he said through clenched teeth.

"Slow and steady, now, Drew," said Mr. Pipes. "Annie, would you be so kind as to carry on at the helm?" he added.

Annie, eager to occupy herself away from where a real live fish might come flopping onto the deck, strewing scales and fish slime everywhere—oh, and after that, all that would happen—she shuddered. Taking the spokes of the wheel in hand, her back on the fishermen, she checked the compass, glanced up at the bulging canvas bold against the blue sky, and strained to see whether she could make out Ireland—anything to distract her from the fishing.

"Ease him in carefully, now," she heard Mr. Pipes say. "Oh, he is a fine specimen—fine indeed."

"He's a whopper!" blurted Drew, his voice high-pitched and cracking in his excitement.

"His will to fight is all but spent," said Mr. Pipes. "But he might try to bolt as you help him aboard—do be careful. I'll gaff him with the boat hook—there, now, don't rush him."

Gaff him? thought Annie, trying desperately to ignore the fish-catching behind her. She began humming loudly.

"We did it!" yelled Drew, above feeble thumping as the fish thrashed at the stern, its strength nearly gone.

Annie broke into song.

"All right, Drew," she heard Mr. Pipes say in a guarded tone, "take up a belaying pin."

"Huh?" she heard Drew reply.

"As a club, my boy," explained Mr. Pipes. "I shall attempt to hold him; you must dispatch him with the business end of . . ."

She couldn't bear it.

"Jib needs adjusting," she called loudly. "I've lashed the helm and I'm going forward to fix things." She resumed singing as she hurried to the bow; the farther from it all, the better.

*

Annie sang a good deal over the next few minutes.

Mr. Pipes and Drew, grateful that Abdul was safely asleep below during the proceedings, cleaned fish and decks as quickly and thoroughly as they could manage. As he sluiced the decks with one last bucket of seawater, Mr. Pipes told Drew that it would never do for Annie or Abdul to stumble across a trace of slime, scale, or blood from Drew's catch.

"Annie," called Drew after Mr. Pipes nodded toward her several times, "isn't it a beauty?"

Annie took a deep breath before turning around. With both hands Drew strained to hold up a fat Atlantic salmon. The bulk of the fish forced Drew to scrunch up his shoulders under the strain; still, its tail nearly touched the deck. Drew grinned, a huge grin, his freckles widening as they stretched around his bulging cheeks.

Annie tried to smile in return.

"Annie, my dear," said Mr. Pipes, "I would be most happy to relieve you of your duties in the galley for the next little while—that is, if you so desire?"

Annie swallowed. "I've never cooked fish before," she stammered. She looked again at Drew's face, plastered with that grin; he looked so ridiculously happy. "But it's time I learn."

Drew took over for Annie at the helm while Mr. Pipes showed her how to cut the fish into steaks and cook them in the broiler. Several times, frantic dashes up the companionway interrupted her cooking lessons; gulping down great lungfuls of the sea air steadied her stomach, and each time she returned to the galley. Soon the savory aroma of fresh-caught salmon, broiling in a special herb sauce that Mr. Pipes had thrown together, drifted throughout the cabin. Drew nearly went mad with the smells wafting out of the companionway, caught by the breeze and blown full in his face. His nose and mouth twitched and his stomach seemed to claw at his insides in anticipation.

Smiling at her brother, Annie emerged from the cabin, set out a checked tablecloth on the cabin roof, and laid out three place settings.

"I'm dying, Annie," Drew moaned from the helm.

"It'll be ready in a jiffy," she said as her blond head disappeared below.

A minute later, with Mr. Pipes steadying a covered platter at her side, Annie pulled a linen cloth off the platter.

"Ta-da!" she said.

Drew, his eyes riveted on the steaming salmon, let go of the helm and licked his lips.

"Lash the helm first," said Mr. Pipes with a laugh.

After Mr. Pipes gave thanks, Annie filled Drew's plate with two large salmon steaks, a mound of sticky rice, and French-cut beans, and then generously smothered all in Mr. Pipes's creamy herb sauce.

"A fisherman's feast, my boy," said Mr. Pipes. "Do you like it?" Rivulets of steam escaped from the layers of pale pink as Drew plunged his fork into the fish. He closed his eyes as he chewed. Mm-mm, the first bite of fish he had eaten for . . . forever.

"Um, ah, um"—he paused and swallowed. "I've never tasted anything better in my life," he said, hoisting another forkful into his mouth. "Twry some," he added to his sister, his cheeks bulging.

Annie's smile disappeared as Mr. Pipes dished up her plate. She managed a smile and a thank-you to their old friend as she took her plate—her first plate of fish. Mr. Pipes had given her, she noticed with relief, the very smallest piece.

"Fish—fresh-caught fish, Annie, my dear—is most eminently eatable," said Mr. Pipes. As if demonstrating, he placed a bit of fish on the back of his fork. Then, his knife and fork working together with the expertise of a long-practiced art, he added beans and some rice, smothered the lot in herbs and sauce, nodded encouragingly at Annie to do the same, and ate.

Watching her brother eat had always disgusted Annie. But watching Mr. Pipes prepare his utensils and take that bite of fish and seeing the glow of delight and satisfaction spread across his tired face as he chewed was almost too much for her. She drew in her breath and looked at her plate. For a moment she hesitated; it was hard to explain; Mr. Pipes made it look so good, and Drew loved the stuff.

Following Mr. Pipes's lead, she lifted a forkful of fish— admittedly, a forkful heavily weighted on the side of rice and bean—into her mouth and began chewing cautiously. Looking up, she saw both Mr. Pipes and Drew staring at her expectantly. She smiled and, without saying anything, took another bite, this time a bite of just fish.

Their cheerful, late-morning breakfast so occupied the threesome that they did not hear Abdul coming up the companionway ladder. Nor did they at first see him staring hard at them with his hands on his hips.

"Avast! Avast!" screeched Virgil from Abdul's shoulder.

All three froze, mid-bite.

"So it's murder, is it?" Abdul's voice boomed suddenly in on the meal.

They turned and stared at Abdul.

"And murder committed on my ship!" he roared on. "If this were the old days, I'd see you all hanging from the yardarm for it!"

"Bilge breath! Bilge breath!" added Virgil.

Abdul stared angrily at them in silence.

Annie and Drew couldn't entirely decide whether he was serious. He certainly looked as though he meant it.

"Forgive me for saying so, Abdul," said Mr. Pipes at last, "but I don't believe catching and eating fish in the old days was considered by seamen to be a crime, and never a crime worthy of death. Come, my man, we approach the Celtic Sea and the waters surrounding the land of your forebears, waters teeming with fish, fish caught and eaten by your Irish today—as for centuries."

"Humph!" Abdul said, spinning on his barefooted heel. "One of you'd better tend the helm. Next thing you'll pile my ship on the rocks, God knows where."

"He does, indeed," said Mr. Pipes.

Abdul made no reply. For the next hour he stormed around the decks, speaking to no one except Virgil and adjusting things that seemed to need no adjusting. Mr. Pipes advised Drew against any more fishing for the time being and cautioned the children in whispers about not upsetting Abdul. Then he went below for some rest.

Annie took her watch at the helm. Off the bowsprit, she watched as the horizon slowly, almost imperceptibly, changed.

Drew rigged the hammock he'd found between the shrouds and the mast on the windward side of the schooner and curled up with his writing journal; he had so much to write about, and it seemed a good plan to stay out of Abdul's way. After several pages telling how long the salmon was, how big, how he'd thumped it with the belaying pin, how good-tasting it was, and so forth, he returned to the hymn he'd been working on. First, rereading Zechariah chapters 9 and 10, he then began writing another verse. After many crossings-out, he cleared his throat, looked around to be sure that no one was within earshot, and read aloud:

> Restored, victorious, gathered in,
>   Their enemies o'ercome;
> God's children worship 'round his throne,
>   And in his name they run!

"I see it!" yelled Annie excitedly, breaking in on his work. She held steady to the helm, straining on tiptoe for a better view.

"See what?" growled Abdul.

"Ireland," she replied. "At least I think it's Ireland."

Abdul looked up from where he had been splicing a line. He unfolded the chart, studied it for a moment, and smiled for the first time that day.

"You're right!" he said, slapping the chart with the back of his hand. "Ireland it is, and I can almost hear the music floating on the wind over the sea. The Emerald Isle, they—I mean *we*— call it; we should see the green soon. Stir your stumps, Drew, and help me hoist the topsails. Let's get more out of this wind."

While Drew helped raise more sail, he asked Abdul, "What did you mean about hearing music coming over the sea?"

"Ireland *is* music; everywhere you go in Ireland, you hear pennywhistles, harps, pipes, singing. If you're Irish, like *I am*," Abdul went on, pausing to hum the strains of some tune that Drew had never heard, "you like music."

"I thought you were American, like we are," said Drew as they rejoined Annie at the helm. Annie scowled at Drew. "By the way, is 'Abdul' an Irish name?" Drew went on. "Doesn't sound Irish to me."

Abdul blinked several times and frowned. Then he snorted. "Once Irish, always Irish; doesn't matter where you're born. I was just born in America, but I'm Irish at heart—always will be."

"So what's Ireland like?" asked Annie.

Abdul's cheeks grew red as he replied. "Green and with music everywhere," he said shortly.

Drew's eyes narrowed as he looked at Abdul.

"Have you ever been to Ireland?" he asked suspiciously.

Again Annie scowled at her brother.

Abdul snorted and gave Drew a sideways look as if to say that the question was so silly, it didn't require an answer. Instead, he pulled a little metal pipe with holes in it out of his pocket and began to play it.

"Here's an Irish tune for you," he said, pausing and looking forward at the horizon.

He played a frolicking melody, his fingers dancing rapidly over the holes. Annie and Drew couldn't help smiling, and if her feet had not been braced for balance at the helm, Annie would have tapped her foot.

They laughed together when, after a blur of fingers and a whistling flourish, he finished the tune.

"You're good," said Drew.

"Or how about this one," said Abdul, beginning a forlorn sort of tune.

Annie sniffed. It sounded mournful and sad, as she imagined an aching deep down in the heart might sound.

"Sounds kind of lonely," said Drew when Abdul finished. "Like wailing; it's almost a little . . . well, a little creepy in places."

"Anguish," said Annie.

Abdul looked at her.

"Huh?" said Drew.

"It sounds like a poet's kind of music," she tried to explain. "Poets use words; the Irish music uses swelling and bending sounds; but it's anguish just the same."

"It does sort of make you think about things," said Drew.

"Couldn't help overhearing your lovely strains, Abdul," said Mr. Pipes, looking rested from his nap and joining them on deck. "And Abdul, you have just illustrated one of the most critical things to remember about music," continued Mr. Pipes.

"I have?" said Abdul.

"What is it?" asked Drew.

"Music is its own message," said Mr. Pipes simply. "But it is a much more objective message than most care to admit. You see, just as letters of the alphabet have little meaning until blended into words, so individual notes have little or no meaning until they are blended together into specific combinations to create music. Just as your first tune was cheerful and evoked smiles and tapping feet, so your second melody evoked a pensive melancholy. And just as words produce objective responses in readers, be certain of this: musical sounds have the power to prompt those who hear to noble or ignoble, good or bad, lofty or base attitudes and deeds. Thus, when one blends musical sounds and words, they must agree. Where they do not, music always crushes the life out of the words."

"Which reminds me," said Abdul with something very close to a sneer, "I picked up a crew member in California a long time ago who called himself a Christian, like you all do—well, sort of like you do. Anyway, he would only listen to *Christian* music; that's what he called it. But frankly, it hip-hopped, be-bopped, and rip-rapped pretty much like all the rest—only not as good."

"Indeed," said Mr. Pipes. "And what did you conclude?"

"Sounded to me like Christians trying to be *with it* and not quite pulling it off and I never could get much from those words. Your hymns—well they're different."

Mr. Pipes smiled at Abdul.

"Drew and I didn't used to agree," said Annie. "But now it all makes sense, and I'm not quite sure why we ever thought otherwise."

"Oh, I know why," said Drew. "It's the sound; it grabs you and won't let you go. But you're right, Mr. Pipes: I never gave a rip about the words; I already got the real message from the music."

"As we always do," agreed Mr. Pipes. "You see, music is not an end in itself," he continued, "nor should it be a means to our own sinful ends. Rather, music is given to assist us in contemplating and expressing the entire range of human emotions and affections; supreme among those affections, music aids us in worshiping God."

"The poet Whittier said the highest use of poetry is the worship of God," said Annie, remembering their snowbound Christmas with Mr. Pipes and Dr. Dudley. "So is it true to say that the highest use of music is the worship of God?"

Scowling, Abdul put his pennywhistle in his pocket and began tossing a belaying pin up and down in his hand.

"What do you think, Annie?" replied Mr. Pipes.

"Well, if man's chief end is to glorify and enjoy God, then everything we do must be to glorify and enjoy him."

"Including music," added Drew.

"And including eating and drinking," added Annie.

"Even eating fish!" said Drew, looking sideways at his sister. She smiled. "All right, I admit it," she said. "It wasn't so bad after all."

"True enjoyment of all God's gifts," said Mr. Pipes, "comes when we do all to the glory of God."

"Even sailing!" said Annie, the breeze playing at her hair as she looked up at the sails with a laugh.

*

Afternoon came, and the sun's rays angled from the west, darkening the blue of the sky and water. Between watches, Drew swung in the hammock and worked at adding more lines to his hymn. Annie sketched Abdul at the helm with Virgil on his shoulder. Clara would never believe a story about sailing with someone who looked so much like a real pirate. Mr. Pipes rested for the night watch—perhaps the last night watch of the voyage.

An awed sort of wonder came over Abdul's face as Annie sketched him, her back to the bow of the ship. She turned to see what he was looking at. With a quick intake of breath, she too gazed at the scene: the blue sky far to the north had grown almost black, and the low rays of amber sunlight illuminated Ireland off their port bow until it seemed to shine—like an emerald, Annie thought. Never had she seen anything more lovely.

Regaining her voice, she called, "Mr. Pipes! Drew! Look!"

Mr. Pipes, his white hair tousled from sleep, joined them. Now all four sailors saw, rising above the blue of the sea, black cliffs shimmering like onyx, crowned with emerald-green fields, rolling like giant illuminated swells. They glowed mysteriously against the dark sky. Though the schooner was still some miles offshore, starlike specks of whitewashed cottages dotting the green hillsides came into view. As the shadows lengthened, the lighthouse miles away on Mizen Head flickered rhythmically.

No one spoke for several minutes.

"There's something special about Ireland," said Abdul at last, his hand relaxed on the helm, the schooner making easy way in the slackened evening breeze.

"Oh, indeed there is," agreed Mr. Pipes, lounging on a sail bag, Annie and Drew joining him in the growing dusk. "Ireland is the land of great storytellers—bards, they called them—and of great stories."

"Oh, won't you tell us one?" asked Annie and Drew.

"How about an Irish fishing story?" asked Mr. Pipes, a twinkle in his eye as he looked at Drew.

"Only if they catch something," said Drew.

"Ah, this is a most successful fishing story, indeed," replied Mr. Pipes with a chuckle and a wink.

Abdul narrowed his eyes at the old man.

"Long, long ago," began Mr. Pipes, "a boy from Roman Britain sailed just where we are sailing now"—Mr. Pipes gestured toward England off their starboard beam—"to Ireland, just there." He nodded toward the green hills to port.

"Sounds good," said Drew, clasping his hands behind his head and settling into the plump sail bag. Waves from the sea slapped rhythmically against the forefoot of the schooner, adding to the enchantment of the evening.

"Oh, I am afraid the young man—Patricius by name—found nothing good about it at the time," said Mr. Pipes.

"Why not?" asked Annie, gazing out over the Celtic Sea as the orange ball of the sun slipped nearer to the green hills of Ireland.

"Brutal Irish pirates had just descended on his home, brandishing swords and screaming furiously in the ancient Irish tongue. They bound him hand and foot and threw him into their boat. Sixteen-year-old Patricius, ripped from his family and home, was on his way to years of cruel slavery in Ireland. He no doubt wept in his despair as the boat carried him here across the sea. Promptly sold to a chieftain named Miliucc, Patricius found himself carted two hundred miles inland, where in bitter isolation he spent the next six years tending sheep. Without proper clothes to hold out the almost incessant Irish rain and cold, and nearly starving for lack of food, Patricius began to pray. Up till then, he had been entirely indifferent to Christianity. But as he prayed, he recounts later in his *Confession*, 'the love and fear of God more and more inflamed my heart.' As he continued praying throughout the loneliness of his days, he wrote that 'the spirit of God was warm upon me.' One night he had a dream. In it he heard a voice telling him that it was time for him to return to his family across the sea."

"But how's he going to get away?" asked Drew.

"He felt confident from his dream that God would provide a ship to take him home," replied Mr. Pipes. "He crept away from Miliucc's service and made his way to the sea, where, sure enough, he found a ship loading Irish wolfhounds for trade across the sea."

"Hold it," said Abdul, shaking his head in disgust. "How's a slave going to make it two hundred miles without somebody catching him? And the bit about the ship waiting just when he gets to the coast—come on."

"Patricius wrote of that later," said Mr. Pipes. "He said, 'I came in God's strength—and had nothing to fear.' At first the sailors, suspicious that he was a runaway slave, refused to give him passage. Dejected, Patricius turned to go; not knowing what to do, he prayed. Suddenly the sailors changed their minds, one of them chasing after him and offering him passage. Some historians speculate that during Patricius's years of tending sheep he had developed a special ability with animals; they may have decided that this boy would provide much-needed help with their cargo of unruly wolfhounds. In any case, once again, God answered Patricius's prayer, and after many trials he was restored to his home and family, just as his longing had expressed itself in his dream.

"Little is known about the next twenty years of his life— though hundreds of years later Roman Catholic biographers filled up those years with grandiose embellishments—but we do know from Patricius's own writings that he had another dream. This time he saw a man from Ireland bearing many letters. While reading one he thought he heard Irish voices from the woods of Flocu, begging him thus: 'We entreat thee, holy youth, that you come here and walk among us.' Stabbed to the heart by this call, with dismay, he concluded that God was calling him back to the hated land of his slavery."

"What a bummer," said Drew.

"That is precisely what Patrick thought," said Mr. Pipes. "Though not in exactly those words."

"Hold it. Did you say 'Patrick'?" asked Abdul. "*The* St. Patrick?"

"I did. And you can only imagine his dismay at the thought of returning to Ireland after the cruelties he had endured there. Again he prayed. He records that God gave him what he did not have in himself, that is, 'a care and anxiety for the salvation of others.' He prayed on until he finally 'did not think of himself,' and immediately prepared for taking Christ back to those who had so brutally torn him from his home and enslaved him. Nothing could stand in his way. Roman bishops from Gaul thought him uneducated and unfit for such a mission. Loved ones reminded him of his own cruel treatment in Ireland; though maps labeled places such as Ireland with warnings, 'Here do be monsters,' he ignored every objection. Patrick was determined to obey the Lord's call. And in A.D. 432, at forty-three years of age, Patrick 'went to Ireland, to pagans, to preach the gospel.' Apparently without pope or counsel, he declared, 'What I am I have received from the Lord.' Saying goodbye to his tearful family, he said, 'I am prepared, most gladly for His name, to give even my life; it is in Ireland that I wish to serve until I die.'

"As he and his helpers sailed toward the northeast coast of Ireland, precisely where we are sailing now," continued Mr. Pipes, his hand sweeping toward the sea and the last rays of amber sunlight all around them, "with a glow of confident expectancy on his face, Patrick said, 'Let us fish well.'"

"He really said that?" asked Drew, sitting up. "So did they catch anything?"

"Drew, Patrick was using figurative language," said Annie. "You know, where Jesus told Peter to be a fisher of men and preach the gospel to everyone."

"Yeah, I knew that," said Drew, slumping back into the sail bag.

"So how was the fishing?" asked Abdul, a mocking lilt in his tone.

"Splendid," said Mr. Pipes. "Though not without discouragement and, from time to time, great trials. Nevertheless, Patrick's single-minded love of God, extended with such meekness and piety to the Irish people, drew many to repentance after hearing him preach. But the Roman Britons across the sea, most of whom claimed to be Christian, scorned the new Irish converts. One Roman chief, Coroticus, sent bands of raiders to Ireland and dragged away many of the new converts for the slave trade.

Patrick wrote an anguished appeal to the 'ravening wolves eating up the people of the Lord as if they were bread.' He pleaded eloquently for the immediate release of the 'servants of God and baptized handmaids of Christ for whom he was crucified.' Perhaps no one but a former slave could have been so feeling in his appeals. To his growing flock he lamented, 'O most lovely and loving brethren and sons whom I have begotten in the Lord, . . . is it a shameful thing that we are born in Ireland?'"

"But he wasn't born in Ireland," interrupted Drew.

"Yes, but Patrick's love for the lost souls of Ireland and his identity with them was so complete that he even speaks of himself as having been born in Ireland. Hereafter, Patrick never again used his Roman name, Patricius; his break with Rome was complete. Furthermore, there is evidence that Patrick, a great lover of the Bible who called every Irish family to read it, may have even translated some of the Bible into Irish."

"I remember when you told us about Martin Luther and the Reformation," said Annie. "The Roman Catholic Church didn't allow translations of the Bible in the languages that people understood. Do you think they let Patrick translate into Irish way back in the 400s?"

"Likely as not, the church in Rome knew and cared little about what Patrick did. Sadly, during his thirty years of faithful ministry he was not highly esteemed by Roman Christians; only later when popes and bishops saw the enormous impact of his missionary work did they claim his gifts and work for Rome."

"Imagine what it was like for those Irish converts, hearing about the Lord Jesus for the very first time," said Annie, her chin cradled in her hands, elbows on the bulwarks as she gazed at the first flickering lights of evening shining from the coastal villages. "They must have had trouble understanding some things, though."

"Indeed, paganism made some truths difficult to grasp," said Mr. Pipes. "Of course, all God's truth is understood by sovereign grace alone. Nevertheless, some truths are more difficult to grasp than others."

"Like what?" asked Annie.

"Think of your own struggles," replied Mr. Pipes, "with the Trinity, for example."

"Well, I'm not an Irish pagan," said Annie, "but it is hard to get my mind around how God can be one and three all at once."

"That is where faith in the unseen is so important," said Mr. Pipes.

"So how did Patrick teach them about the Trinity?" asked Drew.

"I am not entirely sure," said Mr. Pipes, stroking his chin. "And there are so many legends about Patrick. Nevertheless, Irish tradition insists that Patrick plucked a lovely green shamrock from the sod, held it up for all to see, and attempted to explain that though the shamrock had three leaves, it was but one shamrock."

"I've heard that one," said Abdul.

"Of course, it is only an analogy," said Mr. Pipes with a shrug. "Helpful, perhaps, but inadequate to fully tap the depths of the Christian doctrine of the Trinity."

"Did he write any hymns?" asked Annie.

"A sturdy poetic confession of faith called 'St. Patrick's Breastplate' is ascribed to him," replied Mr. Pipes. "In it the poet expresses profound trust in Christ as coequal with the Father and the Spirit—a glorious codifying of the doctrine of the Trinity."

As the orange ball of the sun disappeared at last, Mr. Pipes's clear voice rose above the creak of the rigging and the hissing of the sea against the hull:

> I bind unto myself today
> The strong name of the Trinity
> By invocation of the same,
> The Three in One, and One in Three.

Abdul cocked his ear at the stout Irish melody. Listening closely in the fading light, Annie decided that the next verse was a review of the entire gospel from Christ's coming as a babe to his second coming on the "day of doom."

Mr. Pipes continued singing. The next verse sounded to Drew like Patrick was recounting the many ways in which God had heard his prayers and had worked so powerfully in his own life and ministry:

> I bind unto myself today
> The pow'r of God to hold and lead,
> His eye to watch, his might to stay,
> His ear to hearken to my need,
> The wisdom of my God to teach,
> His hand to guide, his shield to ward,
> The Word of God to give me speech,
> His heav'nly host to be my guard.

Then the melody that Mr. Pipes sang changed: the words were now all about Christ surrounding the Christian in quiet or in danger. Then as the hymn rose to the finish, Mr. Pipes's eyes sparkled in the dusk and his singing took on the deep passion that the children had come to expect—and to love:

> Eternal Father, Spirit, Word.
> Praise to the Lord of my salvation:
> Salvation is of Christ the Lord!

Abdul was the first to break the quiet that followed. "So, that's a nice tune," he said a little awkwardly.

"Set to words of great importance to Ireland's patron saint," said Mr. Pipes, "and to all others who love truth and freedom."

Abdul made no reply.

Mr. Pipes continued, "Patrick preached Christ to all Ireland, to the edge of the world, 'to the point' as he called it late in his life, 'beyond which there is no one.'"

"And where there 'do be monsters,'" said Drew with a grin.

"So the Roman world believed," said Mr. Pipes, smiling. "And while Rome spiraled from peace into chaos and collapse, Ireland under the sweet influence of the gospel of Christ rose out of her chaos into peace. One lasting effect on Ireland—where slavery had been so deeply a part of everyday life—was that slavery was almost completely unknown there by the time of Patrick's death. He died near Armagh on March 17, A.D. 455. But the Celtic church he established flourished throughout the Dark Ages descending on the continent of Europe, in part because Celtic Christians excelled in blending three important Christian priorities all together: they became great scholars, preserving, in beautifully illuminated texts, the manuscripts of antiquity; they led simple lives of devotion to God; and in the generations to follow they continued to spread the gospel. In the century after Patrick's death, Columba, an Irish Christian, established an abbey at Iona in Scotland. From Iona, Celtic missionaries reached much of the rest of Scotland and northern England for Christ."

Mr. Pipes paused. For several minutes they listened to the nighttime sea sounds.

"If the Irish loved music so much," said Drew, breaking the stillness, "they've got to have written more than one hymn."

"Right you are, Drew," said Mr. Pipes. "In the eighth century, about the time St. Brendan embarked on his legendary voyage across the Atlantic, an unknown Celtic Christian, a follower of Patrick, wrote this near-perfect and quintessentially Celtic hymn. Unless you are all too tired, I shall teach it to you. But first, Abdul, might I borrow your pennywhistle?"

"You play?" said Abdul, skeptically, pulling it out of his pocket, eyeing the old man as he handed it to him.

Drew felt his blood rise and was just about to tell Abdul that there wasn't anything Mr. Pipes couldn't do, when Annie caught his eye and silenced her brother with a scowl and a firm shake of her head.

Smiling, Mr. Pipes looked up at the stars twinkling to life above them. He fingered the little pipe soundlessly as if trying to remember something. After a moment, with a nod of satisfaction, he brought it to his lips; a clear melody, which seemed to drift up out of the antiquity of the now-dim green hills slipping by on their port, breathed mysteriously from the pipe. They listened as he played it through several times.

"There, now, do you have the tune fixed in your minds?" asked Mr. Pipes.

It was the kind of tune that Annie and Drew didn't want to ever forget.

"I think I've heard it before," said Abdul. "Here, take the helm, Drew," he added. Mr. Pipes smiled and handed the whistle back to Abdul.

"Do listen to the poetry," he said. Annie and Drew listened as Mr. Pipes sang the words and Abdul played the pennywhistle.

"Now, together, with one voice," Mr. Pipes's voice came from the darkness. "Sing this ancient poem of the most intimate devotion, filled with swords, battles, towers—and a High King victorious over all comers." He paused. "Won't you sing with us, Abdul?"

"Naw," came the reply. "Better keep you on pitch with my pipe."

He made a flourish, his fingers dancing up and down the pipe, and then began playing the tune again. Annie and Drew listened intently as Mr. Pipes sang through the hymn:

Be thou my vision, O Lord of my heart;
Naught be all else to me, save that thou art—
Thou my best thought by day or by night,
Waking or sleeping, thy presence my light.

Be thou my wisdom, and thou my true word;
I ever with thee and thou with me, Lord;
Thou my great Father, I thy true son;
Thou in me dwelling, and I with thee one.

Be thou my battle shield, sword for my fight;
Be thou my dignity, thou my delight,
Thou my soul's shelter, thou my high tow'r:
Raise thou me heav'nward, O Pow'r of my pow'r.

Riches I heed not, nor man's empty praise,
Thou mine inheritance, now and always:
Thou and thou only, first in my heart,
High King of heaven, my treasure thou art.

High King of heaven, my victory won,
May I reach heaven's joys, O bright heav'n's Sun!
Heart of my own heart, whatever befall,
Still be my vision, O Ruler of all.

As the moon rose over England, casting silvery shadows across the sea, Abdul, his eyes closed in thought, held out the last note of the verse. It floated prayerlike over the surrounding sea, creating a sort of breathless pause of anticipation. A thrill spread over Annie as Mr. Pipes, slowing the tempo, began singing the last verse again; then, as Annie and Drew joined in, the piping stopped and Abdul's voice, halting at first, joined them in singing the words out of the darkness:

High King of heaven, my victory won,
May I reach heaven's joys, O bright heav'n's Sun!
Heart of my own heart, whatever befall,
Still be my vision, O Ruler of all.

12
The Voyagers Return

A Hymn of Glory Let Us Sing
(Venerable Bede)

A hymn of glory let us sing;
New songs thro' out the world shall ring:
Alleluia! Alleluia!

Annie gradually became aware of a new motion, accompanied by new sounds: a steel-on-steel clanging and teeth-buzzing rumbling, broken now and then by an eye-popping blare from a horn. That must have been what had awakened her, she decided, squinting at the sunlight catching her full in the face. She looked around the sleeping car of what was clearly a train: Mr. Pipes and Drew lay sound asleep. But what had happened to Ireland, to Abdul and the schooner? How had they gotten on this train?

Then, sketchy and incomplete, memories returned. No one had wanted to go below and sleep last night—their last on board *Euroclydon*. How could they, with the silvery moon shimmering on the sea, the night breezes heeling the vessel as she reached toward England, the companionable mystery of the night sail up the Irish Sea, Abdul's Celtic music played on his whistle, and Mr. Pipes's singing accompanied by the flapping of sails and the creaking of rigging—sleeping was entirely out of the question. Then early this morning—*it must have been this morning*, she thought as she tried getting a better look at the position of the sun, now high in the sky—they had arrived at the bustling harbor of Liverpool. Almost in a trance from lack of sleep, she vaguely remembered saying good-bye to Abdul and then trying to listen as Mr. Pipes and Abdul talked. She had caught such words as "lizard," "truth," and "freedom," but she couldn't remember anything else. At the port-of-entry office, Mr. Pipes had telephoned Dr. Dudley and then ordered a cab. Next she remembered boarding the train, then nothing else until waking just now. She glanced again at Mr. Pipes and Drew; she'd let them sleep.

Sometime later—she couldn't be sure how much later—she woke again with a start. Hissing and screeching, the train slowed. A sign flicked past the window. *Northampton*, she read.

"I am so hungry, I could eat a horse," moaned Drew, stretching and yawning.

"Ah, and you shall," said Mr. Pipes. Undaunted, a twinkle still shone in his weary eyes. "We must gather our things—Drew," the old man broke off, nodding toward the wrinkled mounds of clutter disgorged from Drew's knapsack.

Moments later on the platform they spotted Dr. Dudley, his finger twisted in his black mustache, face and lip stretching off to one side as he pulled viciously on it, his eyes searching faces in the crowd. Drew reached him first.

"Hi!" he said, trying to get Dr. Dudley's attention.

"You will excuse me, young man," said Dr. Dudley, looking past Drew. "I do not want to buy anything; I am waiting for someone."

"But—" Drew started to protest.

"Dr. Dudley!" said Annie and Mr. Pipes at the same moment.

"There, now, you see, I have found them," said Dr. Dudley, replacing his anxious expression with something more like a pout.

"It's me, Dr. Dudley," said Drew, pulling on the sleeve of the man's well-cut suit jacket.

"Oh, so it is," said Dr. Dudley, coolly. Then putting on his sternest face, he asked, "Whatever in the world was that you said on the telephone about a wee bit of sailing? I do not recall anything in your itinerary about sailing."

"Martin, dear man," said Mr. Pipes, "so good of you to pop over and give us a lift home—*home*; a glorious word it is—*home*."

"If so glorious," began Dr. Dudley, blinking rapidly, his chin jutting upward as he supervised the arranging of their things in the trunk of his car, "why do I find it so very difficult to persuade you to remain at said home? And what on earth are these swords doing in your luggage?"

Drew gave Annie a here-we-go-again roll of his eyes.

"Drew," she whispered, "remember, he just cares a lot about him; that's why he always harps at him like this."

"Doesn't seem to care any too much for us," Drew whispered back.

"He always comes around after a bit," said Annie. "Just smile and look friendly."

Drew nodded and, though not entirely convinced, turned a fully toothed grin at Dr. Dudley.

"I, however, know the answer," continued Dr. Dudley guardedly, looking sideways at Annie and Drew. They both watched him mouthing inaudibly in the old man's ear, "It is the blighters, isn't it?" He nodded his head sideways at the children.

"For whose sake, my dear friend," said Mr. Pipes, smiling warmly from Dr. Dudley to Annie and Drew, "I would stop at no extremity."

"Humph! Of course you wouldn't," snorted Dr. Dudley. "Nevertheless, you know how ill disposed I am to interfere," he added with feigned indifference, punctuated by a sniff and a violent thrust of his chin. "Mind you, not that my interference would effect the slightest good."

"Thank you for picking us up," ventured Annie, hoping to help put Dr. Dudley in a better humor. "I can't wait to get back to Olney; it seems almost like home to us, too—though I know it isn't really. How long will it take to get there?"

"At this rate," said Dr. Dudley, slamming the lid of the trunk, "just short of forever."

"We'd better get going, then," said Drew. And they piled into the car.

Dr. Dudley was not the best of drivers—even on his native English roads. Nevertheless, with only one or two near misses, they came to a slight rise in the road and spreading before them at last, like a scene from a storybook, lay the rolling countryside surrounding the little market town of Olney. Flocks of sheep and adolescent lambs neatly trimmed the lush pastures, startled rabbits scurried along the fence line—but towering above it all was the steeple of the parish church of St. Peter and St. Paul's, rising heavenward like a centuries-old beacon in all its sturdy grandeur.

Annie caught her breath. "I'd almost forgotten how—how perfect it all is," she said.

"And that steeple's been pointing up like that," added Drew, squinting as they came closer, hoping to catch sight of a kestrel circling the ancient spire in search of its dinner, "for more than five hundred years. Looks solid as ever, too."

And then they were there—back in Olney. Brick and stone cottages lining the cobbled streets of the village flicked by and then came into focus more clearly as Dr. Dudley pumped the brakes with a succession of jerks, slowing the car to a crawl. Mr. Pipes took in the familiar sights with a contented sigh.

"Ah, yes, home at last," he said softly. "Home . . . the joy of the pilgrimage."

"There it is!" said Drew, excitedly.

"Mrs. Beccles's Bakehouse!" squealed Annie. They waved out the window.

"Oh, please, Dr. Dudley," said Drew, "can't we stop and just say hello to Mrs. Beccles, please?"

"Just say hello, is it?" said Dr. Dudley, driving right past the little stone bakery. "You have more in mind than a polite greeting. I know. You're after more of her jelly fills."

"But—" Drew started to protest.

"Well, in any event, she's not there," continued Dr. Dudley. "I happen to know she's closed up tight for the evening, she has. Besides, I knew Mr. Pipes would be eager for hearth and home—which reminds me. I am not so sure that as you get along in years the damps along the river are so good for your health. Now, I propose you move from the outskirts to the—"

"Never mind that," said Mr. Pipes with a laugh as the car thrummed over the cobblestones of the bridge crossing The Great Ouse, a river that had nourished and amused untold generations of townsfolk, gurgling placidly along the edge of town.

Annie's eyes followed the meandering path of the river, the willow branches bowing gracefully over its banks, leaving silvery trails in the glassy current; late-afternoon shafts of sunlight made their way through the trees, casting bright patches along the shadowy water. As they came to the brow of the arched bridge, just visible from Drew's side of the car, they caught sight of Mr. Pipes's stone cottage nestled along the banks. Annie leaned across, her eyes wide in anticipation.

"And there it is," she said.

"Hey, smoke's coming out of both chimneys," said Drew, studying the twin chimneys rising above the two gable ends of the cottage.

Mr. Pipes smiled at Dr. Dudley. "Oh, you have made ready for us by setting an evening fire—but in the kitchen, too?"

"I don't know what you're talking about," said Dr. Dudley, his eyes watching the roadway. "Looked as lifeless as a tomb to me, indeed, it did."

"We shall see about that," said Mr. Pipes as Dr. Dudley turned onto the grassy track off the main road.

The car had not quite finished jerking to a halt before both back doors flew open and Annie and Drew sprang from the car. For the next several minutes the pair, chattering and laughing together, explored along the staithe, where they had first learned to fish and sail and where their friendship with Mr. Pipes had first been forged. Drew ran his hand along *Toplady*'s keel where she lay turned upside down on the little stone pier.

"Lord Underfoot!" called Annie, turning this way and that, her eyes searching for Mr. Pipes's giant gray cat in the meadow grass and tree branches surrounding the cottage.

"Do you hear 'em?" said Drew, holding up his hand for silence.

"Lord Underfoot?" asked Annie.

"No, silly. The hedge sparrows—there," said Drew, his head cocked as he listened. "That piping sound, *tseep, tseep*. That's hedge sparrows hunting for bugs and flies and other slimy stuff to eat for dinner. I'd almost forgotten about all the birds that live along the riverbank in Olney."

"It is a beautiful song," agreed Annie.

"Oh, but that reminds me of dinner," moaned Drew, a hollow look coming to his eyes.

"I'm hungry, too," said Annie.

"So am I," agreed Mr. Pipes, joining them on the riverbank.

"You must be so happy to be back to all this," said Annie, slipping her hand into their old friend's hand. "I'll never forget as long as I live that first summer and all the fun things you did with us—and all you taught us."

Suddenly, from across the river through the trees on the opposite bank came the gonging of the bells from the parish church, their weighty ringing spreading over the countryside. Amber sunlight glowed warmly from the stones of the steeple rising into the dusky sky above the trees. As they watched, a kestrel darted from the highest louvered Gothic opening in the spire. It soared round and round the steeple, its speckled wings flashing in the sunlight; then, banking to one side, it dipped below the treetops and disappeared from sight.

"Everybody else is having dinner," said Drew, his eyes still searching the sky.

"And maybe Lord Underfoot's inside," said Annie, "eating his dinner."

They turned toward the cottage, now aglow with the warmth of evening emanating from the windows. Dr. Dudley emerged from within and pulled the door closed behind him, a smug grin on his face as he strode toward them.

"Well, I'll leave you to it, then," he said, making as if to leave.

"You will do no such thing," said Mr. Pipes, "depositing us on the doorstep and then being off like this. No, no, that will never do. You must join us for a cup of tea."

"Or dinner," said Drew, hopefully. He sniffed the air as a wave of delicious cooking smells caught his senses—senses relentlessly honed by an adolescent metabolism.

"Oh, I suppose, if you insist," said Dr. Dudley, stepping aside as he opened the door, letting Mr. Pipes and the children enter the cottage first.

It took them a moment to process what happened next. As Annie and Drew followed Mr. Pipes into the dining room of the little cottage, they each noticed something different. Annie saw the smiling faces of Mrs. Broadwith, their landlady of that first summer in Olney; Mrs. Beccles, her full cheeks bulging and rosy with merriment; Mrs. Willow's reserved but friendly smile and nod; Mr. and Mrs. Howard, their children—and her friend Clara, more grown up and beautiful than Annie even remembered.

Drew saw a table spread with the most delicious-looking food, steam rising tantalizingly from steak and kidney pie; Cornish pasties—Mrs. Beccles's contribution, no doubt; roast beef surrounded by Yorkshire pudding; jacket potatoes smothered in cheddar cheese and shrouded with strips of crispy bacon; a platter of pike, generously dribbled with gutted gooseberry and butter sauce and sprinkled with parsley. And a sideboard loaded with Manchester raspberry tart and clotted cream; almond and cherry trifle; and a cheese board heaping with Cheshire, Blue Stilton, and the deep orange of Leicester cheese. Then he noticed the people, including grinning Bentley Howard standing nearly as tall as his father.

"Three cheers for the returning mariners!" Bentley shouted, followed by a chorus of *hip, hip—hurrah*s!

For the next moments everyone talked at once. Surrounded by all their old friends, Annie felt almost too excited to think about eating; even Drew found himself more interested in talking with old friends—for a few moments. Still, he was relieved when everyone was seated around the table, and the room grew quiet as all eyes turned to Mr. Pipes.

"Thank you all," he said, pausing to smile at each of his friends around the table. "A greeting such as this must be very like that promised homecoming we long for in heaven—with a meal very much like this one you have spread before us this evening. May I propose that we sing a hymn of glory to God before we eat this most lovely and welcome meal?"

"I'll get the hymnals," said Drew, jumping up from his place.

Mr. Pipes sat down at his harpsichord. He announced the hymn, and after a shuffling of pages, he played it through once. Then with one voice the cottage swelled to the ancient strain:

A hymn of glory let us sing;
New songs thro'out the world shall ring:
Alleluia! Alleluia!
Christ, by a road before untrod,
Ascendeth to the throne of God.
Alleluia . . . !

The holy apostolic band
Upon the Mount of Olives stand;

Alleluia! Alleluia!
And with his followers they see
Jesus' resplendent majesty.
Alleluia . . . !

To whom the angels, drawing nigh:
"Why stand and gaze upon the sky?"
Alleluia! Alleluia!
"This is the Savior," thus they say,
"This is his noble triumph day."
Alleluia . . . !

"Again shall ye behold him so
As ye today have seen him go,
Alleluia! Alleluia!
In glorious pomp ascending high,
Up to the portals of the sky."
Alleluia . . . !

As Mr. Pipes sang, his eyes took on that clear, faraway look that always made Annie and Drew think he was seeing something—or someone—real and beautiful and grand. Sometimes Drew would even try to follow his gaze.

The room grew silent as Mr. Pipes prayed. And as all who knew him had grown accustomed, his prayer was full of Scripture and hymns, and his voice was full of longing as he thanked the Lord for "'his glorious triumph day,'" and "for good food and fellowship, a gracious foretaste of that to be enjoyed someday—soon—in 'the portals of the sky.'" He said *Amen*. Then, amidst *ooh*s and *ah*s, platters of scrumptious food made their way around to everyone.

Drew wanted to ask Mr. Pipes about the hymn and who had written it, but just at that moment he preferred to eat. While they ate, their friends fired questions at Mr. Pipes, at Annie, at Drew, and then back to Mr. Pipes. They all laughed heartily at the thought of the old man dressed in medieval costume—including tights. As the story of the robbery and their nighttime flight through the streets of Milan unfolded, Dr. Dudley clucked his tongue disapprovingly.

When she could eat no more, Annie felt a soft tickling on her leg and then an impatient batting of a large paw—claws velveted, for the moment—on her knee. Then Lord Underfoot, with an irritated meow, jumped up on her lap. Annie laughed, rubbing his ears and stroking his thick gray back and twitching tail. Rumbling with contentment, he worked his paws up and down, twisting his head and leaning toward her to get the fullest benefit of her attention.

When the last fork and knife were laid down in resignation, Mrs. Beccles's voice rose above the rest.

"We have dearly missed your playing on the organ these Sabbaths while you've been abroad, no doubt playing all those fancy organs in all those highbrow Italian churches."

"He didn't play a one," said Drew. "Though I sure tried to get him to let 'em have it in Milan."

"Never a one?" said Mrs. Beccles incredulously.

"No, though I missed it sorely," said Mr. Pipes.

"Well, that settles that," she said, nodding her head decisively, and tying on her apron. "You and the young ones—but my, how they have grown since I first laid eyes on 'em. As I was saying, you and the young ones'll be wanting to ankle your way up to the church, then."

"Whatever for?" asked Dr. Dudley, scowling.

Annie caught Clara's eye. They had so much to talk about; but it might just have to wait.

"To play at his organ, Dr. D.," said Mrs. Beccles. "Now, run along, then, the three of you, while we tidy up the place a wee bit. That's it, run along." With that, she shooed them out the door.

The full moon cast a silvery sheen over the river as they walked slowly toward the church, its steeple bathed in pale light as it pierced the night sky. From the grass and reeds along the riverbank, crickets and toads called back and forth in a night-time antiphon. For several minutes the three friends walked in companionable silence, enjoying the muted night sounds and the cool air.

As they neared the crown of the bridge and looked back on Mr. Pipes's cottage, moonlight reflecting from his slate roof, Annie said, "This has been a celebration to remember."

"Indeed," said Mr. Pipes.

"Best food I've eaten for weeks," said Drew.

"Except for your ... your salmon," said Annie, generously.

"It is so lovely to be reunited with dear ones," said Mr. Pipes.

"Isn't that what the hymn was about?" asked Annie.

"All about the ascension, wasn't it?" asked Drew, "when Jesus went back to heaven after the resurrection?"

"Yes," replied Mr. Pipes. "And about our seeing him again in his resplendent majesty, when we too shall rise and be forever united with our Lord in heaven."

"Where I think we'll sing only the best hymns of glory to God," said Drew.

"We should never offer him less," said Mr. Pipes, as they made their way down narrow, winding Main Street, brick and stone cottages snuggled on either side.

"Who wrote it?" asked Annie.

"Chap known as Venerable Bede," replied Mr. Pipes.

"Who would name their kid 'Venerable'?" asked Drew.

Mr. Pipes laughed. "His mother and father did not name him that; Bede came to be known as 'Venerable' for his piety and scholarship. In fact, he was one of the most brilliant minds of his day."

"When did he live?" asked Annie.

"A.D. 673 to 733," replied Mr. Pipes. "And though he wrote many books, he is best known for his *Ecclesiastical History of the English People*, written in 731, and our source of most of what is known about ancient Anglo-Saxon Britain. In his history he traces the progress of Roman Christianity in Britain, espe-

226

cially from the work of Augustine of Kent whom Pope Gregory sent to England in A.D. 597."

"Those were the guys who sang the *Te Deum* on the beach," said Drew.

"The very same," said Mr. Pipes.

"So did Mr. Bede write about Patrick?" asked Annie.

"And that other Celtic missionary named Columba?" asked Drew.

"I am afraid that Bede, like the rest of Roman Christians in his day, did not think much of Celtic Christianity. Alas, he does not even mention Patrick, I fear, and reserves some rather uncomplimentary remarks for Columba."

Drew frowned.

"Nevertheless," continued Mr. Pipes, "in spite of his failings, Bede appears to have been an earnest Christian whose hope was in a crucified and risen Savior."

"Who ascended to heaven and will come back," said Annie, "as he wrote in his hymn."

"Precisely," agreed Mr. Pipes. "Bede also includes in his history the account of a shy, unlearned cowherd, Caedmon, who is credited with writing the first hymn in English—Old English, that is, though Bede first copied it down in Latin."

"Hold it," said Drew, halting for a moment on the pavement. "If Caedmon was so unlearned, he wouldn't have been able to read or write. So how could he have written anything, let alone a hymn? You know, it's not easy work writing a hymn."

"There are problems with the story, to be sure," agreed Mr. Pipes. "For example, it is recorded that Caedmon, in an ecstasy of devotion and inspiration, sang his hymn out spontaneously. But I doubt it."

"Why?" asked Annie.

"For many reasons," said Mr. Pipes. "But mostly because worthy poetry doesn't just happen; it is the result of thought, skill, learning, and, of course, devotion."

"Let's hear it," said Drew, as they turned onto Church Street.

227

"I know no tune to which it is set. But I will recite the earthy Anglo-Saxon poetry in the English we understand today. Here it is, the oldest hymn in our English tradition:

Now we must praise the Ruler of Heaven,
The might of the Lord and his purpose of mind,
The work of the Glorious Father; for he,
God Eternal, established each wonder,
He, Holy Creator, first fashioned the heavens
As a roof for the children of earth.
And then our guardian, the Everlasting Lord,
Adorned this middle-earth for men.
Praise the Almighty King of Heaven.

"I agree with you, Mr. Pipes," said Drew. "Caedmon didn't just come up with it out of thin air."

"And why is that, my boy?" asked Mr. Pipes.

"It has a pattern," said Drew. "Begins with 'Ruler' and ends with 'King'—a kind of ruler."

"And it has seven names for God," said Annie. "If I counted right, that is."

"You did, indeed," said Mr. Pipes.

"So was Bede, the guy who wrote all about Caedmon—was he a good guy or a bad guy?" asked Drew.

"Judging from his priorities," replied Mr. Pipes, "I am compelled to think well of him."

"What priorities?" asked Annie.

"The Bible," said Mr. Pipes simply. "Though none of it survived the Viking invasions, Bede translated parts of the Bible into Anglo-Saxon; he spent his last days on his deathbed translating the gospel of John. Bede, who often referred to the day of someone's death as his heavenly birthday, spent his heavenly birthday singing psalms, giving thanks to God as long as his strength remained."

"Sounds like the best way to celebrate your heavenly birthday," said Annie. "Considering that's what we'll all be doing in heaven—singing."

"Here comes Mr. Newton's house on the left," interrupted Drew.

"'Amazing Grace,'" said Annie. "I love his story, and that other hymn of his you taught us, 'Glorious Things of Thee Are Spoken.' And to think, he lived right here."

"And wrote right up there in his study," added Drew, pointing to the right-hand gable poking out of the roof.

Suddenly, out of the stillness they heard a muffled *thump, thump* of hooves on grass, and out of the shadows the moonlight shone full on a white pony trotting expectantly toward them.

"Lady Lulu!" called Annie, clambering onto the stone wall surrounding the pasture. Reaching toward the pony's scruffy mane, she said, "Oh, Dr. Dudley's been starving you, poor thing."

"I believe her ladyship is somewhat rounder when you two are in town," said Mr. Pipes with a chuckle.

"She needs chocolate now and then," said Annie, scratching the pony under its chin.

"Yeah, she's gotta keep her strength up," said Drew. "Jelly-filled doughnuts would do the trick."

"Do you think we'll have time to ride her before we go back . . . back home?" asked Annie, hesitantly.

"I was wondering more about fishing—and sailing *Toplady?*" said Drew.

"Perhaps we shall have time," said Mr. Pipes, distractedly, as he led them through the eerie stillness of the churchyard, moonlight casting shadows from the worn gravestones lining the pathway.

The clinking of keys broke the stillness as Mr. Pipes fitted a large skeleton key into the lock. As she waited, Annie ran her fingers over the pocked stone-carved features of one of the somber faces holding up the Gothic passage into the church. She couldn't help remembering that first meeting with Mr.

Pipes. It seemed like only yesterday that she had heard him playing the organ from this very spot.

The heavy oak door groaned open, and Annie and Drew followed Mr. Pipes into the high-vaulted stillness of the parish church.

People have been coming here to worship for way more than six hundred years, Drew thought as he looked down the central aisle of the nave, moonlight shimmering through the stained-glass windows, falling in dim shafts on the pews and worn stone floor.

Mr. Pipes walked faster toward the altar. He pulled back a velvet curtain to the right of the lectern. A sliver of moonlight caught his white hair for an instant as he gazed from the rows of pipes and back at the keyboards; a smile spread across his face as if he were greeting an old friend.

"Well, then," he said as if he were picking up a conversation left off only yesterday, "how fares my Battleship Binns this evening?"

Annie and Drew watched in silence as he clicked on the light above the music stand and ran his hands over the familiar oak console. Then, with a *thunk, thunk,* he pulled several stops, rubbed his hands together, and closed his eyes. Moments later, the ancient walls echoed with music. Annie and Drew smiled at each other as their old friend played louder and louder. Watts blended into Newton, Waring to Bonar, Luther to Heermann, Palmer to Davies, Kelly to Patrick, Francis to Ambrose; they recognized hymn after hymn, and still Mr. Pipes played on, as if to make up in one sitting and in one grand medley all the weeks spent away. At some point as he played (so enchanted were Annie and Drew that later they could not quite remember when), they were all singing. And as their voices had risen that first afternoon, which seemed so long ago, again they sang along with their old friend.

Then he stopped.

"I feel like I've died and gone to heaven," said Drew when all was still again.

Annie looked at Mr. Pipes and then frowned at her brother.

" 'Twill be very like this in heaven," murmured Mr. Pipes. "Our Great Lord, victorious over all, shall one day welcome us into the glory—the grandeur—of his presence. And on that great day, when we see our Lord Christ—and all our loved ones"—he paused, looking intently at Annie and Drew—"we shall sing like never before; even times such as this will seem as nothing."

"I can't wait," said Annie, her eyes glistening in the moonlight.

"Me either," said Drew, quietly.

"And we won't ever have to leave you," stammered Annie.

"No, indeed, you will not," said the old man, smiling at them both.

"And in heaven we will . . . how did Thomas Ken put it?" said Annie, frowning in thought, " 'incessant sing and never tire.' That was it, wasn't it?"

"Precisely," replied Mr. Pipes, exhaling contentedly.

"Do you think we will sing Watts in heaven?" asked Drew. "Or any other hymns you've taught us?"

"What we sing in heaven," said Mr. Pipes, "will be the very finest words and music to sing before our Holy and Great Sovereign; how could it be anything less? Therefore, what we offer to him in song now must be appropriate to the transcendent splendor of his being. From age to age, what we sing to God must be nothing less than the very finest."

He placed an arm around both of them. "I shall not always be here to tell you these things, and so it falls to you to know, to love, and to help preserve all that is grand and worthy in these hymns." He paused, lowering his head as he looked intently at them over his glasses, his full eyebrows splaying upward. "And it falls to you, as your gifts allow, to add high praises to that hymnody. Which reminds me, Drew," he continued, "I would be most honored if you would show us the poetry that has occupied your time whilst on our voyage—oh, yes, I have been watching you."

"Yeah," said Annie, "remember Bede's hymn: 'New songs throughout the world shall ring.' Come on, Drew, I had to show mine. Let's see it."

For a moment Drew's eyes darted from side to side like a rabbit trying to find a place to hide.

"Well, it's nothing like Andrew of Crete or Ambrose," said Drew, fumbling in his knapsack.

Mr. Pipes's eyes narrowed as he studied the page from Drew's journal; at several places his eyebrows rose and fell rhythmically, and from time to time as he read he tipped his head and smiled, nodding in approval—at least Drew hoped it was in approval.

"You have taken my advice and used scriptural poetry," he said at last.

"Yeah, I used Zechariah," said Drew. "So . . . is it okay?" he asked, cautiously.

"It is by no means perfect," said the old man, looking unsmiling at Drew.

"Oh," said Drew, grimacing.

Mr. Pipes smiled. "But then, what human poetry is perfect? Your poetry has a strong martial character to it—sounds like a young man wrote it, a young man whose strength is the Lord's. This is fine, indeed," said the old man, squeezing Drew's shoulder. "And you must continue your efforts, striving always for the best."

"Could you read it out loud?" asked Annie. "I love the way poetry sounds when you read it to us."

When Mr. Pipes had finished reading the poem aloud, he said, "Now, my boy, you have also followed my advice to write in a common hymn meter. Might I suggest that we choose a tune and sing it together to your words?"

"Yes, let's," said Annie.

"If you think so," said Drew a little doubtfully.

"I believe this might just sound perfect to a tune of the English composer Jeremiah Clarke, *St. Magnus*. Though, Drew, I am afraid it is frightfully old, written in 1701." Mr. Pipes's eyes twinkled as he continued. "And I do recall how ill you used to think of all that's old and gray."

"Only 1701?" snorted Drew. "That's nothing!"

The ancient sanctuary filled with *St. Magnus*, rising to a victorious climax of praise at its ending. Then the three friends sang Drew's hymn together:

> The Lord, Great Sovereign, shall appear,
>   His wand'ring sheep he'll bring,
> From distant lands, through surging seas,
>   To shout before their King!
>
> Deceitful shepherds, false and vain,
>   Have led his flock astray;
> God's enemies he'll trample down,
>   Their lies he will repay.
>
> With trumpet blast, the Lord appears,
>   His arrows flashing 'round;
> He shields his flock, destroys his foes;
>   Glad vict'ry shouts will sound.
>
> He makes his children mighty men,
>   They bend the battle bow;
> So in God's strength, against the proud,
>   His foes they overthrow!
>
> Restored, victorious, gathered in,
>   Their enemies o'ercome;
> God's children worship 'round his throne,
>   And in his name they run!
>
> God's bless'd, redeemed, and chosen ones,
>   His children, shout and sing!

"All praise to Christ, the Cornerstone,
    Triumphant, glorious King!'"

When they finished and all was quiet again, Mr. Pipes said,
"When you return home in a few days' time, show this to your
mother and father. I think they will be pleased, and I shall mention it in my next letter to them."

"Oh, I agree," said Annie. "It's really good—better than mine."

"No, it's not," said Drew, smiling at his sister, in spite of
himself.

They sat in silence for several minutes, listening to the faint
calls of the crickets outside. No one wanted to be the first to suggest that they return to the cottage. Annie and Drew couldn't
help feeling that every moment spent with Mr. Pipes might be
their last with him.

"Well, my children," said Mr. Pipes, his eyes shining as he
looked intently from one to the other, "let me leave you with
this." He hummed a few bars of a tune. Then his fingers strayed
to the keys of the organ. At last he sang:

Even down to old age all my people shall prove
My sovereign, eternal, unchangeable love;
And when hoary hairs shall their temples adorn,
Like lambs they shall still in my bosom be born,
Like lambs they shall still in my bosom be born.
          ("K" in Rippon's *Selections*, 1787)

"I get it," said Drew, after another silence. "I get it!"

"What is it you get?" asked Mr. Pipes, looking intently at
Drew.

"It's not time or place, language or age that matters," said
Drew. "God's truth, his law, his love, his grace, his worship—
none of it changes; it can't change!"

"'Thy truth unchanged hath ever stood,'" quoted Annie,
softly.

"'While unending ages run,'" added Mr. Pipes.

"'Evermore and evermore,'" said Drew.

"Amen to that," said Mr. Pipes, switching off the organ and rising to go.

Glossary of Nautical Terms

abaft: Toward the rear (astern, see below) of the ship.

abeam: At right angles to the keel of the ship or boat.

aboard: On board or within the boat.

adrift: A boat is adrift when it is no longer on its moorings.

aft: Toward the stern or rear of the boat.

aground: When a boat is touching or held fast to the bottom.

ahoy: Traditional seaman's greeting when hailing a vessel.

alee: Opposite the direction of the wind.

aloft: In the rigging; above the deck of the boat.

amidships: The center region of a boat.

astern: In back of the boat, opposite of ahead.

athwartships: At right angles to the centerline of the boat.

batten down: Secure hatches and loose objects throughout the vessel.

beam: The widest part of the boat.

bearing: The heading or direction a boat is going, or the true bearing as shown on the chart.

bilge: The lower part of the hull usually covered by floorboards.

bow: The forward part of the boat.

bowsprit: A sprit or timber projecting forward of the bow.

bowline: A knot used to make a secure but not permanent loop in the end of a line.

brightwork: Varnished woodwork or polished bronze or stainless steel.

bulkhead: Vertical partition that separates compartments.

cabin: Space below decks or the living quarters for passengers or crew.

companionway: Main access from the cabin of a vessel to the deck.

capsize: To turn over.

cast off: To release mooring lines.

chafe: The wearing of lines and rigging from constant motion.

chart: A map showing navigators sea depth and contour.

cleat: A metal fitting to which lines are tied or made fast.

cockpit: A recessed opening in the deck where the helmsman steers the boat.

coil: To gather a line in a series of loops ready for future use.

course: The compass bearing on which a boat is steered.

current: The horizontal movement of water.

dead ahead: Immediately ahead.

dead astern: Immediately aft (behind).

deck: The permanent covering over the hull of a boat.

disembark: To get off the boat or ship.

dock: A wood or concrete structure where vessels are moored; a pier, float, or wharf.

draft: The distance from the waterline of a vessel to its deepest part below the water.

fathom: Six feet.

fix: Establishing the position of the boat with compass or sextant.

flood: An incoming current resulting from a rising tide.

following sea: An overtaking sea coming from the stern.

fore-and-aft: A line running parallel to the keel.

forecastle or forepeak: A compartment in the bow of a ship or boat.

forward: Toward the bow of the boat.

freeboard: The vertical distance from the waterline of a boat to its gunwale (see below).

galley: The kitchen of a boat.

gangway: The area where people board and disembark a ship.

grab rails: Hand-holds fitted on cabin tops and sides used for personal safety.

ground tackle: A term denoting the anchor, chain, rode, and associated gear.

gunwale: The upper edge of a boat's sides.

hatch: An opening in a boat's deck or house secured with a watertight cover.

heading: The direction in which a vessel's bow points at any given time.

headway: The forward motion of a boat. Opposite of stern-way.

helm: The wheel or tiller that controls the rudder.

helmsman: The person who steers the boat.

hold: A cargo compartment below deck.

hull: The main structure of a vessel.

inboard: The center or inside of a vessel.

jetty: A masonry structure projecting out from the shore usually designed to protect a harbor entrance.

keel: The structural backbone of a boat running fore and aft.

knot: A measure of speed or distance based on one nautical mile (6,076 feet).

knot: A fastening made by tying ends of rope.

latitude: The distance north or south of the equator measured in degrees.

lee: The side of a boat or promontory sheltered from the wind.

leeward: The direction away from the wind. Opposite of windward.

leeway: The sideways movement of a vessel usually caused by either wind or current.

line: Rope used on a boat.

log: A device to measure speed, or a record of a voyage or maintenance operation.

longitude: The distance in degrees east or west of the meridian running north and south through Greenwich, England.

marlinspike: A tool for opening the strands of a rope while splicing.

midship: The location on a boat more or less equally distant from the bow and stern.

mooring: The act of securing a boat with lines to a mooring buoy or a pier.

nautical mile: One minute of latitude, approximately 6,076 feet (statute mile is 5,280 feet).

navigation: The art and science of guiding a vessel safely from one location to another.

navigation rules: The steering and sailing rules governing right of way.

overboard: Referring to someone or something going over the side of the boat.

pier: A non-floating structure extending from the shore, traditionally used for loading cargo.

pile: A wood, metal or concrete pole driven into the bottom.

piling: A support made of several piles for wharves, piers, and ferry docks.

port: The left side of a boat looking forward. Also a harbor.

quarter: The part of a boat aft of amidships, as in port quarter, starboard quarter.

quartering sea: A following sea with wind or current on a boat's quarter.

rat lines: Rope ladders for climbing up the mast and rigging.

Rigging: The cable and rope supports used to secure the mast of a sailboat.

rode: The anchor line.

rope: As soon as this comes aboard a boat it is called line, rode, halyard, sheet depending on its function.

rudder: A vertical board mounted at the stern of a boat used for steering.

running lights: White, red, and green lights required on boats operating between sundown and sunup.

schooner: Traditionally a gaff-rigged sailing vessel with at least two masts, the forward-most shorter or equal in height to the mizzen or after mast.

scope: The ratio of anchor rode to the vertical distance from the bow of the boat to the holding at the bottom.

scuppers: Drain openings on deck or in bulwarks to facilitate spray water runoff.

seamanship: The skills of boat navigation, steering, maintenance, rigging, sail handling.

seaworthy: A boat designed, built, and equipped to withstand the sea conditions.

sextant: An instrument derived from the ancient quadrant used for finding the ground position of the sun or another heavenly body.

sole: Cabin or saloon floor.

sounding: Measuring the depth of the water.

squall: A sudden, violent storm of short duration.

starboard: The right side of a boat when looking forward.

stem: The structural member at the bow of a vessel.

stern: The back or after part of a boat.

stern line: A docking line securing the stern of a boat.

stow: To put an item in its proper place.

thwart: Seat on a rowing boat.

tide: The global rise and fall of oceanic water levels.

tiller: A bar that controls the angle of a boat's rudder.

topsides: The sides of a vessel between the waterline and the deck.

transom: The flat stern of some boats.

trim: The precise adjustment of sails or cargo for optimum balance.

underway: Said of a vessel in motion.

wake: Moving track of waves created when a boat moves through the waters.

waterline: The painted line on a hull showing where a properly trimmed vessel should rest in the water.

way: Any movement of a vessel through the water: headway, sternway, leeway.

windward: The side of a vessel toward the wind.

yacht: The name traditionally reserved for sailing craft, especially racing sailboats. Americans use the word to indicate size and luxury, more often referring to power boats.

Hymns Sung in *The Accidental Voyage*

Shepherd of Tender Youth

Shepherd of tender youth,
Guiding in love and truth
Through devious ways:
Christ, our triumphant King,
We come thy Name to sing;
Hither our children bring,
To shout thy praise.

Thou art our holy Lord,
The all-subduing Word,
Healer of strife:
Thou didst thyself abase,
That from sin's deep disgrace
Thou mightest save our race,
And give us life.

Thou art the Great High Priest,
Thou hast prepared a feast
Of heav'nly love:
While in our mortal pain,
None call on thee in vain:
Help thou dost not disdain,
Help from above.

Ever be thou our Guide,
Our Shepherd and our Pride,
Our Staff and Song:
Jesus, thou Christ of God,
By thy perennial Word,
Lead us where thou hast trod;
Make our faith strong.

So now and till we die,
Sound we thy praises high,
And joyful sing:
Infants, and the glad throng
Who to thy church belong,
Unite to swell the song
To Christ our King.

Hail, Gladdening Light

Hail, gladdening Light, of His pure glory pour'd
Who is th'immortal Father, heav'nly, blest,
Holiest of Holies, Jesus Christ, our Lord!
Now we are come to the sun's hour of rest,

The lights of evening 'round us shine,
We hymn the Father, Son, and Holy Spirit Divine.

Worthiest art Thou at all times to be sung
With undefiled tongue,
Son of our God, Giver of life, Alone:
Therefore in all the world
Thy glories, Lord, they own.

O Light That Knew No Dawn

O Light that knew no dawn,
That shines to endless day,
All things in earth and heav'n

243

Are lustred by thy ray;
No eye can to thy throne ascend,
Nor mind thy brightness comprehend.

Thy grace, O Father, give,
That I may serve in fear;
Above all boons, I pray,
Grant me thy voice to hear;
From sin thy child in mercy free,
And let me dwell in light with thee:

That, cleansed from stain of sin,
I may meet homage give,
And, pure in heart, behold thy beauty while I live;
Clean hands in holy worship raise,
And thee, O Christ my Saviour, praise.

In supplication meek
To thee I bend the knee;
O Christ, when thou shalt come,
In love remember me,
And in thy kingdom, by thy grace,
Grant me a humble servant's place.

Thy grace, O Father, give,
I humbly thee implore;
And let thy mercy bless
Thy servant more and more.
All grace and glory be to thee,
From age to age eternally.

Of the Father's Love Begotten

Of the Father's love begotten
Ere the worlds began to be,
He is Alpha and Omega,

He the source, the ending he,
Of the things that are, that have been,
And that future years shall see.

This is he whom heav'n-taught singers
Sang of old with one accord,
Whom the Scriptures of the prophets
Promised in their faithful word;
Now he shines, the long-expected;
Let creation praise its Lord.

O ye heights of heav'n, adore him;
Angel hosts, his praises sing;
All dominions, bow before him,
And extol our God and King;
Let no tongue on earth be silent,
Ev'ry voice in concert ring.

Thee let age and thee let manhood,
Thee let boys in chorus sing;
Matrons, virgins, little maidens,
With glad voices answering;
Let their guileless songs re-echo,
And their heart its music bring.

Christ, to thee, with God the Father,
And, O holy Ghost, to thee,
Hymn, and chant, and high thanksgiving,
And unwearied praises be,
Honor, glory, and dominion,
And eternal victory.

Te Deum

O God, we praise thee; and confess
That thou the only Lord

And Everlasting Father art,
By all the earth adored.

To thee all angels cry aloud;
To thee the pow'rs on high,
Both cherubim and seraphim,
Continually do cry:

O holy, holy, holy, Lord,
Whom heav'nly hosts obey,
The world is with the glory filled
Of thy majestic ray.

Th' apostles' glorious company,
And prophets crowned with light,
With all the martyrs' noble host,
Thy constant praise recite.

The holy church throughout the world,
O Lord, confesses thee,
That thou eternal Father art,
Of boundless majesty;

Thine honored, true, and only Son;
And holy Ghost, the Spring
Of never-ceasing joy:
O Christ, Of glory thou art King.

O Trinity, Most Blessed Light

O Trinity, most blessed Light.
O Unity of sov'reign might,
As now the fiery sun departs,
Shed thou thy beams within our hearts.

To thee our morning song of praise,
To thee our evening prayer we raise;
Thee may our glory evermore
In lowly reverence adore.

All praise to God the Father be,
All praise, eternal Son, to thee,
Whom with the Spirit we adore
Forever and forever more.

Let All Mortal Flesh Keep Silence

Let all mortal flesh keep silence,
And with fear and trembling stand;
Ponder nothing earthly-minded,
For with blessing in his hand,
Christ our God to earth descendeth,
Our full homage to demand.

King of kings, yet born of Mary,
As of old on earth he stood,
Lord of lords, in human vesture,
In the body and the blood.
He will give to all the faithful
His own self for heav'n ly food.

Rank on rank the host of heaven
Spreads its vanguard on the way,
As the Light of light descendeth
From the realms of endless day,
That the pow'rs of hell may vanish
As the darkness clears away.

At his feet the six-winged seraph,
Cherubim, with sleepless eye,
Veil their faces to the presence,

As with ceaseless voice they cry,
Alleluia, alleluia,
Alleluia, Lord, Most High!

Christ Is Made the Sure Foundation

Christ is made the sure Foundation,
Christ the Head and Cornerstone,
Chosen of the Lord and precious,
Binding all the church in one;
Holy Zion's help forever,
And her confidence alone.

All that dedicated city,
Dearly loved of God on high,
In exultant jubilation
Pours perpetual melody;
God the One in Three adoring
In glad hymns eternally.

To this temple, where we call thee,
Come, O Lord of hosts, today:
With thy wonted loving-kindness
Hear thy people as they pray;
And thy fullest benediction
Shed within its walls alway.

Here vouch-safe to all thy servants
What they ask of thee to gain,
What they gain from thee for ever
With the blessed to retain,
And hereafter in thy glory
Evermore with thee to reign.

Laud and honor to the Father,
Laud and honor to the Son,
Laud and honor to the Spirit,
Ever Three and ever One,
One in might, and One in glory,
While unending ages run.

Christian, Dost Thou See Them

Christian, dost thou see them
On the holy ground,
How the pow'rs of darkness
Rage thy steps around?

Christian, up and smite them,
Counting gain but loss,
In the strength that cometh
By the holy cross.

Christian, dost thou feel them,
How they work within,
Striving, tempting, luring,
Goading into sin?

Christian, never tremble;
Never be downcast;
Gird thee for the battle,
Watch and pray and fast.

Christian, dost thou hear them,
How they speak thee fair?
"Always fast and vigil?
Always watch and prayer?"

Christian, answer boldly,
"While I breathe I pray!"

Peace shall follow battle,
Night shall end in day.

Hear the words of Jesus:
"O my servant true;
Thou art very weary—
I was weary too"—

But that toil shall make thee
Some day all mine own,
And the end of sorrow
Shall be near my throne.

All Glory, Laud, and Honor

All glory, laud, and honor
To thee, Redeemer, King,
To whom the lips of children
Made sweet hosannas ring!
Thou art the King of Israel,
Thou David's royal Son,
Who in the Lord's name comest,
The King and blessed One!

The people of the Hebrews
With palms before thee went;
Our praise and prayer and anthem
Before thee we present:
To thee, before thy passion,
They sang their hymns of praise;
To thee, now high exalted,
Our melody we raise.

Thou didst accept their praises;
Accept the prayers we bring,
Who in all good delightest,

Thou good and gracious King!
All glory, laud, and honor
To thee, Redeemer, King,
To whom the lips of children
Made sweet hosannas ring!

Jesus, Thou Joy of Loving Hearts

Jesus, thou joy of loving hearts,
Thou Fount of life, thou Light of men;
From the best bliss that earth imparts,
We turn unfilled to thee again.

Thy truth unchanged hath ever stood;
Thou savest those that on thee call:
To them that seek thee thou art good,
To them that find thee, all in all.

We taste thee, O thou living Bread,
And long to feast upon thee still;
We drink of thee, the Fountainhead,
And thirst our souls from thee to fill.

Our restless spirits yearn for thee,
Where'er our changeful lot is cast;
Glad when thy gracious smile we see,
Blest when our faith can hold thee fast.

O Jesus, ever with us stay;
Make all our moments calm and bright;
Chase the dark night of sin away;
Shed o'er the world thy holy light.

Jerusalem the Golden

Jerusalem the golden,
With milk and honey blest,

Beneath thy contemplation
Sink heart and voice oppressed.
I know not, O I know not,
What joys await us there;
What radiancy of glory,
What bliss beyond compare.

They stand, those halls of Zion,
All jubilant with song,
And bright with many an angel,
And all the martyr throng.
The Prince is ever in them,
The daylight is serene;
The pastures of the blessed
Are decked in glorious sheen.

There is the throne of David;
And there, from care released,
The song of them that triumph,
The shout of them that feast;
And they who with their Leader
Have conquered in the fight,
For ever and for ever
Are clad in robes of white.

O sweet and blessed country,
The home of God's elect!
O sweet and blessed country
That eager hearts expect!
Jesus, in mercy bring us
To that dear land of rest;
Who art, with God the Father
And Spirit, ever blest.

All Creatures of Our God and King

All creatures of our God and King,
Lift up your voice and with us sing
  Alleluia, alleluia!
Thou burning sun with golden beam,
Thou silver moon with softer gleam,
  O praise him, O praise him,
  Alleluia, alleluia . . .

Thou rushing wind that art so strong,
Ye clouds that sail in heav'n along,
  O praise him, alleluia!
Thou rising morn, in praise rejoice,
Ye lights of evening, find a voice,
  O praise him . . .

Thou flowing water, pure and clear,
Make music for thy Lord to hear,
  Alleluia, alleluia!
Thou fire so masterful and bright,
That giveth man both warmth and light,
  O praise him . . .

And all ye men of tender heart,
Forgiving others, take your part,
  O sing ye, alleluia!
Ye who long pain and sorrow bear,
Praise God and on him cast your care,
  O praise him . . .

Let all things their Creator bless,
And worship him in humbleness,
  O praise him, alleluia!
Praise, praise the Father, praise the Son,

And praise the Spirit, three in one,
    O praise him . . .

Fierce Was the Wild Billow

Fierce was the wild billow,
Dark was the night;
Oars labored heavily,
Foam glimmered white;
Trembled the mariners,
Peril was nigh—
Then said the God of God,
"Peace! It is I."

Ridge of the mountain-wave,
Lower thy crest!
Wail of Euroclydon,
Be thou at rest!
Sorrow can never be,
Darkness must fly,
Where saith the Light of Light,
"Peace! It is I."

Jesus, Deliverer,
Come thou to me;
Soothe thou my voyaging
Over life's sea:
Thou, when the storm of death
Roars, sweeping by,
Whisper, O Truth of Truth,
"Peace! It is I."

St. Patrick's Breastplate

I bind unto myself today
The strong name of the Trinity

By invocation of the same,
The Three in One, and One in Three.

I bind this day to me for ever,
By power of faith, Christ's Incarnation;
His baptism in the Jordan river;
His death on Cross for my salvation;
His bursting from the spiced tomb;
His riding up the heavenly way;
His coming at the day of doom:
I bind unto myself today.

I bind unto myself today
The virtues of the starlit heaven,
The glorious sun's life-giving ray,
The whiteness of the moon at even,
The flashing of the lightning free,
The whirling wind's tempestuous shocks,
The stable earth, the deep salt sea
Around the old eternal rocks.

I bind unto myself today
The pow'r of God to hold and lead,
His eye to watch, His might to stay,
His ear to hearken to my need,
The wisdom of my God to teach,
His hand to guide, His shield to ward,
The Word of God to give me speech,
His heav'nly host to be my guard.

Christ be with me, Christ within me,
Christ behind me, Christ before me,
Christ beside me, Christ to win me,
Christ to comfort and restore me,
Christ beneath me, Christ above me,

Christ in quiet, Christ in danger,
Christ in hearts of all that love me,
Christ in mouth of friend and stranger.

I bind unto myself the Name,
The strong Name of the Trinity;
By invocation of the same,
The Three in One, and One in Three,
Of whom all nature hath creation,
Eternal Father, Spirit, Word.
Praise to the Lord of my salvation:
Salvation is of Christ the Lord.

Be Thou My Vision, O Lord of My Heart

Be thou my vision, O Lord of my heart;
Naught be all else to me, save that thou art—
Thou my best thought by day or by night,
Waking or sleeping, thy presence my light.

Be thou my wisdom, and thou my true word;
I ever with thee and thou with me, Lord;
Thou my great Father, I thy true son;
Thou in me dwelling, and I with thee one.

Be thou my battle shield, sword for my fight;
Be thou my dignity, thou my delight,
Thou my soul's shelter, thou my high tow'r:
Raise thou me heav'nward, O Pow'r of my pow'r.

Riches I heed not, nor man's empty praise,
Thou mine inheritance, now and always:
Thou and thou only, first in my heart,
High King of heaven, my treasure thou art.

High King of heaven, my victory won,
May I reach heaven's joys, O bright heav'n's Sun!
Heart of my own heart, whatever befall,
Still be my vision, O Ruler of all.

A Hymn of Glory Let Us Sing

A hymn of glory let us sing;
New songs thro'out the world shall ring:
Alleluia! Alleluia!
Christ, by a road before untrod,
Ascendeth to the throne of God.
Alleluia . . . !

The holy apostolic band
Upon the Mount of Olives stand;
Alleluia! Alleluia!
And with his followers they see
Jesus' resplendent majesty.
Alleluia . . . !

To whom the angels, drawing nigh:
"Why stand and gaze upon the sky?"
Alleluia! Alleluia!
"This is the Savior," thus they say,
"This is his noble triumph day."
Alleluia . . . !

"Again shall ye behold him so
As ye today have seen him go,
Alleluia! Alleluia!
In glorious pomp ascending high,
Up to the portals of the sky."
Alleluia . . . !

Douglas Bond, a high school history and English teacher, has done extensive research on hymnody and has traveled to many of the places featured in the *Mr. Pipes* books. He is the author of *Duncan's War, King's Arrow,* and *Rebel's Keep,* as well as the *Mr. Pipes* series of children's books. Bond has earned an M.I.T. in education from St. Martin's College. He lives with his wife and six children in Washington state. Visit Bond's website at www.bondbooks.net.